WHALES' ANGELS

A husband and wife battle whalers
in a seagoing adventure of
international intrigue and murder

A Novel

Paul J. Mila

Bloomington, IN Milton Keynes, UK

authorHOUSE

AuthorHouse™
1663 Liberty Drive, Suite 200
Bloomington, IN 47403
www.authorhouse.com
Phone: 1-800-839-8640

AuthorHouse™ UK Ltd.
500 Avebury Boulevard
Central Milton Keynes, MK9 2BE
www.authorhouse.co.uk
Phone: 08001974150

First published by AuthorHouse 5/17/2006

ISBN: 1-4259-3937-6 (sc)

Library of Congress Control Number: 2006904500

Printed in the United States of America
Bloomington, Indiana

This book is printed on acid-free paper.

DEDICATIONS

*This book is dedicated to the memory
of two special people:*

*Robert Mila, my big brother and
my larger-than-life hero,
WW II Veteran of the Pacific and father of five.
Recently learning he was seriously
ill, Bob philosophically said,
"Well, I've lived a good long life,
and I had fun doing it."
No one could ask for more than that.*

And,

*Alan Catalano, my good friend, a true gentle-man,
and the ultimate good neighbor.
During his 56 years and 11 months on earth,
Al enriched our lives simply by his presence.
Alan faced his final adversity with
more grace and courage
than any man I have ever known.
I miss you, buddy.*

Acknowledgments

I would like to thank those who read the original manuscript, and whose comments and suggestions significantly improved the final book.

Amanda Baxter, Bonnie Cardone,
Alan Catalano, Carol Catalano, Alison Dennis,
Nick Fittipaldi, Terry Gallogly, Carol Mila,
Christine Mila, Laura Mila, Challis Moore, Lisanne Lange,
Leon Rutman, Jack Sheedy, Ankie Stiasny

I am especially grateful to four friends, who generously devoted a great amount of their time to edit and correct the manuscript.

Tish Dace, *Writer and Diver, Bonaire, Netherlands Antilles*
Judith Hemenway, *author of* The Universe Next Door,
Best Publishing Co., 2003
Jessica Koenig, *Westbury Library, Westbury, NY*
Brian Paradine, *future author and tennis coach par excellence*

Any remaining errors and shortcomings in the book are totally the author's fault.

Technical assistance relating to medical issues:
Lisanne Lange, *M.D.*

Technical assistance relating to police procedures:
Lieutenant Alan Catalano, *Lake Success NY Police Department, Retired.*

<u>*Special Thanks!*</u>

To Ankie, for introducing me to the whales of the Silver Bank.

To Kieran Mulvaney (Author of The Whaling Season, *Island Press/Shearwater Books, 2003), whose patient e-mail correspondence provided invaluable firsthand insights regarding whaling and efforts to save whales.*

To Mary Whalen and Deollo Johnson, for allowing me to use the lyrics of their song, <u>The Whales' Delight</u>, which they composed during our whaling adventure to the Silver Bank.

Foreword

To the many readers who enjoyed *Dangerous Waters* (AuthorHouse, April 2004), and suggested a sequel developing the relationship between Terry Hunter and Joe Manetta, here is *Whales' Angels*.

Reviewing *Dangerous Waters* for the *Playa Maya News*, Challis Moore wrote, *"Terry Hunter is a woman who faces many life-altering changes, and she is a woman who you really want to see succeed. Her story is dramatic and her quest for happiness and peace can strike a chord with us all."*

Whales' Angels continues Terry's quest.

In *Whales' Angels* Terry and Joe embark on a globetrotting odyssey, from the sunny Mexican Caribbean to Iceland's frigid north Atlantic. Their adventure leads them into a dark world of danger, mystery, and international intrigue, where fate has the last word. Actual events provide background into the international politics of whaling, and the ongoing conflict between those commercially exploiting whales versus those fighting to save whales from extinction.

The photo plates, including the cover, are my own dive photos. They were used to illustrate the beauty of scuba diving in our undersea world and the thrill of free diving with the largest animals ever to roam the earth.

I hope you enjoy the story.

Paul J. Mila
Long Island
June 2006

Prologue

The Pacific Ocean, North of the Hawaiian Islands

*T*he jubilant crew of the *Sea Angel* had just finished dinner. They concluded the evening with several rounds of toasts, celebrating their success in preventing whalers aboard the Japanese whaling ship *Hakudo Maru* from slaughtering a sperm whale pod. "Quiet down, mates! Let me read this e-mail we just received from England!" said Karel, the forty-three-year-old first mate.

"To the entire *Sea Angel* crew. The Peaceful Seas Conservation Organization salutes your gallant and successful efforts in confronting the *Hakudo Maru* on the high seas today. All civilized human beings applaud your dedication to saving the lives of the ocean's peaceful and intelligent inhabitants. We are proud of your efforts to establish truly peaceful seas around the globe. We wish you continued success.

Signed, Sir Adam Raleigh, Chairman, Peaceful Seas Conservation Organization."

"Hip, hip hooray!" cheered a British seaman.

"Hip, hip hooray!" replied the multinational crew of young men and women.

"Let's watch the video again!" shouted Marie Brighton, who piloted the eighteen-foot Zodiac outboard in today's action.

"Okay, okay, let me pop in the cassette," Karel replied. He pressed the play button and the blue screen on the giant television monitor transformed into a panoramic ocean view, showing a large object moving through the water directly ahead of the Zodiac. As ship's cameraman Lester Phillips zoomed in, details emerged: a disproportionately large head, dark grey wrinkled skin, triangular flukes frayed at the edges. The object was clearly recognizable as a large sperm whale. The whale raised its tail flukes and dove. Lester panned the camera around. The gunmetal-grey steel bow of the *Hakudo Maru* came into view, slicing the water like an angry knife, bearing down less than fifty yards astern of the tiny craft. He panned the camera up to the prow, where a sailor manned a deadly harpoon cannon. He zoomed in, focusing on the menacing tip of the harpoon's explosive warhead. Marie yelled above the noise of the wind and waves, "Les, whale's up, at two o'clock!" He whipped the camera around toward a spot of ocean just right of the Zodiac, where the mist of the whale's breath formed a momentary rainbow in the sunlight.

The audience heard Phillips shouting on the video, "I see it!" The camera panned dizzily across the sky as he lost his balance when Marie turned sharply right, following the whale, anticipating the larger ship's next move. He swung the camera in a wild arc as he steadied himself and videoed the *Hakudo Maru* also turning starboard. Phillips focused on the bow again, where the harpooner aimed his weapon for the kill. But Marie skillfully maneuvered the Zodiac into his line of fire, blocking the shot. The cat-and-mouse move and counter-move sparring between Marie, in her eighteen-foot craft, and the captain of the 150-foot *Hakudo Maru* lasted for thirty minutes. Finally, the captain cut his engines and the audience applauded as the larger ship fell behind the speeding Zodiac, breaking off the chase. "You did it!" exclaimed Lester.

"Yes!" Marie shouted on the tape as Les panned the camera back to the whale, flukes raised high, signaling another deep dive, as if saluting its benefactors. Then Lester shot the cheering crew of the *Sea Angel* lining the starboard rail, waving and snapping photos of the dramatic encounter. Before returning to her mother ship, Marie spun a victory lap around the *Hakudo Maru,* now sitting dead in the water. She looked up at its stone-faced crew and waved. Wet ringlets framed her smiling face. The sailors returned her gesture with scowls and shook angry fists. This part of the tape elicited the loudest peals of laughter from the audience. Marie stood and took a demonstrative, exaggerated bow, eliciting more laughter, applause, whistling and enthusiastic cheering.

As Karel removed the tape, Marie asked, "Who'll pilot the Zodiac tomorrow, Karel?"

"Well, Marie, I think tomorrow it will be Albert. I fear these whalers are getting bolder and more aggressive. I prefer another seasoned person out there again. Besides you, he's had the most experience compared with the other three pilots."

"You mean besides *you,*" said Albert, deferentially.

"Yes, besides me," he smiled. "You know, I've confronted Russian whalers in the western Pacific years ago, and more recently the Japanese. I do miss being out there on the water, between them and the whales, only meters in front of their ships, fucking with their minds," he said wistfully. "But now it's time for you youngsters to hone your skills. This is a deadly business, and we need new blood to carry on the fight." Karel sighed. "Well, it's late and I'm tired. I'm going on deck for some fresh air, look for some shooting stars, and then turn in."

"Good night, Pops," some crewmembers shouted, good-naturedly.

Karel turned around and replied with a wink and smile. "Good night, kids. Busy day on the sea tomorrow. Get your rest." Leaving, he thought, *Boy, sometimes they really make me feel like the old man.* Up on deck, he gazed at the stars, shining as if someone had thrown a handful of glitter against black velvet. Karel loved astronomy—a useful hobby for a seafarer. He knew the constellations and could name many of the stars composing them. In the clear night sky, Karel easily picked out the Big Dipper, part of the constellation Ursa Major, The Great Bear. His eyes scanned the Dipper. He found Alkaid, the star at the end of the handle. Then he looked for the two "pointer" stars on the opposite end of the Dipper, Dubhe and Merak. He drew an imaginary line through them, which pointed to Polaris, the North Star. Light from the full moon shone on the water, creating a silver path leading toward an unseen enchanted land, somewhere over the barely visible horizon. He also noticed the lights of the *Hakudo Maru,* less than a mile away. That puzzled him. *Hmmm, surprised they're still in the area. Figured after we've been harassing 'em all week they'd try to lose us during the night.*

After stargazing and savoring the salty night air for almost an hour, Karel went below to his small cabin. Though cramped, its privacy was a benefit of his seniority. *Nice not having to share a berth with the kids,* he thought, smiling. It was his last conscious thought. Several hours later, while Karel and the entire crew slept, dawn was breaking. As the first rays of the sun pierced the eastern horizon, an enormous explosion rocked the *Sea Angel,* ripping out her bottom. She sank quickly, flooding from the stern, pitching bow-up at such a severe angle that only the watch on deck and three other crewmembers sleeping near the bow escaped. The four survivors desperately clung to bits of wreckage as the *Sea Angel* slipped below the surface, trapping Karel, Marie, Lester, Albert, and the rest of the young crew in a watery grave. Shouting desperately for help, they watched the *Hakudo Maru* disappear over the horizon.

Chapter 1

Cozumel, Mexico
Three Years Later

August 12th

    *T*erry Manetta looked over her shoulder at the rooster-tail wake of the *Dorado* as the twin Yamaha-65 outboards powered her twenty-eight-foot dive boat through the water at twenty-five knots. "Hey, that's quite a flotilla," she remarked, watching the numerous boats following close behind. "That hurricane kept everyone in port the last four days. They look like school kids running out for recess."

    "Is that unusual for this time of year?" asked one of the divers.

    "Well, most hurricanes hit down here August through November, but we can get a big blow anytime after June," explained

Joe Manetta, Terry's husband. "So, early August certainly isn't out of the question. And whenever the wind really blows hard, the port closes and smaller boats like ours aren't allowed out. The sea gets very choppy, and it's not safe unless you're in a larger boat. And even then it's not a pleasant ride."

"Sure are a lot of boats out here today," commented another diver.

"Yeah, reminds me of Manhattan at rush hour," said Joe.

"Hey, you from New York?"

"Yeah. Brooklyn, originally."

"Me too. Everybody's from Brooklyn, originally. So you and your wife relocated down here?"

"Yep. Well, I did. Terry's originally from California."

"No foolin'. And you two met down here? I bet there's a story behind that."

"Oh yeah," replied Terry, smiling. "Quite a story, but too long to tell right now. Looks like we're at the dive site, right, Manuel?"

"*Si,* Terry. Yucab Reef."

"Okay," said Joe. "Since all of you requested two easy dives for the first day of your trip, we're diving Yucab first and Santa Rosa Shallows for the second dive. Here's our plan: We'll all descend slowly to the bottom, at about forty to fifty feet. Make sure you equalize the pressure in your ears. You don't want to start off your vacations with perforated eardrums or middle-ear damage. If you run into a problem, don't try to force it by over-pressurizing. Go up a couple of feet, equalize and then keep coming down. Once we're all down, just follow me. The current is pretty weak today, just about one knot. So, even though we'll be drift diving, you'll be able to kick your fins against the current without too much effort and stop if you want to explore something that catches your eye. After about forty-five minutes, or if someone's air gauge indicates seven hundred pounds of air pressure, we'll slowly ascend to fifteen feet and hang for a three-minute safety stop to expel some of the nitrogen build-up."

"Yeah, wouldn't want to start the vacation with a case of the bends either," commented one of the divers.

6

"All right, once everyone is suited up inflate your BC vests [**B**uoyancy **C**ompensating devices] so you float easily until you're ready to descend. We'll sit three on each side of the boat. When Manuel counts to three, we all do a backward roll into the water together. Let's get into position."

"One, two, three, go!" shouted Manuel, as the six divers, seated on opposite sides of the *Dorado,* rolled backward into the warm, clear water. They popped to the surface a moment later and checked their equipment one final time, ensuring that facemasks were in place, regulators were delivering air properly, and weights were secure and comfortable.

"Everyone ready to go down?" asked Joe. Everyone indicated they were ready, so Joe said, "Okay, let's go!"

Each diver raised the inflation/deflation hose and pressed the "deflate" button. As air escaped, they slipped below the surface, into a liquid world far different from the one above. Descending slowly, the divers equalized the pressure in their ears, squeezing their nostrils shut with their fingers and gently blowing air into the Eustachian tubes and middle-ear area to offset the growing pressure of the seawater pressing against their eardrums.

The divers followed Joe as he led them through the dive. Two honeymooners held hands as they cruised along with the current. Two other divers who had buddied up were middle-aged men, friends on a vacation away from their wives, and many years removed from their respective honeymoons. The sixth diver hung back from the group, closely observing Joe and carefully noting his performance on this, his first dive as a certified dive master. Terry wanted to make sure Joe performed his duties efficiently, thoroughly, and properly. The divers' safety was in Joe's hands and, as his instructor, his wife wanted to confirm she had taught him well. He had come a long way from being a novice diver only a little more than two years ago. Terry had also come a long way in that time. Two years ago, her name was Terry Hunter. An NYPD detective named Joe Manetta saved her life after she had inadvertently stumbled into his drug-smuggling investigation and became the target of the local drug kingpin.

Terry felt slightly envious watching the honeymooners. She and Joe had been married just over a year, and she felt as though they were still on their honeymoon. She wanted to hold his hand too, as they drifted weightless through the delightfully warm, gin-clear Caribbean water. However, Terry was the consummate dive professional. She shook the romantic idea from her head, reminding herself she was "on duty" today. *Okay, he got everyone down in good shape. Now, keep track of everything he does. Is he asking everyone how much air they have left on a regular basis? Is he checking to see the group is together, not too spread apart? Is he keeping track of the depth and dive time? Okay, good job so far, Joe.*

Everyone's air consumption was good, and after forty-five minutes Joe signaled the group to ascend to the fifteen-foot level for their safety stop. It was a good dive and Terry was happy for Joe that it had gone so well. In addition to the interesting corals and sponges, they had seen two large nurse sharks, each about seven feet long, swimming slowly along the bottom, looking for a lobster dinner. They also found a southern stingray camouflaged in the sand. Then, they crossed paths with a hawksbill turtle. The normally shy sea turtle surprised them by swimming with the group for several minutes. The friendly hawksbill created a great photo-op for the two men, and they took turns posing as the cooperative turtle swam between them.

Manuel had followed the divers' bubbles as they drifted below with the current, ensuring the boat would be close when they surfaced. He expertly maneuvered next to the floating divers and Pepe, the mate, lowered a ladder over the side. Terry and Joe climbed up after everyone else was safely aboard. The other four divers traded enthusiastic observations and impressions of the dive. Terry was delighted because she knew they would tip generously, and especially because Joe had performed so well in his first outing as dive master. She stepped over and gave him a gentle peck on the lips. "Nice job, partner," she said coolly.

"Thanks, I thought it was a great dive," Joe said, deliberately downplaying his excitement and personal satisfaction in his own performance. Neither of them wanted to give their customers the impression that Joe was anything other than a very experienced dive master.

After a fifty-minute surface interval, to allow their bodies to expel excess nitrogen, they arrived at Santa Rosa Shallows for their second dive. Once again, Terry let Joe take charge and observed his demeanor. She was pleased he exuded confidence explaining the dive plan. "Okay, Santa Rosa is usually a deep wall dive, but today we're going to stay in the reef plateau, forty to fifty feet. The current is pretty mild right now, so you can fin to the wall's edge and feel like you're flying over the edge of the abyss. Just don't descend below fifty feet. We'll see some interesting coral formations as we drift north, also horse-eyed jacks, and a variety of other fish. After about forty-five minutes, or when someone is down to seven hundred pounds of air, we'll move into the shallow, sandy area and ascend to fifteen feet for a three-minute safety stop. Okay?" Everyone nodded affirmatively, so he said, "Let's go diving!"

The second dive was uneventful but enjoyable. On the way back, Terry and Joe smiled at each other as the divers exchanged comments about the good diving. They dropped their customers at the Allegro Hotel pier and then headed to their final destination, Puerto de Abrigo, where Manuel moored the *Dorado*. On the way back, Joe asked, "Well, now that the paying customers are gone, how'd I really do?"

"Actually, you did great, Joe," Terry said, searching her mental notebook for her assessment.

"Hey, you sound surprised! Don't forget, I had the best instructor in Cozumel!"

"Wow, flattery is even better than an apple for the teacher," Terry replied, smiling coyly.

"Here's something even better than flattery," Joe said, hooking his arm behind Terry's neck, pulling her close and kissing her sensuous lips. They embraced, wet suit-to-wet suit, and Manuel and Pepe smiled at each other, pretending not to notice.

Back in port, everyone shared the not-so-glamorous job of hauling air tanks and other gear from the boat, rinsing it for the next day's diving, and other mandatory prep work. They drove into the town of San Miguel, dropped off Manuel and Pepe and then headed home, just north of town. As they drove away, the two crewmen waved. "It is nice to see they are so much in love," Manuel said.

"*Si*. Let us hope it is for a long time, amigo."

Joe and Terry were indeed very much in love. They had been attracted to each other from the first moment they met. That was two years ago, when Joe interviewed Terry in the local hospital after she had survived the first attempt on her life by the local drug lord, Oscar. Terry assisted Joe in his investigation, which required teaching him to scuba dive. It had been an exciting, dangerous adventure, though her involvement had almost cost Terry her life. But, more importantly, it had brought them together.

The hawksbill created a great photo-op for the two men, and they took turns posing for each other with the unusually cooperative turtle swimming between them.

Photo by Paul J. Mila

Chapter 2
The Western Atlantic, off New England

September 1st

    *S*he always enjoyed swimming off Cape Cod, especially in late summer. The sun had warmed the water to a comfortable temperature and the currents were still mild. She enjoyed renewing acquaintances, and especially introducing her new son to his extended family of aunts, uncles, and cousins. But she had to head south now, ahead of the family. She felt the unmistakable fluttering of life in her womb, a familiar signal she should leave as quickly as possible. The family would understand her early departure, and they knew they would soon meet again.

    So the fifty-foot, forty-ton female humpback whale decided to have one last feast of sand lances and krill, the tiny fish and shrimp that were a mainstay of her diet. Then, she would begin her 1,500-mile journey to the birthing and mating grounds for this humpback population, the waters of the Silver Bank, off the coast of the Dominican Republic. The northern waters were still plentiful with food, not only krill but also other small, schooling fish such as herring and capelin. The whales always consumed prodigious amounts before starting their annual migration. While wintering in the southern Atlantic they would not eat for several months, living off fat reserves stored in their blubber before returning to the waters off Long Island and New England next spring.

The female humpback noticed a huge congregation of krill just ahead of her, hundreds of feet across, near the surface. She accelerated, rhythmically pumping her powerful flukes vertically as she lunged, mouth open, into the dense cloud of small crustaceans. Ventral grooves, extending from the tip of her lower jaw lengthwise to the middle of her body, streamlined her. Now they opened like the pleats of a woman's skirt, allowing her throat to expand and take in hundreds of gallons of seawater containing thousands of krill. Then, using her tongue as a giant piston, she forced the water out through hundreds of thin, two-foot long baleen plates hanging from her upper jaw. The baleen strained the shrimp from the escaping water like a giant sieve. Her reward was a hundred pounds of shrimp, which she consumed in a single, leisurely gulp. Then she watched her seven-month-old calf consume his share. He had recently stopped nursing, and by observing her feeding behavior he was becoming more efficient at feeding himself. The surface roiled as the two whales made repeated passes through the krill, gorging themselves on thousands of pounds, until the school was reduced to a few survivors, not worth the effort to consume.

The pair then headed south at a leisurely pace for several miles when a third whale, a large bull who would serve as their escort, joined them. This was not the father of her current offspring, but he had mated with her last year and fathered the baby whale she was carrying. Although his presence provided protection, his motives were far more basic – to position himself closer to her than other competing males, thus increasing his chances of mating again, as soon as she was receptive. But her receptivity this year was not a foregone conclusion. Two pregnancies in consecutive seasons were unusual, and three would be out of the question. Whales, like humans, preferred a respite from having babies. Consequently, the male escort would likely finish this year's mating season frustrated, unless he found a new paramour.

Several days later, the trio adjusted their heading southeast toward a shallow area farther out in the Atlantic. Humans called the area *Bermuda*. The whales knew it only as a good place to obtain more food to sustain them for their journey and long winter fast.

Chapter 3
The North Atlantic, off the Iceland Coast

October 6th

    *T*he Icelandic whaling ship *Arctic Wind* closed fast on a pod of six whales, and the crew prepared for the slaughter. A century and a half ago an epic battle would have ensued between leviathan in the sea and men in small wooden boats. But this was not the nineteenth century. These twenty-first-century whalers — little more than pirates — were illegally hunting an internationally protected species. The *Arctic Wind*'s crew pursued whales that nineteenth-century whalers could not have caught. These were fin whales, also called finbacks, reaching 80 feet and weighing up to 260,000 pounds, surpassed in size only by blue whales. They sped so fast, whalers called them *greyhounds of the ocean*. Capable of twenty-five knots for short bursts, they had eluded whalers trying to row after them until the late 1800s. But the advent of steam power and the explosive harpoon made finbacks one of the most hunted whale species. By the 1980s, close to extinction, they were declared endangered and listed as whales that should not be hunted.

The *Arctic Wind* continued gaining on the whale pod. The whales accelerated, attempting to escape the steel monster hounding them. Forty-two-year-old Captain Ulf Swenson maneuvered his ship just behind the whales, giving his harpooner a good shot. Swenson presented a formidable figure at the helm. A huge man, with a shock of red hair barely contained in a short ponytail and a full beard, his piercing blue eyes flashed as he focused on the kill. Norse blood coursed through his veins, and he would have looked perfectly natural standing at the bow of a twelfth-century Viking man-of-war, dressed in animal skins and battle helmet.

He shouted encouragement to his harpoon gunner, positioned at the bow. "Soon Gudmund, soon! Pick out a big one!"

Harpooner Gudmund Vikinsson lined up the shot through the sight of his cannon. He had selected the largest whale of the pod as his victim, a seventy-footer, but it dove for the safety of the deep. He relaxed and waited for the whale to surface. Years of experience enabled Swenson to think like a whale. Watching the effort a whale expended to outrun his killing machine, he knew how long it could stay submerged. When the whale dove, he could somehow sense if it would maintain a straight heading or turn. Consequently, the desperate beast surfaced to replenish the air in its cavernous lungs just where Swenson expected, and he had maneuvered the *Arctic Wind* into perfect position for the kill. Vikinsson smiled as he swiveled the harpoon cannon and took aim again. The cannon roared and the 160-pound harpoon, fitted with an explosive grenade, sped a hundred feet in less than a second. The whale had no time to react to the pain of a metal spike driving into its body. The harpoon's explosive warhead detonated, pulverizing the finback's massive lungs and car-sized heart, killing it instantly.

The *Arctic Wind* came alongside the dead fin whale to claim its prize. After the crew finished securing it to their ship, the *Sea Angel II* came abreast, less than one hundred feet away. Owned by Peaceful Seas, *Sea Angel II*'s mission was to disrupt the whale hunt. "Bloody murdering bastards!" roared Captain Jan Shalken through his loudspeakers. He had been shadowing the whaler for several days but had fallen behind, since his old boat could not match the *Arctic Wind*'s speed. Consequently, the *Sea Angel*'s crew had missed their opportunity to launch their Zodiacs and maneuver between the harpooner and the whales, preventing a kill. The blue-green sea between the two ships turned crimson, as gallons of blood flowed from the dead whale while the crews taunted each other. Lara Shalken, Jan's wife, documented the bloody scene on video while other crew members took still photographs. "Make sure you get plenty of footage and still shots," exhorted Jan. "We couldn't save this whale, but at least the world will know what transpired on the high seas today."

"Keep a respectful distance unless you want my gunner to place the next harpoon up your ass!" bellowed Captain Swenson, furious at the unwelcome intrusion and the unwanted publicity he knew would result. "We'll do as we please while conducting scientific research in international waters." Gudmund Vikinsson leaned against his weapon, patting the barrel as he laughed derisively at the *Sea Angel II*'s crew.

Jan's face remained icily defiant and he bit his lip, fighting to contain his anger. Through tears, Lara continued shooting video as she watched the dead fin whale wallow in the bloody wake between the two ships.

After keeping pace with the *Arctic Wind* for thirty minutes, the *Sea Angel II* veered away. Lara raced up to the wheelhouse, furious. "What the hell are you doing, Jan? We just can't let them kill more whales! Scientific research my ass! The Japanese use that same loophole in the Whaling Commission's rules as a cover for slaughtering whales that end up on their dinner tables! And you read that Iceland announced it would resume commercial whaling next year. We just cannot . . . ."

"Calm yourself, Lara. They'll be busy butchering their prize. Besides, it's almost dusk. There won't be any more hunting tonight. I'd rather use our time productively. Let's activate the satellite link so we can broadcast our pictures and inform the civilized world about today's tragedy. Documenting this illegal kill may increase public support for intensified conservation and bring international economic sanctions against Iceland. The publicity worked when they tried to resume whaling twenty years ago and they cancelled their plans."

"Yes, you're right. It's just that I feel so damned helpless, so powerless to . . . ." Her hands balled up into fists and, as Lara cried in frustration, Jan stepped over and embraced her. He admired her devotion to their cause. Her passion was a trait that had always attracted him. To Jan, Lara seemed even more beautiful when she was inflamed about some issue. Her blue eyes blazed with an intensity that could pierce a man's soul, and her skin, smooth and clear, glowed from the blood rushing through her veins. He imagined he could see flames extending from the tips of her golden hair. Jan was her ideal counterbalance. While he felt as passionately about the same issues as Lara, he exuded an icy calm that belied his true feelings. Jan had been a champion tennis player in his youth and his role model had been Bjorn Borg, the Swedish tennis star, whose steel composure and icy self-control never revealed his emotions during a difficult match. Consequently, even when his opponents were on the verge of winning, Borg defeated them because his demeanor and steady play eventually broke their will. Jan Shalken had also broken the will of most men who had challenged him, not only on genteel Dutch tennis courts, but also in other aspects of life. The only chink in his otherwise impervious personal armor revealed itself when anyone threatened Lara. Then, he would explode like an angry volcano. Nevertheless, Lara found in Jan an inner strength that fortified her during difficult moments. They complemented each other perfectly and were very much in love.

Lara and Jan also loved the ocean. They had met five years ago, on an unusually warm late-August afternoon along a secluded beach in Holland. Lara was walking the shoreline, flip-flops dangling from her fingers, letting the cool surf splash her toes. She noticed a tall man in the distance, facing the ocean. Jan was watching the North Sea preparing another winter assault on Holland's dikes. His feet sank deeper into the sand as each wave threw itself onto the shore and receded. He looked down at his covered ankles and smiled. A shore breeze whipped the spray off the crest of the crashing waves and Jan smiled again, watching the setting sun create a transient rainbow through the sea mist. He closed his eyes and drew a deep breath, feeling he could draw life from the ocean. Lost in meditation, he never saw or sensed the onrushing wave that knocked him flat. He coughed and rolled over on all fours, as the spent wave ran back to the sea. Trying to catch his breath, he heard gentle laughter. "Mother ocean, are you mocking me?" he said aloud, shaking sand and water out of his hair. Jan was still on his hands and knees when a pair of feet materialized in front of him. He blinked and raised his eyes, following the feet to well-toned legs, an athletic figure, and then to the clearest blue eyes he had ever seen, framed by golden hair reflecting the setting sun. "Mother ocean, you've sent a beautiful mermaid to rescue me!" He heard her laugh above the sound of breaking surf, and then she spoke.

"Oh, I don't live in the ocean. I'm from Amstelveen." Lara reached down and her long hair brushed Jan's face. He inhaled the fragrance. "Let me help you." He grasped Lara's hand, impressed by her strength as she pulled him to his feet. Lara was tall, almost six feet, and she was equally impressed by Jan's robust six-foot-six frame.

"I'm lucky you happened along."

"Yes, I've never come to this beach before," she replied. She reached up and brushed Jan's wet hair, the color of sand, from his eyes. He smiled and his blue eyes sparkled. Lara felt she was looking into the depths of the ocean. "My name is Lara."

"I'm Jan," he replied. His mind raced. *Say something intelligent, you fool. Witty, funny, anything, before she leaves your life as quickly as she entered!* His mind went blank. Suddenly, he shivered.

"Oh, you must be cold, soaked as you are. Is your car near?"

"Yes, behind those dunes."

"Mine too. Come. I'll walk you to your car." They reached a flat rocky area where two cars were parked. They paused, then Lara extended her hand. "Nice to meet you, Jan. Make sure you change quickly when you get home."

"Yes, I will, Lara. I enjoyed meeting you too." He was struck by the warmth and softness of her skin. She turned and walked toward her car. *This is your last chance, you idiot. Another minute and you'll never see her again!* Still blank. Jan sighed and reached into his pocket. Empty! He looked toward the ocean and exclaimed, "Oh no!" Lara wheeled.

"What's wrong, Jan?"

"My car keys! They must have fallen out of my pocket when the wave knocked me over."

"Do I have to rescue you *again?*" she laughed.

"Would you mind giving me a lift? I live less than two kilometers from here. I have a spare set of keys at home."

"Sure. Hop in my car." Jan ran over and jumped in. "I guess this is my day to rescue little boys in trouble."

"Would you like to make a habit of it?" he said, grinning. Lara smiled back. *Not bad, Jan,* said his inner voice.

They married a year later. At their ceremony, they exchanged matching gold bracelets in addition to conventional wedding rings. They engraved a humpback whale, their favorite among the leviathans, on the outside of each bracelet. Inside, they engraved a mutual proclamation of love. Lara detected a tear in Jan's eye when he read the inscription she had engraved in his bracelet: *Dear Jan, my eternal love for you is deeper than the ocean. Love, Lara.*

Lara and Jan fit together like two puzzle pieces, and they never were apart for long. They joined various conservation projects and eventually left their Dutch homeland to work with Peaceful Seas. That was two years ago and they never regretted their decision. The organization's activist policy, directly confronting those polluting coastal waters in courtrooms and whale killers on the high seas attracted them.

Their passion for their causes was only matched by their passion for each other. Now their next dream was only months away from being fulfilled. Prior to leaving on this voyage, Lara's doctor informed her she was one month pregnant. She and Jan had talked frequently about starting a family. Lara planned to tell her husband the good news, but she decided this was not the right time. Later in the voyage, during a happier moment, she would tell him he was going to be a father. And she would see the joy in his sparkling blue eyes.

Chapter 4

Tokyo, Japan

October 23rd

"*S*o tell me about this boat captain of yours," thirty-two-year-old Oshura Haigata asked his counterpart from Iceland, in a hostile tone. Though relatively young in diplomatic circles, Haigata was the senior official of the powerful Fisheries Agency of Japan (FAJ) and Japan's senior delegate to the International Whaling Commission. "If he was an American, *I* would call him a 'cowboy'! What would *you* call him?" he pressed on, raising his voice. Haigata adjusted his glasses, waiting for an answer. The other members attending the unofficial clandestine meeting, from Norway and Finland, shifted in their seats, embarrassed for their fellow diplomat from Iceland, Jon Andresson.

Andresson replied in his best diplomatic-speak, "Well, I agree the captain of the whaler *Arctic Wind* seems out of control, but my government will handle the situation internally. And I apologize to the rest of you for the difficulty this has caused to our efforts."

"'Difficulty' is a mild term for what we are facing now, Mr. Andresson!" Haigata hammered on, undiplomatically. "Our goal to convince the International Whaling Commission to rescind the commercial whaling ban has been seriously jeopardized because of the news accounts and gruesome video of that dead whale broadcast around the world!"

"Jon, can you offer more concrete action, such as revoking his license or having him removed from his position as captain?" Stig Carlson from Norway gently suggested, steering the meeting back to a comfortable diplomatic tone. Before Andresson could reply, Eric Braunnel, the delegate from Finland, tried to minimize the damage, reminding the group to address the larger picture and not dwell on a single incident. "Gentlemen, the uproar this Icelandic cowboy caused distracts us. Let us maintain our focus on a global plan of action."

"I agree wholeheartedly," said Andresson, wiping perspiration from his brow, grateful for the Finland delegate's assistance in diffusing Haigata's diatribe and moving the group to more productive ground.

Haigata pursed his lips in frustration, but decided to discuss the issue with his Icelandic counterpart privately. "Let us move on then," he said. "Our original strategy was to submit our plan to the Whaling Commission at the annual meeting, which begins June 15, I believe." Heads nodded in agreement. "We will propose eliminating the commercial whaling ban for most whales and suggest quotas for the whales we seek to harvest in order to sustain the populations. As I recall, Eric, you suggested requesting a very high quota so we could negotiate down to the numbers we really want and still appear reasonable to the *whale huggers*." He spat out the term in obvious disdain. "So, what do you suggest now, Eric?"

"Well, I have a strategic plan which Stig and I have discussed, and we would like to present it to the group for consideration. But why don't we take a short break first?"

"Fine," said Haigata, "we will reconvene in fifteen minutes." As the delegates left the room to make phone calls and attend to personal matters, Haigata pursued Andresson into the men's room and strategically waited, knowing he would have a captive audience. "Jon, you cannot let this happen again!" he hissed. "Because of this situation, we have an uproar from those sanctimonious sons of bitches in the United States, demonstrations in Britain, and riots in the streets of your own country! My own sympathetic contact on the Whaling Commission privately advised me to delay our efforts for a year, which I cannot do. I have many people here in my country demanding to eat whale meat. Japan has an economic infrastructure in place, whalers, distributors, and restaurateurs, all ready to satisfy the demand. But no whales to catch! Our Ministry of Agriculture, Forestry and Fisheries is depending on me to change the situation!"

Andresson regretted having drunk so much coffee. He was not close to finishing at the urinal and could not escape Haigata's tirade. "Oshura, I understand your situation, which you have made painfully clear. I promise to resolve the problem." Privately, however, Andresson knew that dealing with Ulf Swenson, captain of the *Arctic Wind,* raised issues for him that the Japanese diplomat could not even begin to imagine. *Haigata thinks we are dealing merely with a lowly sea captain whom I, as a deputy prime minister and Iceland's senior delegate to the IWC, should be able to quash like a bug,* he mused. Haigata, a skilled international negotiator, noticed the equivocation in Andresson's eyes as he spoke, piquing his curiosity. "Jon, who is this boat captain causing us such grief?"

"His name is Ulf Swenson, a very experienced whale hunter from my country. He has hunted whales in all the world's oceans, sailing vessels under the flags of several nations." Andresson, himself a skilled negotiator and reader of people, noticed Haigata's eyes widen, ever so slightly, and saw his jaw muscles tense when he heard Swenson's name. *Now there's an interesting reaction,* he thought. He decided to probe. "Do you know him, Oshura?"

"Of course not. Why would someone such as myself ever have a reason to know a vulgar, uncouth boat captain from Iceland? I will accept your personal pledge to resolve the problem. I'll see you inside. I hope Eric and Stig have put together an effective plan to get us back on track," he said, turning on his heels and slamming the door as he left the lavatory. *For someone who supposedly doesn't know Ulf Swenson, that was an unusually accurate description,* reflected Andresson.

Chapter 5

October 24th

"*L*et me summarize our strategy and action plan," Oshura Haigata began, as he opened the final session of the clandestine meeting the following morning. "Please correct me if I misstate facts or fail to mention any significant points. First, I want to thank the delegates from Norway and Finland for their excellent presentation yesterday." He smiled directly at Stig Carlson and Eric Braunnel, but his gaze turned steely as he glanced briefly at Jon Andresson.

"We will wait three months to allow public emotion to cool from this latest incident involving killing that fin whale. Hopefully, there will not be any repeat performances to fuel our detractors' efforts." He paused, looked up briefly from his notes, and threw another withering glance toward Andresson, who inhaled audibly while maintaining eye contact with Haigata. He continued, "Our four nations will jointly petition the IWC to vote at the June meeting in Iceland on our proposal to resume unrestricted commercial whaling. The only exception will be for whale populations that have been *scientifically* proven to be in danger." Haigata stressed the word "scientifically," since he and the group knew this would be an important strategic loophole they could exploit at their convenience. "We will not mention quotas but we will negotiate this point and agree to quotas, demonstrating our combined nations' sensitivity with a conciliatory and reasonable approach. Have I summed up our overall position accurately?" All three delegates nodded affirmatively.

"Fine. Now, here are the specific action items that we have agreed upon. Again, if I misstate anyone's position, please correct me. The government of Japan will use its influence in Asia, Central America, and the Caribbean, to persuade countries in those regions to vote favorably toward our position." Haigata continued, "My government will use financial incentives and other positive economic and political inducements wherever possible. However, we are prepared to use negative inducements for leverage, withdrawing economic aid if necessary. We will also utilize our public relations assets within the United States to blunt American opposition efforts by exploiting a weakness in their position, which they themselves have created. I am referring to the United States permitting native Alaskan populations to harvest whales as part of their traditional heritage. We can keep them off balance pointing out the hypocrisy of the U.S. government granting internal citizens permission to kill whales while opposing whaling by other countries.

"Stig Carlson, you will ensure the Norwegian government continues to block the development and establishment of the DNA registry of whales that are sold. As long as this registry is not in effect, no one can prove with certainty what kinds of whales are being killed. Japan can also provide assistance here, if needed."

"Thank you, Oshura. We appreciate any assistance you can provide."

"Eric and Jon, you will request that the governments of Finland and Iceland lobby other members, arguing that whales are responsible for dwindling fish stocks, and killing more whales will result in an increase in the availability of fish for all countries. In addition, my contact at the IWC has informed me they are considering something called a 'Revised Management Scheme,' for controlling whaling. You may hear it referred to as the RMS. We need you to join the working committees to find out what measures are being proposed so we can advocate proposals ensuring all whaling bans are lifted and that enforcement provisions in the rules are weak or non-enforceable."

"We are prepared to handle those assignments," said Eric Braunnel, from Finland, looking at Jon Andresson from Iceland for confirmation.

"As can we," said Andresson.

"That is all I have," concluded Haigata. "Does anyone have anything else to add?" As his eyes scanned the room, there was only silence, indicating uniform assent to the plan. "Then we can adjourn. Thank you all for attending, for your cooperation and your support. With our united efforts, I firmly believe we will succeed in June. I will arrange to have the meeting minutes distributed before you leave tomorrow. Please treat these documents as highly confidential. No leaks! It must appear to the world community that our countries have arrived at these conclusions and developed these proposals as the result of independent, scientific analysis. For a celebration, I have arranged dinner at a wonderful restaurant tonight. It has been reserved only for us, to ensure total privacy, and they serve the best whale steaks in Japan. I will see you all there at eight o'clock."

At the mention of the evening's menu, the other three delegates exchanged glances. Except for Oshura Haigata, none of them had ever tasted whale meat.

Chapter 6

Cozumel

December 11th

Terry and Joe enjoyed a pleasant breakfast on the front portico of their home, overlooking the channel, facing west toward the Yucatan mainland. The angle of the sun, rising behind them from the east, lit the scene like a bright painting. "I never get tired of this view," said Joe. "Look at those amazing colors!" The early-morning air, not yet laden with the steamy moisture from the day's coming heat, was crystal clear, creating a vivid tapestry. "I don't think I've ever seen the sky so blue."

"You said that two mornings ago," Terry countered playfully.

"Look at the different shades of blue and green in the water. So beautiful it's almost unreal, artificial!"

"I recall you also said *that* three days ago."

"Well, what if I did," Joe replied, a little defensively. "It's still fantastic, and I love it!"

"I know. I love it too. And you too," Terry said, leaning across the small table and kissing Joe. A loud splash interrupted the moment. They looked toward the shoreline and saw a brown pelican in the water, shaking its head as it maneuvered a captive fish in its basketlike bill after a successful dive. The pelican finally aligned the hapless fish with its gullet, swallowing it in a single gulp. "Well, I guess it's his breakfast time too," said Terry.

They watched the dive boats heading to the various reefs, sporting their colorful dive flags, brilliant red severed by a diagonal white stripe. "I love watching Cozumel come to life each morning," she sighed. "But I'm glad we scheduled today off. I need a break. You coming to the doctor with me?"

"Sure. I just hope we get good news for a change." They had started trying to have children shortly after they were married a year ago, but Terry had suffered a miscarriage in the first trimester and had been unable to become pregnant since. Joe was thirty-five years old and missed the lively day-to-day chaos of family life. Four years earlier, he had lost his family. An SUV-load of stoned kids speeding in the wrong direction late one night on a Long Island highway killed Joe's pregnant wife, Jenny, and three-year-old twin boys, Bobby and Andy. Ever since, he had hoped for the opportunity to raise a family again. Terry, twenty-nine years old, expected she would have children with Mark Stafford, her late fiancé. But during a research expedition in the Channel Islands off Southern California, a great white shark ended her dream. She and Joe felt grateful that fate had thrown them together, granting them a second chance.

"Well, Terry, I wish I had better news for you today," began Doctor José Ortega. "But, unfortunately, the tests indicate you are still not pregnant." Joe held Terry's hand firmly and her eyes began to tear, as Doctor Ortega continued. "But the good news is that you are a healthy young woman, not even thirty years old, and there are no reasons why you cannot successfully conceive again and carry a baby to full term."

"Then what can I do, Doctor?" Terry pleaded, as much with her eyes as with her voice. "We've been trying for months."

"Well, look. You are extremely stressed over this situation, and you work very hard, even though you enjoy what you do. I recommend you both take a vacation. Relax and see what happens. You know, our bodies work much better when we are in harmony with our surroundings and with ourselves. If nothing happens in the next few months, there are other things we can explore. But let's try this idea first, yes?"

"That sounds like a prescription we can handle," Joe said cheerfully to Terry as she forced a smile. "Thank you, Doctor. We'll follow your advice and send you a postcard from an exotic location."

"Then I look forward to receiving one, from a remote, deserted paradise. Just have a good trip and give fate a chance to work its magic."

Neither said much on the ride back home, each lost in private thoughts. Finally, Terry broke the silence. "What do you think about what Dr. Ortega said, Joe?"

"About what, Ter?"

"You know, his comment about letting fate work its magic. Do you believe that strongly in fate?"

"Gee, I don't know. I've always believed in taking charge, controlling your own destiny. I don't know how much room that leaves for fate. What do you think?"

"I never thought too much about it until now. But sometimes things happen, and it seems like they were just meant to happen. Is that fate?" Before Joe could answer, they arrived home. Upon entering the spacious, quiet house, their eyes subconsciously wandered toward the empty rooms they hoped one day would be children's bedrooms. Joe took Terry's hand and led her into their bedroom and held her tightly. They continued their embrace, letting their bodies react to each other. Joe ran his hands through Terry's long, auburn hair and gently pulled her head back so he could look into her deep, green eyes. After holding his gaze for several long seconds, Terry leaned forward and kissed Joe, sliding her tongue along his lips and then into his mouth. The sensation hit Joe like a surge of electricity and Terry felt his body shudder. Joe pulled Terry down on the bed next to him.

"I love you, Joe."

"And I love you, Ter. Very much." They spoke no other words for many passionate minutes.

Chapter 7

The Silver Bank, Dominican Republic

January 8th

*T*he trio of whales finally reached the warm, shallow waters of the Dominican Republic's Silver Bank after a three-month journey from New England. Mariners had named the location for the sunken treasure of silver-laden Spanish galleons that foundered on the Bank's coral reefs during the seventeenth century. The bull escort broke away from the pair to join other males. They would form into "rowdy groups" that would joust, sometimes violently, to establish dominance. The female whale's young offspring, now a forty-thousand-pound one-year-old, would leave his mother more frequently to socialize with other juvenile whales in rough horseplay, the precursor to mating battles he would fight upon reaching sexual maturity in several years. Now, his mother sought the company of other female humpbacks as her delivery time approached. It was a time to relax and conserve energy in the warm, calm waters of their naturally protected environment.

Several nights later, as the female humpback glided silently just below the surface, rising only to breathe, she felt a brief stab of pain. Her brain recognized the familiar sensations of contractions. She sensed her time had come. She continued swimming until she found the location for which she was searching. It was a quiet area of the Silver Bank, a location memorized from past visits. Only sixty feet deep and sheltered on three sides by large coral heads rising within ten feet of the surface, it formed a broad horseshoe a quarter mile across. The space was too confining for groups of young, rowdy males who might otherwise come barreling through, and it was protected from ocean swells, which were dangerously powerful on windy days. It was the perfect place to birth a baby whale.

Cruising along the surface, she rolled slightly and looked up at a bright, full moon that bathed the nighttime ocean in silver light. She felt another contraction and knew that before the sun rose in the morning, her baby would be born. After several more contractions she drifted down to twenty feet. Slowly but forcefully, she began pumping her flukes, gently pushing the baby whale through the birth canal. After two hours of labor, a pair of small flukes emerged. Unlike human babies, whales and dolphins are born head-last to prevent drowning, while the placenta continues supplying oxygen. Two more hours of hard labor passed and half a small whale was squirming outside its mother. Another hour passed and then with one last giant push and a gush of blood, the baby whale, a very healthy fourteen-foot fifteen-hundred-pound female was born.

The mother humpback quickly wheeled around and came up under her baby, gently nudging her to the surface for her first breath. The pair continued swimming and breathing in unison even though the mother whale did not have to breathe as frequently as her baby. The newborn whale quickly learned swimming was easier close to her mother. She dropped back, next to her mother, and enjoyed an effortless ride in her mother's slipstream. Every few minutes, her mother rolled to one side, exposing her teats and, after a short while, her baby found the source of nourishment, the richest milk on earth.

Specialized breast muscles enabled the mother humpback to actually pump milk into her baby, adding pounds to her each day.

During the following days, the pair enjoyed the post-partum bonding experience, which involved continuous rubbing and brushing up against each other, frequent nursing, and nuzzling chins and heads together. Cetaceans are extremely tactile creatures and, as mammals, have hairs growing from bumps in the head and jaw area, which pick up sensations the same way as a cat's whiskers. Rubbing and caressing not only felt enjoyable, but also reinforced the bond between mother and baby. They spent their days enjoying floating weightless in the warm water, and gently rubbing their sensitive skin as the baby whale swam alongside, under, and on top of her mother.

The bull whale that had escorted the pregnant whale and her offspring to the Silver Bank was not in the immediate area, so she would not likely be the object of male competition for sexual favors this year. She needed a season away from the effort and resulting consequences of mating. For the next month, life was good for the two whales. The baby satisfied her natural curiosity by examining her environment, learning that most coral was rough, and sponges soft. She also realized the small, strange creatures splashing into the water from strange, noisy objects at the surface seemed to be friendly, and very curious about her as well.

They spent their days enjoying the sensation of floating weightless in the warm water, and gently rubbing their sensitive skin as the baby whale swam alongside, under, and on top of her mother.

Photo by Paul J. Mila

Chapter 8

The North Atlantic

January 23rd

*U*lf Swenson maneuvered the *Arctic Wind* through sleet and rolling ocean swells as he followed a large finback whale. Finally, he was in position for the kill, when his first mate interrupted him. "You must take this call, Captain."

"Damn it! Can't you see I'm busy?"

"I'm sorry, Captain, but it's urgent, from the capital."

"Give me the goddamn phone," he snarled, grabbing the receiver from the mate. "Swenson here!" He listened for a minute, while watching the harpooner aim for a shot. "Fire the cannon! What the hell's wrong with you?" he shouted to the gunner, while listening to the angry tirade coming through the phone. "So, what the hell do I care if Andresson got his ass reamed at a meeting?" he said to the caller. After listening for several minutes he slammed the receiver down in disgust. "Political assholes," he hissed. "Gudmund, I have the ship in perfect position! What's the problem out there?"

"I can't shoot, Captain," replied his harpooner. "A Zodiac is in the way."

Swenson looked ahead and saw Lara Schalken's long blonde hair blowing in the salt spray. She was expertly piloting the Zodiac, keeping herself and two fellow crewmembers between the deadly harpoon gun and the whale, essentially acting as human shields. On the back of her orange slicker, Swenson recognized a familiar emblem he hated: an angel holding a shield, riding on a whale's back. After weaving between the *Arctic Wind* and the targeted whale for twenty minutes, Lara and the crew aboard the Zodiac worried that the harpooner would recklessly fire his weapon in frustration. Finally, they watched, relieved, as the *Arctic Wind* broke off the chase. Swenson turned the rudder sharply to port, glaring at the Zodiac's crew as they whooped and cheered. Lara looked back over her shoulder and saw Swenson watching her. She smiled, defiantly thrusting her fist high in triumph. No whale would be killed this day. Watching the action through his binoculars from a mile away, Jan Shalken slammed his fist on the helm in a burst of emotion. "Way to go, Lara!" he shouted.

"We'll see what happens next time we meet," muttered Swenson. "Take over. I need a drink," he told the first mate as he stormed from the wheelhouse, intent on soothing his raging temper with strong brandy from his private liquor stock. Stomping to his cabin, he brushed past a young seaman in the narrow hallway, pinning him against the wall with a heavily muscled forearm. "Watch where the hell you're walking, lad."

"Sorry sir, I mean Ca-Captain," stammered the petrified seaman, looking up into Swenson's fierce blue eyes, blazing with anger. "It won't happen again, Captain."

"Stupid little son of a bitch," he heard Swenson mutter as he disappeared into his cabin. In the ship's galley, the young seaman, shaken after his encounter with Swenson, met Gudmund Vikinsson, who was relaxing with a cup of hot tea, still angry after being stymied by the Zodiac's crew.

"What's wrong, Erwin? You look like you've just run into the devil."

"I wish I had, Gudmund. It was worse. I accidentally bumped into the captain in the hallway. I thought he was going to kill me!"

"Oh, he'll get over it soon enough, Erwin. Trust me. He'll forget he even saw you. He doesn't like having his plans upset, especially by a woman."

"He scares me, Gudmund. He looks so fierce with that shark-tooth necklace he wears. Where did he find such huge shark teeth?"

"He found them in the jaws of a great white he killed several years ago." Vikinsson watched Erwin's eyes grow large. "We'd been having a run of bad luck. Hadn't even seen a whale for several days. We were all getting anxious about the prospect of returning with almost nothing to show for our efforts. Everyone was staying clear of Swenson. He was in a very foul mood. Late in the afternoon our lookout spotted a pod of minke whales. I harpooned a decent-sized whale, thirty-five-footer. We were securing it alongside the ship when this huge great white came up, like something from the depths of hell. It started ripping out chunks of flesh. We tried hitting it with long poles, even shooting at it with a rifle. It just ignored us. The shark was huge, six meters at least, maybe seven. Furious, Swenson ran to his cabin and grabbed an old, rusty nineteenth-century harpoon from the wall. Then he ran back and jumped over the side of the ship onto the whale's floating body. He rammed the harpoon into the shark's head again and again, until he killed it. We heard him yelling at the shark. He was a madman, shouting something about how dare it try to steal his whale. Just before the dead shark sank into the sea, he reached into its mouth with his bare hands and tore out several teeth."

"With his bare hands?"

"Aye. It was a sight we'll never forget. There was blood in the water from the shark and from the whale. Swenson's clothes and arms were covered with blood because he slashed his hands ripping out the shark's teeth. I wish I had a camera. He had a wild look in his eyes, too. The doctor gave him over sixty stitches to close the wounds. Swenson never said a word, never felt a thing. He made the necklace and he's worn it ever since. The story has become a legend of sorts in the whaling community, and the necklace has been an amulet to him. He feels it brings him good luck and his enemies bad luck. And he has more than a few enemies. Anyone even *thinking* about challenging him just looks at that necklace, the four large shark teeth, and they back off. It reminds them of the violence he's capable of when angry."

"Then I'm glad I didn't make him any angrier than I did," remarked the young seaman. "Has he always been such an evil-tempered man?"

"Well, as long as I've known him, and I suppose I've known him longer and better than anyone else. He never talks about his boyhood, but I sense he had a difficult time growing up. He mentions his mother occasionally but never his father. I think he grew up poor, perhaps abandoned by his father, always fighting for whatever he got. I'm not sure which made him angrier, the grinding poverty or his father's rejection. But I'll give you this piece of advice, lad. Steer clear of him, no matter what his mood."

Chapter 9

Cozumel

January 25th

"*W*hat's on the board for today?" asked Joe, washing down the remains of a scrambled egg breakfast with refreshingly cold orange juice while Terry listened to a new voice mail message on their answering machine.

"Well, we already have a group of four divers for a two-tank dive this morning, but I just got another message from someone who wants to do a single dive this afternoon."

"Just one diver? Can't we combine her with this morning's group or another group tomorrow?"

"Well, there's no time to pick her up now, and she's flying home to the Netherlands tomorrow night. This afternoon's the only time she can dive before she leaves."

"Can't we just blow her off?" asked Joe. "We don't break even, taking one diver."

"Oh I know, hon, but I feel sorry for her. She said she had a horrible week with the dive shop she booked. Said it was like a cattle car, too many divers, very disorganized, and not much fun. Let's do it for her."

"Hey, you're the boss. I'm just the silent partner."

"Oh, and such a sweet partner too," Terry cooed, kissing his cheek. "I'll call her back and tell her we'll pick her up at two o'clock this afternoon."

"Okay, I'll be in the truck," said Joe as he took the keys and went downstairs.

The morning's dives went smoothly. Terry led the first one, a deep dive to eighty feet on Santa Rosa Wall. The group spent their required forty-five minute surface interval relaxing and discussing the sponges, coral and fish they had observed along the wall. Joe was the dive master on the second dive, shallower, to sixty feet at Paso Del Cedral. After dropping the four divers at their hotel pier, Terry and Joe remained on the *Dorado* and had lunch with Manuel and Pepe before picking up their lone customer. "Any vacation ideas?" asked Joe.

"Nope. I checked our calendar and we only have a small group next week and then we can clear out for a few weeks of R&R. We can refer any dive customers to my buddy Enrico while we're away. But I don't have any preferences on where we go, do you?"

"Not really. Let's figure it out over dinner tonight."

"Sounds like a plan. How about Pancho's Backyard?"

"It's a date," said Joe, remembering when he and Terry had their first dinner at Pancho's. He recalled it was the first time he had felt any real attraction for another woman after the death of his wife. "Hey, we better get moving if we're going to pick up our solo diver. Manuel, Pepe, let's shove off!"

Fifteen minutes later the *Dorado* arrived at the Reef Club pier, where a tall woman with short-cut light-brown hair, dressed in a wet suit, carrying fins, mask, and snorkel, waited. "Are you Femke van der Zee?" asked Terry.

"Yes, you must be Terry, from DiveWithTerry?"

43

"That's me," said Terry, in typically upbeat fashion. "And this is my husband and partner, Joe."

"Pleased to meet both of you," said Femke. "And thank you so much for agreeing to squeeze me in today. I really appreciate your service."

"Hey, no problem for a fellow diver," said Terry. "I believe you said you needed a regulator, BC and weights. Correct?"

"Yes, I have everything else, including my own dive computer." She passed her fins and mask to Terry, gripped the railing supporting the canvas top of the boat, and jumped into the pitching boat. *She seems pretty athletic, so she probably can handle herself in the water,* Terry noted. Femke reached into a small waterproof bag. "Here's my certification card," she said, handing it to Terry for inspection.

"Thanks. Any preference on where you'd like to dive?"

"Oh no, anywhere where I can see something interesting. I have an advanced rating, so I think I can handle any of the dive sites here."

"Well, we can get to Chankanaab Reef quickly. There's always plenty of diverse sea life there. It's not too challenging, pretty easy actually. Since you only have time for one dive, that would be my recommendation for an interesting dive."

"Fine by me. You're the expert."

"By the way, your English is very good," interjected Joe. "Have you always lived in the Netherlands?"

"Well, my father worked for a major international oil company. We moved around the world quite a bit when I was young and I spent a lot of time in English-speaking countries. And I was also an au pair in the Midwest of your country for several years when I was a teenager. I learned a lot about American customs, slang, and so forth. But that was many years ago."

"That can't have been too many years ago," said Terry.

"Oh, you're very kind. I'm in my early fifties, and . . ."

"Really?" said Joe. "You're in great shape, and you seem very fit for your . . . ah," Joe said, groping, trying to rescue his well-intentioned compliment from the minefield into which he had verbally blundered.

"My *age,* you mean," laughed Femke, finishing Joe's sentence for him.

"I always go around apologizing for my husband," interjected Terry, good-naturedly. "You'll have to excuse him. He doesn't get out socially very often. By the way, is there a translation for your name?" she asked, smoothly shifting the topic.

"Yes. In Dutch, Femke van der Zee means, 'Woman of the Sea.' My sister and I were, I should say, *are,* real ocean lovers. My parents made sure we could swim almost before we could walk, and everyplace we lived was always near the ocean. We spent many happy days on many beaches together. We were two water rats. No one could ever get us out of the water," she laughed.

"Sounds like you two were very close. Do you still see each other frequently? asked Terry.

"Unfortunately, no. My sister married the love of her life and travels quite a bit, so I don't see her as often as I'd like. But we are still close, if you know what I mean." Terry nodded and smiled, as Femke continued. "I'm still looking for the right guy, but I feel fulfilled. The ocean sustains me. I've dived all over the world, in the Red Sea, the North Atlantic, the Pacific, but my favorite place is the Caribbean. I think it's the most beautiful location on earth."

"Wow! That's an impressive diving résumé," said Joe.

"Yes, I've been fortunate to dive in many diverse environments." As she spoke, Joe noted that her light eyes, contrasting against her tan skin, seemed to change color, depending on the reflection of the ocean, from pale blue to sea-green.

"We're here!" exclaimed Terry. "Let's go diving!" As they suited up, Terry gave a simple dive plan. "We'll descend to forty feet and cruise along the bottom, which slopes to sixty feet. It's a long reef, with good coral formations broken by large patches of sandy areas, so we have a chance to see eels, rays, large grouper, almost anything. Plan for about fifty minutes bottom time and a three-minute safety stop at fifteen feet. When we surface, Manuel will have the boat nearby."

"Sounds fine," said Femke.

"Okay, we'll do a backward roll into the water when you're ready."

The trio descended quickly and Terry saw by Femke's relaxed demeanor that she was an accomplished diver. *Swims like a fish and she's not breathing rapidly; she knows her stuff,* thought Terry. The current was mild, making it easy to stop and examine interesting small animals living on the reef community of coral and sponges. They saw tiny shrimp, feathery Christmas-tree worms, which looked like little flowers until Femke reached out with her finger, causing them to retract in the blink of an eye. They encountered numerous juvenile fish, hiding in crevasses to avoid becoming a meal for larger predators. Then both women saw Joe pointing excitedly and swam over and saw a large green moray eel poking his head from under a small rock outcropping, a perfect ambush spot for catching an easy meal. They hovered over the eel and watched it rhythmically open and close its mouth, revealing needle-sharp teeth. While the eel's behavior appeared menacing, they knew the moray was just breathing by pumping water through its gills.

As they watched the eel, Terry felt a familiar tingling sensation through her mid-section. Realizing what it was, she whirled around. Suddenly, two grey torpedo shapes buzzed the group, startling Joe and Femke. It was a pair of bottlenose dolphins. Terry saw a familiar notch in the tail of the larger dolphin and realized it was Notchka and her year-old female calf, whom Terry had not yet named. Terry never ceased to marvel that Notchka trusted humans enough to bring her new calf to play with them after a human had brutally killed her first offspring. Terry thought she would never see her again. Joe was mesmerized watching the two dolphins, but Femke immediately reacted, undulating her body, swimming in dolphin-like fashion and turning barrel rolls. Terry saw the dolphins were amused and that Femke's actions had caught their attention. She was also surprised the dolphins stayed so close, knowing snorkelers have better encounters because the bubbles from scuba divers usually scare dolphins away. She watched, enthralled, as Notchka presented Femke with a long string of seaweed, so they could play the dolphin version of "keep-away." Terry watched as Femke swam with the seaweed, followed by the dolphins, who swiped the seaweed only when Femke purposely let it go after an appropriate period. She realized that Femke was playing the game according to dolphin rules. Terry wondered, *where did she learn about dolphin culture?*

Soon they heard the metallic sound of someone banging on a scuba tank for attention. They saw Joe pointing to his dive watch and then to his air gauge, indicating they had been down for the planned time and reminding them to check their air supply. Terry nodded, checked her air and gave a thumbs-up sign, indicating they should ascend slowly to fifteen feet for their three-minute safety stop before surfacing. Ascending, they waved goodbye to the dolphins, who had grown bored playing with the humans and were leaving the area. Bobbing on the surface waiting for the *Dorado* to pick them up, Femke was overjoyed. "Oh, what a thrill! I never expected to see dolphins today!" she exclaimed.

"Awesome!" yelled Joe, as Terry laughed at him.

Back on board, Terry said to Femke, "Looks like you know your way around dolphinville."

"Yes, I've swum with them many times, in Hawaii, Florida, the Bahamas, and other places. I feel that if I call to them, they'll come. I feel a oneness with their spirit, that I can communicate with them, and they with me. I also believe they can greatly influence our lives."

"Really," said Joe, exchanging glances with Terry and not knowing what to say to Femke regarding her views on dolphins. She intercepted their glances and laughed.

"Oh, I can see you don't believe me. You think I am, how do you say it in English, 'way out there.' But I think it's true. They really can affect us and our lives."

"You know, just before I saw them I got this strange sensation in my stomach," Joe said, changing the subject.

"They were scanning your innards with their sonar, dear. I guess they wanted to see what you ate for breakfast," joked Terry.

"Can they do that? See inside you, I mean?"

"Yep. They can actually use sound waves to see inside objects. They could see your internal organs and know if something was wrong."

Joe looked at Femke, who nodded her head affirmatively, confirming Terry's statement about dolphin capability. "Good thing they aren't MDs," he said. "I might get a bill in the mail."

"Yes," joked Femke, laughing, "Take two aspirins and mail me a tuna."

Twenty minutes later they arrived at the Reef Club pier, and exchanged brief hugs and handshakes. "Have a good flight home," shouted Terry as the *Dorado* pulled away.

"Thanks, it was great diving with you."

"And now that you have our number, call us next time you plan diving in Cozumel."

"You can count on it! You saved my vacation with one superb dive. Thanks again."

"She's a real nice lady," Joe said, waving.

"Yes, I hope we see her again one day," replied Terry. "Well, let's get back home and change for dinner. That was a long day and I'm famished! I'm in the mood for Pancho's Backyard."

Chapter 10

January 25th

*T*erry and Joe parked their car and entered Pancho's Backyard, their favorite restaurant. It was located on a quiet section of the waterfront thoroughfare, Rafael Melgar, just past the bustling T-shirt palaces, jewelry shops, and other stores selling everything from trinkets to Cuban cigars. Pancho's was tastefully decorated. Low lighting, tables separated by natural vegetation and a real open-air backyard provided authentic Mexican ambiance. They were surprised to see every table filled and a crowd waiting. "Gee, I never thought to make a reservation. This place is never this crowded," said Joe.

"Well, dear, I guess it's getting more popular. You haven't been telling the tourists how good the food is, have you?"

"Hey, you know me. Loose lips sink ships."

"And create crowded restaurants too, I guess," said Terry, glancing at the full tables. After a fifteen-minute wait sipping margaritas on the rocks with salt, they were escorted to their table. Terry glanced toward the door and saw Femke van der Zee. "Look Joe, there's Femke. She's alone and she'll never get a table for one person with this crowd. Okay with you if I ask her to join us?"

"Sure, why not."

"Femke, over here," Terry called, waving. Femke was surprised to see them. She smiled and waved back. "You won't get a table by yourself. How about joining us?"

"Are you sure you don't mind?"

"Of course not," said Joe, stepping over and pulling out a chair.

"Isn't he gallant?" teased Terry, as Femke laughed.

They toasted each other with a round of margaritas. "Here's to a safe trip back home," said Joe.

"And to many more good dives, hopefully with you good friends again one day," replied Femke, clinking glasses. Waiting for the waiter to bring menus, Femke asked, "So, how did you two meet? I take it you're from different parts of the United States?"

"You're right about that. How did you know?" asked Terry.

"Well, I cannot place your accent, but Joe's accent I recognize as from the New York area."

"You got me," confessed Joe. "Born and bred in New York. Grew up in Brooklyn and moved to a suburban area called Long Island. Hey, you're pretty sharp. You should've been a cop."

"Was being a policeman your profession?"

"Yes ma'am, NYPD. Also known as New York's finest. Made it all the way up to detective-lieutenant, gold shield and all."

"Yes," interjected Terry, "they promoted Joe for cracking an international cocaine smuggling ring and, *especially* for rescuing a damsel in distress."

"You, I presume?"

"None other," said Joe.

"Oh, how romantic!" exclaimed Femke. "I always dreamed about being rescued by the brave knight on a white horse."

"Well, in this case, it was more like the scared cop on the speedboat. And the real hero was the dolphin that you met today, Notchka."

"Really?"

"Yes," said Terry. "My white knight was running a bit late and the bad guy, Oscar, was trying to kill me. Notchka dispatched him by ramming him and pulverizing his vital organs. Unfortunately, Oscar had already fatally stabbed her son, Lucky, and he was preparing to do the same to me when she killed him."

"Oh, how dreadful! But at least it brought you two together. And Terry, you came from?"

"From sunny California," said Terry.

"Oh, were you what they call a *surfing girl?*" laughed Femke, restoring a more lighthearted mood at the table.

"Well, not exactly. I was studying marine biology at the University of Santa Barbara, living with my boyfriend, Mark, who was also a graduate assistant there. We were on a research expedition to the Channel Islands, about a hundred miles off the California coast. We were documenting certain aspects of shark behavior. During our final dive, a great white shark attacked and killed him. I had too many memories in Santa Barbara so eventually I moved to Monterey Bay, where I became a dive instructor. After a couple of years I needed a fresh start, so I came to Cozumel and began my life anew. I worked for a dive shop for several years. Eventually, I left and opened my own operation, *DiveWithTerry.*" While Terry was telling her story, Femke saw she was unconsciously fingering a gold diver charm on a chain around her neck. Femke noticed a diamond set where the diver's faceplate would have been and made a logical assumption.

"And he was also your fiancé?"

"Well, he had planned to give me the ring at the end of the trip, but he never got the chance. I didn't learn about his intentions until his mother told me after his memorial service. She gave me the ring and I had the diamond set here," Terry explained, showing Femke the charm.

"My my, that's quite a story. And Joe, you decided to leave the police and return to be with your new love?"

"Not immediately, but eventually I did. After we put the bad guys away, I stayed on the force for a while. I gained quite a bit of international experience working that case, so they gave me more challenging assignments. I met interesting people in international law enforcement, even some from your country. But after being separated from Terry, I realized how much I missed her and how much I needed her. She was the only woman I ever met who reached me as deeply as my late wife. I knew I couldn't live without her."

"So," Femke, summed up, slowly, "you two came from entirely different backgrounds, separated by over four thousand kilometers, you each suffered personal tragedies in your lives, and were given the chance to be united . . . .by a dolphin."

Joe and Terry just stared at each other in silence. Each knew the other was reflecting on what Femke had said earlier about dolphins affecting people's lives. After several seconds of pensive silence, Joe said, "Well, I never thought about . . . ."

"Excuse me," the waiter interrupted, "here are your menus. Let me tell you about our specials."

After selecting dinner, Terry asked, "What kind of work do you do, Femke?"

"Well, I was a social worker but now I'm retired. Actually, I should say semi-retired. I still work several days a week with handicapped children."

"That sounds interesting, said Joe."

"Yes it is, and very fulfilling. When I stopped working I drifted aimlessly for a several months. I felt like a ship without a rudder. Then, one day my sister called me and told me about this position. I applied and with my social service background got the job. Some of the children have physical handicaps but most have various degrees of autism and other learning disabilities. We find that having them interact with animals improves their socialization skills."

"Really?" Remarked Terry.

"Yes. In fact we even use dolphin therapy with some of the children. It's absolutely amazing to see the effect dolphins have on them. The most withdrawn child all of a sudden opens up and communicates after a session with a dolphin."

"I think I read about that therapy being used in some parts of the U.S.", said Joe.

"Well, no wonder you are so in tune with dolphins," said Terry. As Femke smiled, Terry noticed she was wearing a silver tail on a braided silver chain. "What a beautiful charm. I didn't notice it under your wet suit. Is that a dolphin tail?"

"No, actually it's a humpback tail."

"So, I gather you're a whale lover as well as a dolphin lover," asked Joe.

"Yes, I usually swim with them for about a week in the Dominican Republic every year," Femke replied. Terry blinked and shook her head, not believing what she had just heard.

"Excuse me. You do *what*, with *whom, where?"*

"I swim with the humpbacks every year, usually for a week during February or March, in the Dominican Republic," Femke replied, matter-of-factly.

"I love it!" exclaimed Joe. "She says it like, 'Oh I take a walk to the grocery store to buy a quart of milk every so often.'"

"I didn't know you could do that," Terry said. "I thought whales were protected and only scientists with special permits could approach them in the water."

"Well, the area is a whale sanctuary, a breeding and mating area. As far as I know, it's the only place in the world where ordinary people can do it. Only boats with special permits from the Dominican government are allowed to bring tourists there. It's very regulated."

"Tell me more," said Terry, her natural curiosity piqued.

"Well, if you go to this website you can get all the details," she said, writing down the dot-com address.

"Suddenly I have a funny feeling I know where we're going on our vacation," said Joe, smiling at Femke.

"Joe, this is amazing. Imagine, swimming with humpbacks, in the water, right next to them!"

"Is it dangerous?" he asked.

"Well, if one of them breached or did a tale slap or pec fin slap on top of you it would certainly ruin your day, but the crew is very careful. They only let you in the water when the whales seem calm."

"Interesting," said Joe, pensively. "Well, the food's here. Enjoy!"

After a leisurely dinner, Joe and Terry dropped Femke at her hotel, where, after another round of goodbye kisses, they bid each other farewell. Joe and Terry returned home after midnight. They were exhausted after a long day of diving, but Terry was pumped about the prospect of swimming with whales. "I'm hitting the sack," said Joe, wearily.

"Oh, please take me to see the whales, pretty please," Terry said playfully, following him into the bedroom and putting her arms around him. "If you say yes, I'll make it worth your while, I promise," she cooed softly in his ear, kissing him and then slipping her hand down Joe's leg and around to his inner thigh, while staring seductively into his eyes.

"You certainly have an effective way of waking a guy up, lady," said Joe, pulling her close against him, kissing her lips passionately. Their tongues danced around each other for several seconds, when Terry said, "You're right about my interesting techniques, mister, but you're wrong on the other count."

"What's that?" asked Joe, breathing heavily, slipping his hands under Terry's blouse, enjoying the feel of her soft skin and gently caressing her breasts.

"This is no time for me to be a lady," she said, quickly slipping out of her skirt and kissing him as she rolled on top.

Chapter 11

The North Atlantic

January 26th

*T*he *Arctic Wind* had slipped away from the *Sea Angel II* one foggy evening, attempting to hunt whales without interference. The following morning, the sun had burned off the fog and the windless sea was unusually calm. Jan Shalken scanned the horizon from his ship's bridge, trying to locate the whaler. "Lara, over there off the starboard bow!"

"Looks like a pod of sperm whales," she said. "See how their blows rise at an angle, not straight up like other whales?"

"Aye, I see it. That gives them away every time. And it looks like someone else has spotted them too," he said ominously, handing Lara the binoculars. She panned the horizon and saw the *Arctic Wind* bearing down on the whales, but it was closer and on a more favorable heading.

"We're too far away to intercept them in time, Jan. This ship is too damn slow! We can't wait. Let me take the Zodiac now. I'll take an extra can of gas in case I need it."

Jan knew she was right, but did not feel comfortable letting the small Zodiac stray so far from the ship. But he also knew that Lara would not be dissuaded. "Okay, Lara. Take Peter and Carl with you, but be careful. No foolish chances."

"I'll be careful, my love. Wish us luck."

"And Godspeed," he replied. They kissed and she ran down to the main deck and launched the Zodiac. Several minutes later, Lara, Peter, and Carl were bounding over moderate swells, three to five feet, racing to intercept the *Arctic Wind* and prevent a slaughter. As the pirate whaler closed on the sperm whale pod, Ulf Swenson shouted to the harpooner, Vikinsson, poised on the ship's prow, "Pick out a big one, Gudmund!"

The first mate on the bridge interrupted Swenson. "Sir, a Zodiac is rapidly approaching from the port side."

"Shit!" exclaimed Swenson, clenching his teeth. He squeezed the helm so tightly his knuckles turned white as he watched the Zodiac closing fast, cutting off his angle on the whales. Vikinsson was hunched over his weapon, preparing to shoot a large bull sperm whale directly ahead of the ship. He stood erect as the speeding craft interrupted his line of fire. Now began the maneuvering and weaving of the Zodiac and the *Arctic Wind.* Lara Shalken and Ulf Swenson tried to anticipate each other's moves, playing a dangerous battle of chess on the high seas. The whales turned right, following the bull leader, and the whaler followed, but the quicker Zodiac cut in front once again, shielding the whales. They were on a heading directly away from the *Sea Angel II,* which could not match the pace of the faster boats. Jan Shalken could only watch, helpless as the deadly game moved farther and farther away. Soon the combatants became mere specks in the distance. Then they disappeared over the horizon.

"Shoot, goddamn you!" ordered Swenson.

"I can't get a clear shot, Captain!" replied the gunner. Frustrated, Swenson repeatedly changed his angle of attack while keeping the whales in harpoon range. But each time, Lara, in the more nimble Zodiac, blocked the shot.

"Take the wheel!" Swenson finally ordered his first mate. He left the bridge, jumped down to the main deck and ran to the bow, pushing the gunner aside. "If you're too afraid, I'll shoot!" he exclaimed. Vikinsson, startled, watched as Swenson grabbed the cannon's handles with his massive hands, swiveled the weapon, and lined up the shot. At that critical moment, the bow of the *Arctic Wind* dipped into the trough of a swell, disrupting Swenson's aim. "Ulf, no!" exclaimed Vikinsson. The first mate at the *Arctic Wind*'s helm lost his balance and slipped to the wheelhouse floor as the ship pitched. He regained his footing and watched in horror as the tiny Zodiac stalled in the water, and then disappeared under the ship's bow as it plowed through the waves. The deckhands heard screams in the water below.

"My God, what have we done?" cried Vikinsson in anguish. Swenson turned ashen momentarily, but quickly recovered his composure.

"*We* have done *nothing!* Do you understand?" shouted Swenson, shaking the seaman by his jacket collar. "Nothing!" He turned, facing the crew assembled on deck to watch the hunt, and shouted. "Do you *all* understand what has just happened?" He scanned their faces as he continued his tirade, making a mental note to remember which crewmembers had witnessed the tragedy: Gudmund Vikinsson, the harpooner; Alfred Haggar, the ship's cook; Thor Rodale, a maintenance engineer; and two young apprentice seamen, twin brothers whose names Swenson could never seem to recall. "What happened was the result of reckless, careless seamanship by the Zodiac's crew. They lost control of their craft during a dangerous and illegal maneuver, creating an unavoidable, tragic accident! That is what I will officially record in this ship's log, and that is what you will say to anyone investigating this accident. Do you all understand? Are there any questions?" His statement to the five men was met with silence. He saw the blank stares of men in shock after witnessing the violent death of fellow seamen. *What are they thinking? Can I trust them?* Swenson maintained eye contact with them, using each man's eyes as a conduit into his soul. He was uncomfortable with what he saw. In that split second, they ceased to be human beings, just loose ends of a problem he needed to tie up. He thought, *I'll deal with them later. For now, we have work to do.* "All right then. Let's search for survivors and recover the dead."

Several miles away, Jan Shalken had no idea what had transpired as he tried to coax maximum speed from the *Sea Angel II*'s aging diesel engines. He noticed he was rapidly catching up to the *Arctic Wind,* which meant she must have stopped. *Why? Had Lara been unsuccessful preventing them from killing another whale?* Approaching, he looked in vain for the Zodiac. His blood ran cold when he saw floating wreckage. He watched the whaler's crew in a lifeboat searching the water and recovering debris floating behind the *Arctic Wind,* now dead in the water. When he closed within fifty yards of the scene, he recognized the wreckage as the Zodiac's remnants. Fearing the worst, he felt an icy dagger pierce his stomach. He grabbed a bullhorn and ran to the railing, shouting to the whaler's crew. "Where is my wife! Where is my crew? What happened?" Looking toward the whaler, he saw what appeared to be three shrouded bodies on the deck. Stunned, he could not believe his eyes. Then, he saw a familiar orange slicker draped over one of the shrouded bodies. On the slicker was an emblem he could not yet make out, but which he knew would be an angel holding a shield, riding on a whale. Realizing he had lost his beloved Lara, Jan let out a blood-curdling scream, and he collapsed against the railing, sobbing.

"I regret to inform you that there has been a terrible accident," shouted Ulf Swenson with icy precision, through his loudspeaker. "We have recovered three crew members from your Zodiac. One is a female, who I assume is your wife, Captain Shalken. I'm very sorry." Jan was standing at the rail, supported by two crewmen, tears streaming down his face. The lifeboat that had recovered the bodies came alongside to transport him to the *Arctic Wind.* Jan stepped into the small boat without saying a word. Climbing aboard the *Arctic Wind,* he pushed past Swenson and ran to the rear deck where three shrouded bodies lay, side by side. Jan stood over his fallen crew, and then knelt by his wife's body. Lara's left hand protruded from under the shroud and he noticed a pale ring of skin on her wrist, where her gold wedding bracelet should have been. He looked for a moment at his own matching bracelet and held her hand. He gently removed Lara's gold wedding band. The coldness of her flesh pierced his heart. Then he pulled the shroud back, uncovering her face. He gasped when he saw a horrific neck wound, but recovered his composure and gently closed Lara's open eyes, frozen in the shock of her violent death.

Standing, head bowed, he quietly asked, "How did this happen?"

"They maneuvered directly in front my ship, preventing us from taking a shot," replied Swenson. "Apparently, she lost control of the Zodiac trying to make a sharp turn and capsized in a swell. There was no time for us to take evasive action. I am sorry to say this to you, but her actions were reckless."

Jan swallowed hard and fought back tears. He knew they would come later, again and again. "I have notified the authorities and they will meet us when we return to Reykjavik. They will investigate and make a report."

"I will take the bodies of my crew back to my ship."

"Captain Shalken, I understand your wishes, but I think it is best they remain here. They are, well, considering what happened to them, I think the bodies will remain in better shape if they are not moved. Do you understand me?"

Jan swallowed hard and took a deep breath. He squeezed his eyes shut for a moment, visualizing the suffering his wife and two crewmen had endured in their final moments.

"As you say, Captain Swenson, it is probably best they remain here. But I promise you one thing," Jan said, glaring at Ulf Swenson with cold determination. The two huge men, both six-foot-six and thickly muscled from years of hard work at sea, maintained eye contact inches from each other. Jan continued, "I will make sure there is a full and thorough investigation. Lara's seamanship was too good to have lost control of a Zodiac, even in these conditions. If it turns out, as I suspect, that the cause was other than you have described, you will answer to me, personally. Do you understand *me?*" He paused, letting his words sink in. Swenson stared back impassively, neither flinching nor acknowledging the threat. Jan turned and looked toward Lara's covered body. He stepped over to her and gently removed her bloodstained slicker from the shroud. He folded it reverently, stopping momentarily as he stared at the emblem of an angel riding on a whale's back. He tucked the slicker under his arm and returned to the *Sea Angel II*.

Vikinsson, the harpooner, had been standing nearby, listening to the exchange between the two captains. After Jan left, he stepped over to Swenson. "I think Shalken appreciated your consideration for the remains of his wife and crew, Captain."

"Ah, I don't give a rat's ass about their bodies, Gudmund. This whole mess happened in international waters. According to international maritime law, Shalken could make a good case to have the investigation handled in Holland, where the *Sea Angel* is registered, and where he and his wife are citizens. But I need to have the matter settled in Iceland, where I know I can influence the investigation. Having the bodies onboard the *Arctic Wind* when we arrive in port will give us leverage to ensure the investigation will occur in Reykjavik. Have the crew move them into a refrigerated compartment."

"Aye, Captain," said Vikinsson quietly. He grimaced, watching Swenson walk away, sickened by his insensitivity. He thought, *after all these years, I felt I knew this man, but he is still a mystery to me.*

Chapter 12

Puerto Plata, Dominican Republic

January 27th

    *T*erry and Joe landed at Puerto Plata airport on a breezy, warm, sunny afternoon. "Gee, the Dominican Republic feels a lot like Cozumel," observed Joe.

    "Well, don't forget, we *are* still in the Caribbean," Terry reminded him. "Let's get through customs and immigration and find our meeter-greeter." Hauling their luggage and following the directions sent by SeaVenture Adventures, they looked for someone holding a sign that read "Carlos." Finally, Joe saw a hand waving a sign just above the crowd, and guided Terry towards the sign. They met a young man, about twenty-five, wearing a colorful tropical shirt. "Are you Carlos, who will take us to the *SeaVenture*?"

"*Si señor,* that is me. I am also waiting for two more people. My van is over there. The white one, next to that large bus. Please wait there."

After several minutes, they spotted Carlos walking toward them with another couple in tow. Joe helped Carlos load their luggage into his van and made introductions.

"Hi there, nice to meet you. I'm Jim Duncan and this is my wife Janice. We're from St. Louis," he said, shaking hands too enthusiastically for Joe. After a lifetime of living in New York, he still maintained a New Yorker's natural defense mechanism, which is to maintain a reserved distance from strangers until getting to know them better.

"I'm Joe Manetta, and this is my wife, Terry. We're originally from the States, but we live in Cozumel now. We own a dive operation."

"Hey that's great, where is that exactly?"

"In Mexico, just south of Cancun," answered Terry, who had learned from experience the most efficient reply to questions about Cozumel's location.

"Okay, I know about Cancun. It's a wild party place. That's great! I'm in sales. Computers, actually. Hey, do you use computers to manage your business? You know my company has a new line that's perfect for small businesses. We . . . ."

"Not now, dear, this is a vacation," said Janice, gently squeezing her husband's arm. Joe smiled politely, thinking, *Could be worse. He could be selling life insurance!*

"Isn't this scenery beautiful? Look at those mountains," said Terry, trying to distract the group, and wondering if she and Joe could endure a week on a small live-aboard boat with Jim and Janice. After a half-hour van ride, they arrived at the pier where the *SeaVenture*, a 100-foot twin-engine catamaran, was moored. The crew helped them aboard and instructed them to proceed to the dining room, where Terry and Joe were relieved to meet the other eager whale enthusiasts.

At dinner, everyone was formally introduced to the crew. Captain Phil Rogers, a tall, lanky young man, was in charge of the *SeaVenture.* He would occasionally pilot one of the boat's two

Zodiacs when it was time to find the whales. *Reminds me of a young Jimmy Stewart,* thought Joe. Two other crewmembers, Bob Johnson and Adam Fischer, performed miscellaneous shipboard duties but their main responsibility was to pilot the Zodiacs and search for whales. Phil's wife, Elaine, was the cook, and there were two other helpers assigned to cabin service. During dinner, Elaine explained the boat's housekeeping rules and then her husband addressed the guests.

"First, I want to thank you good folks for joining us. You're in for some amazing and unique experiences this week. The humpbacks you'll be seeing arrived here from the northwestern Atlantic, around New England, about a month or two ago. Whales have some of the longest migratory routes of any animals, certainly the longest of any mammals."

"How do they manage to navigate such long distances?" asked Janice, the salesman's wife.

"Good question. We aren't totally sure. However, geologists know deposits of magnetite, which is a ferrous ore, are buried under the sea floor. These deposits run in roughly a north-south pattern. Autopsies on dead whales have revealed minute traces of magnetite in their brains. So, one prominent theory among scientists is that whales have developed some kind of magnetic navigational system over their eons of evolution."

"Oh Jim, isn't that amazing?"

"So," replied her husband, trying to be clever, "whales are really like giant compass needles, right Captain Rogers?"

"Well, not exactly, Jim, but I see you get the idea," he replied politely, trying not to offend a paying guest, but thinking, *is this guy for real?*

"We could be in for a long week with Jimbo around," Joe whispered to Terry.

"I hope you remembered *not* to bring any scuba equipment," emphasized Rogers. "Scuba is not permitted in the whale sanctuary, so you'll be snorkeling and free-diving. The government doesn't want scuba divers harassing the whales. Besides, they don't like the bubbles from scuba gear. In whale etiquette, bubble blowing sometimes signals aggression. Trust me, you really don't want to piss off a fifty-ton whale.

"I would also suggest you get to bed early, because the boat leaves tomorrow morning at six sharp." Joe was already nodding off after a grueling travel day and Terry jabbed his ribs to keep him awake. "We have an eighty-mile trip to the Silver Bank. We call it 'the crossing,' because we cross through some rough ocean water. The *SeaVenture* can do twenty knots, so we'll make the crossing in about four hours. If you have seasick pills, take one tonight and another one just before we leave in the morning. Don't wait until you're sick, because by then it'll be too late. Are there any questions? Okay, I'll give you another briefing tomorrow afternoon just prior to going out to meet the whales. In the meantime, get a good night's sleep and I'll see you all tomorrow morning. Enjoy your dinner and have a good night."

They finished dinner at 8 o'clock, so the group broke up and went to their assigned cabins. Everyone had been traveling for a day, in some cases two, and all were tired. Most traveled from the United States, but several came from Europe. There was also a couple from Australia and another from Hawaii. As Terry and Joe walked down the narrow corridor, they noticed all the cabins had bunk beds. Terry looked over her shoulder and said to Joe, "I'll flip you for the bottom bunk."

"This could be a *real* long week," he replied, massaging the back of her neck as they proceeded to their cabin. When they opened their cabin door, they were pleasantly surprised to see a queen-sized bed. "Hey," Joe said, perking up, "We won the lottery!"

Captain Rogers, walking past their cabin, heard Joe's enthusiastic comment. "You two lucked out, booking your trip late. We had a last minute cancellation, and the only available cabin had a queen-sized bed." Terry and Joe slipped into bed and relaxed as the gentle rocking of the ocean provided a soothing sensation. Terry closed her eyes and said, "Wow, doesn't that feel wonderful?"

"Yeah, the ultimate waterbed," said Joe, drifting off to sleep.

"See you in the morning," she said, as the sound of snoring filled the darkened cabin.

Chapter 13

The Silver Bank, Dominican Republic

January 28th

*B*y 10 AM, the *SeaVenture* had been pounding through four-to-six-foot ocean swells for almost four hours. It was a sunny but breezy morning and salt spray covered those bold enough to venture on deck for the ride, stiffening their hair and clothes as it dried. Joe leaned over the portside railing near the stern, feeding his partially digested scrambled egg breakfast to the fishes. "Hey buddy, you look a little green around the gills," said Terry, playfully.

"Can we go home so I can die?" muttered Joe. "I never felt so sick in my life," he moaned. "I should have taken one of those damn seasick pills."

"Poor baby," said Terry, teasing, but also commiserating, because she knew from experience seasickness is one of the worst feelings in the world.

"I feel dizzy, sick to my stomach. Why can't I just die?" he pleaded, hunched over the railing, head down. His stomach muscles ached after heaving for twenty minutes. Terry leaned over and rested her chin on his shoulder while patting his back gently, distracting him from his torment. She was looking out at the passing sea when several hundred yards away, a submarine-launched Polaris missile appeared to erupt from the ocean. "Look! Over there!" she exclaimed. Joe raised his head too late to see the large humpback whale fall back into the ocean with a resounding splash. The loud droning of the *SeaVenture*'s twin engines muffled the sound. "Did I miss something?" he asked weakly. They both looked toward the disturbed ocean, and the whale breached again, this time closer. It rose until its flukes cleared the water, and then the massive, fifty-foot, forty-ton body fell back again, disappearing in a huge splash of foam and spray. "Wow, I've seen pictures of whales breaching before, but I never saw one in person!" said Terry. "Impressive!"

They watched other whales breaching in the distance, one pirouetting as it rose from the water, spreading its long, white pectoral fins like the arms of a ballet dancer. "Looks like they're having a grand old time," said Joe, holding his unsettled stomach. Fifteen minutes later, they felt the engines reduce power and the droning vibration subsided. The *SeaVenture* slowed to half speed, about ten knots. Captain Rogers's voice came over the loudspeakers. "You can see whales breaching and tail-slapping off both the port and starboard sides. That means we're entering the Silver Bank. We're required to reduce speed to avoid collisions with whales in the sanctuary, so we'll reach our destination in thirty minutes." Joe felt better as the calm water of the sheltered reef reduced the *SeaVenture*'s rocking motion substantially.

"Feeling like a human being again?" asked Terry. She was going to kiss Joe, but when he turned to face her, she decided it would be more prudent to take a handkerchief and just wipe his lips. "Well, I guess love has its limits," he joked, managing a wan smile. Thirty minutes later they noticed the outline of a ship on the horizon, directly in the path of the *SeaVenture*. As they got closer, they saw it was the rusted hulk of an old freighter that had run aground on the reef years ago and been left to rot. "Look!" Terry exclaimed. "That's the ship pictured in the sales brochure they sent us. We're here!"

Captain Rogers cut the engines and the *SeaVenture* drifted toward one of several mooring buoys. A deckhand dragged a buoy with a long hook and secured a line from the boat. Over the loudspeaker, Captain Rogers announced, "Okay, we've arrived. We'll serve lunch at noon, and then we'll take you out to meet some whales. In the meantime, you can swim, snorkel off the stern, or just relax."

Chapter 14

Reykjavik, Iceland

January 29th

Jon Andresson was at his desk preparing a report when his secretary buzzed the intercom. "Yes, Anna?"

"Mr. Andresson, your conference line is ready."

"Thank you, Anna," he said, taking a deep breath before starting what he knew would be a stressful and contentious conference call. "Jon Andresson here," he began. "Are the representatives from Norway, Finland, and Japan on the line?"

"Stig Carlson, Norway, here."

"Eric Braunnel, Finland."

He stared at the speakerphone, hearing his own heart beat over the low hissing static of empty air, when a female voice broke the silence. "I'm sorry, Minister Haigata is on his way. He will join the call in just a minute."

"Thank you, we'll wait. Please ask him to announce himself when he arrives," Andresson said, enjoying the temporary reprieve.

Several silent minutes were punctuated by occasional coughs and other background noises. Then the speakerphone crackled and Haigata immediately put Andresson on the spot.

"Haigata here. Please accept my sincere apologies for being late. I was briefing my superiors regarding the latest situation, or should I say, Jon, *calamity?*" The other participants watched their speakerphones intently, as if the small boxes were animated beings, wondering how Andresson would reply.

"Yes. Well, there will be a full investigation into the accident. Until that investigation is finished, we cannot . . . ."

"The *obvious* facts are," Haigata said, interrupting him sharply, "that you have been totally ineffective in controlling your whaling *cowboy.* As a result, several softheaded whale huggers were killed while he was attempting to catch whales. Isn't that the essence of the situation?"

"Yes, I'm afraid three people are confirmed dead and authorities are investigating specific circumstances surrounding the incident."

"Well, Jon," interjected Stig Carlson, "I suppose we may safely assume the authorities will finally curtail the whaling activities of this, ah, Captain Swenson?"

"You are correct, Stig. They have impounded his ship, the *Arctic Wind,* secured his passport, and restricted him to the immediate area. In addition . . ."

"Too little, too late!" interrupted Haigata.

"Before we try to estimate how this latest incident will impact our efforts, I would like an update on our progress regarding our action plan since our last meeting," said Eric Braunnel, restoring civility and a positive tone to the meeting.

"Excellent idea," said Carlson. "Oshura, what has your government done?"

"We have already held individual meetings with Mexico and three Caribbean nations, who have asked not to be identified publicly at this time. In exchange for their votes at the next IWC meeting, we have offered the following incentives: To Mexico, direct investment in two desalinization plants to be constructed on their Pacific Coast. We have also offered to build an automotive factory and the Mexicans are in the process of deciding where it would have the most favorable impact, politically as well as economically. To three Caribbean nations, we have offered direct grants, which they can use as they see fit. We have also scheduled meetings with two other nations regarding the extension of substantial, low-cost credit lines. Finally, we have initiated a media campaign within the United States concerning the unfairness and inconsistency of U.S. government policy permitting certain Native American tribes to continue whaling while simultaneously assuming a sanctimonious position opposing other nations harvesting whales."

"Yes," said Stig, "I noticed one of your initiatives in Alaska backfired on you when the local news media gave most of the attention to the anti-whaling forces. Did any of you see the picture in *Time* magazine, showing the sign one protester carried? It read, 'Save a whale, eat an Eskimo today'."

The laughter erupting from the speakerphones broke the tension momentarily, until Haigata replied. "Yes. Well, obviously we still have much work to do, especially in the area of public opinion. How about the rest of you?"

Eric Braunnel gave his report next. "Jon Andresson and I have been successful convincing scientists in our respective countries to publish reports supporting our position that too many whales are eating too many fish, causing economic hardship for our fishing industry, and higher consumer prices. In addition, while we have not yet been assigned to working committees developing rules for the Revised Management Scheme, which I believe Oshura called the RMS, we have been assured access to meeting minutes. We will continue to lobby committee members to place us on the working groups. That's all I have for now."

"That's accurate," confirmed Andresson. "And Stig, how about your efforts?" he asked.

"My government has provided me with assistance developing position papers explaining why the whale DNA registry is not needed, but there is tremendous pressure to implement it. I believe our best strategy may be to propose reducing penalties for being caught with whale meat proven by the registry to come from protected whale species. I will advise you of our progress."

"Fine," said Haigata. "It sounds as though we are making good progress toward our goal, but we must not let our efforts flag. Now let's address the main issue. What do we do about this latest situation involving the death of these activists from that anti-whaling organization . . .uh . . ."

"Peaceful Seas," said Stig. "This situation will obviously create sympathy for the opposition. We must skillfully use media contacts sympathetic to our position and put our own, as the Americans say, *spin,* on the situation.

"We may need a more direct approach," disagreed Haigata. "Jon, we will rely on you to apprise us of developments in your country, but you may also have to consider taking direct action."

"What do you suggest?" asked Andresson, warily.

"You may have to influence the investigation as it develops."

"Oshura, my government does not look kindly on anyone obstructing justice, especially in life-and-death matters." The silence from the other two participants was palpable, as they listened to a political, cover-your-ass exchange between two senior diplomats.

"Jon, I merely suggest that you take a creative and proactive approach, not that you break any laws," Haigata said, skillfully distancing himself from any suggestion of illegality or impropriety, should anyone record the meeting minutes. "Unfortunately, there is little Japan can do to assist you in this matter, occurring as it did in international waters," he said, for public consumption. "I'm afraid we must leave this matter in your hands. Please keep us informed and ensure it does not adversely impact our efforts toward achieving our objectives."

Andresson stared at the speakerphone while Haigata spoke. The continued silence of the other participants left him feeling naked and alone. "I will keep you all informed," he said curtly.

"Then I think we can adjourn," concluded Haigata. "My secretary will contact you to arrange our next conference call. Thank you all for participating. This was very productive, and thank you for your combined efforts." As they signed off, Haigata thought, *well, so much for my public position on this crisis. But if I do not take direct action, that weakling Andresson will doom our efforts.*

Chapter 15

The Silver Bank, Dominican Republic

January 29th

*C*onversation was animated during lunch aboard the *SeaVenture,* as the group anticipating swimming close to the largest creatures ever to roam the earth. Captain Rogers arrived and addressed them in a high-spirited tone. "Well, is everyone ready for the most amazing experience of your lives?" After a rousing cheer, he continued. "After lunch, change into your swimming and snorkeling gear and assemble at the stern. We randomly broke you into two groups, about ten people to a Zodiac. Check the list posted by the door as you exit the dining room to see which boat you're in. During the week you can change boats. I don't care, as long as we don't have more than twelve in one boat. Every day you'll assemble after breakfast, at about 9 AM, and head out to find whales. You'll return to the boat at about noon for lunch and then head out at 2 o'clock, and return at 5 o'clock.

Okay, here's the protocol for whale encounters. Number one rule is the whales are in charge. You stay with them if they want to stay with you. If they swim away don't chase them. You couldn't catch them anyway. They may touch you, but you do not initiate contact. Just relax and enjoy your encounters, which may last from two minutes to an hour or more, depending on what the whales decide. Your best encounters will occur with mothers and babies. Solitary whales and groups of males seem to have better things to do than hang out with humans, but babies are curious and will approach you, usually with mom close by. Any questions?"

"Is being close to the baby dangerous if the mother is near?" asked Jim, the salesman.

"Not as long as you don't make any movement she may interpret as aggressive. For the most part, you'll find them gentle and trusting. Anything else?"

"What would happen if you got hit with a fin?" asked Terry.

"Well, if you're merely brushed by a fin, probably nothing, although you could get a nasty scrape from barnacles attached to the whales. But, if a whale whacks you with a full stroke, you'd be seriously hurt. Their tail flukes are especially powerful. Think about how much energy is required to hurl forty tons of whale clear out of the water. It wouldn't take much to end up with broken bones, or worse." Terry pondered this, realizing that, despite all her diving experience and animal encounters, she had never been in the water with creatures this large. She unconsciously squeezed Joe's hand.

"Okay, any other questions? One last thing that will help you locate whales. When you're in the Zodiacs, the bow is always 12 o'clock. The stern is 6 o'clock. Directly to the right is 3 o'clock, so what do you call out if you see a whale directly to the left of the boat?"

"9 o'clock!" exclaimed Jim, enthusiastically.

"Okay, looks like you have the idea. I'll meet you all at the stern in about twenty minutes."

As Joe and Terry passed the assignment sheet on the wall, they saw they were in boat one, piloted by Bob Johnson, while Jim, the salesman, and his wife, Janice, were assigned boat two. Terry looked at Joe and smiled. Joe acknowledged with a subtle wink. Bob brought the Zodiac next to the *SeaVenture* and Joe jumped in first so he could assist Terry and several other boat mates. They shoved off as boat two loaded up. Johnson headed in a westerly direction, where he had seen several blows. Their mood was decidedly upbeat as he fed gas to the Yamaha-60 outboard engine. The part-inflatable part-rigid craft accelerated, plowing through and over the waves, with the group perched along the pontoon sides. After two hours trying to approach whales, which proved uncooperative this afternoon, the group was discouraged. They were sunburned and thirsty. Some had sore hands from holding the safety rope to avoid being pitched into the sea. A woman sitting next to Joe asked, "Are we having fun yet?"

But they perked up when Bob announced, "Hey, there's a whale right under us!" Standing up while driving the boat, he had a better angle of vision into the water. He spotted the whale's long, white pectoral fins as it rested on the bottom, fifty feet below. He cut the motor and drifted for a moment, to see what the whale would do. "Looks like it's sleeping. If you slip over the side quietly so you don't spook him, you'll get a good look."

Terry and Joe slipped over the side, barely raising a ripple, and adjusted their masks and snorkels. Staring down, neither could believe what they saw. Terry raised her head out of the water. "Joe, look how big it is!"

"Yeah, he's just hanging down there with his pecs spread out. Looks like somebody sunk a 747."

The group spread out on the surface and watched the whale intently for several minutes. Then, it slowly began moving. Without perceptible movement of its fins or flukes, it changed position from horizontal to a forty-five-degree, heads-up angle and drifted slowly to the surface. Its head broke the surface and it explosively exhaled and refilled its massive lungs in less than two seconds. As it settled toward the bottom, excited squeals from several snorkelers reached its sensitive ears, and it opened its eyes. Using its fifteen-foot-long pectoral fins like giant arms, it swung its body around and slowly, rhythmically, began pumping its ten-foot-wide flukes. Swimming in a lazy arc, it passed directly under Joe and Terry, who were looking down, holding hands to maintain their position in the two-foot waves. They were so intent on looking at the details of the whale's head, only several feet below, that they didn't notice they were in direct line of the approaching flukes, breaking the surface at the top of each stroke, only forty feet away. Joe startled Terry as he squeezed her hand and pointed toward the rear of the whale. Realizing there was no time to avoid the approaching flukes, now within twenty feet and closing, they folded their arms across their chests, bracing for the impact. They watched in relief, and awe, as the flukes stopped in mid-stroke as the whale glided under them and then continued the vertical, upstroke-downstroke pattern after it passed. Several seconds later the huge whale disappeared, dissolving into the blue mist. The group was ecstatic.

"Wow!"

"Unbelievable!"

"Joe, did you see what it did?"

"Yeah and I'm glad it did it, too."

"I mean, that whale knew we were there! It purposely stopped its flukes so it wouldn't hit us."

"Yeah, pretty amazing. He was clearly annoyed at our intrusion and left for peace and quiet, but still was careful not to hit us. Pretty thoughtful of him, if you ask me."

As the group clambered aboard the Zodiac, Bob said, "Well, folks, how was your first whale encounter?" What followed recreated the scene at the Tower of Babel. "Whoa, one person at a time." Looking at Joe and Terry, he said, "You two are pretty quiet. How was it?" Terry described what had transpired, and Bob just listened and smiled, knowingly. "Yeah, they're pretty considerate creatures." Looking at his watch, he said, "Well, it's almost 4 o'clock. We'll head back to the *SeaVenture* and maybe we'll see some more whales on the way." They didn't, but no one cared. Boat one arrived at the *SeaVenture* ahead of boat two, so the group showered and changed into comfortable clothes for dinner. They looked forward to hearing how their shipmates on the other Zodiac had fared.

Chapter 16

Evening on the Silver Bank

January 29th

*J*oe and Terry entered the dining room hungry after chasing whales all day. They anticipated the animated conversation of compatriots sharing the day's exciting experiences. Instead, they encountered total silence and tearful eyes. Somber faces were tinted an eerie blue by the glow from the ship's television. They turned toward the screen, and watched the CNN satellite news feed.

The attractive, blonde newscaster appeared visibly shaken beneath her usually cool, professional demeanor. " . . . . and this morning, the Icelandic whaling ship *Arctic Wind* pulled into port carrying the bodies of three members from the activist conservationist group, Peaceful Seas. Tomorrow afternoon, the *Sea Angel II,* flagship of the Peaceful Seas organization, will arrive in Reykjavik, piloted by Captain Jan Shalken, husband of one of the victims, Lara Shalken, pictured here in happier times."

As Lara's pretty face filled the screen, Joe's eyes narrowed as he studied the image. His policeman's subconscious, indelibly imbedded by years of experience even after retirement, kicked in. He vaguely heard Terry say, "Gee, she looks familiar, something about her eyes." Then, pictures of the other two victims, Peter Wilson and Carl Schaefer, were displayed on the screen and they listened to the broadcast.

"As international protests mount over the deaths, Prime Minister Stefan Valsson of Iceland promised an investigation would commence immediately. When pressed on the related issue of hunting whales, Prime Minister Valsson provided this comment." A short video clip showed him responding to a reporter's question. They watched as the broadcast cut to a tall, handsome man, conservatively dressed in a blue suit. His red hair was just beginning to turn silvery-gold as grey was setting in. *Just crossing to the wrong side of middle-age,* Joe guessed. Valsson's clear blue eyes looked directly into the camera as he spoke.

"We are scientifically studying the issues surrounding whale harvesting, with an intention toward maintaining the sustainability of these international resources as well as maintaining the economic viability of critical fish stocks which whales consume, clearly affecting many of our interrelated economies."

The camera returned to the blonde newscaster. "In other parts of the world . . . ."

"What the hell did that guy just say?" remarked Jim the salesman.

"Total bullshit, mate," exclaimed one of the Australians.

"Now that's what I call real *politico-speak,*" said Terry.

"Yeah, say a lot and nothing, all in the same sentence. Looks like he's refined it to a fine art," said Joe. "What happened? What did we miss before we came in?"

"Well," said Bob Johnson, "it seems the Icelandic whaler *Arctic Wind* was hunting whales, even protected fin whales. They still had butchered carcasses in the ship's hold. Evidently, a crew from the *Sea Angel II* in a Zodiac were acting as human shields between a sperm whale pod and the *Arctic Wind*'s harpoon gun, betting they could pull off saving the whales safely."

"I guess they bet wrong," said Joe grimly.

Dinner featured pot roast with mashed potatoes, drowning in warm gravy, with vegetables. Few people enjoyed the carefully prepared meal, and conversation was markedly subdued. Instead, the crew and guests reflected on the dichotomy between their uplifting experiences earlier on the ocean and their sorrow over what they had witnessed tonight on television. After dinner, Terry suggested, "Joe, let's go outside. I need some fresh air, and it looks like a beautiful night."

"Sounds like a good idea, hon, let's go," agreed Joe. They bid good night to the other guests and went outside, arm in arm, climbing a metal stairway to the top deck. They spent several quiet moments gazing at the ocean, smooth as a black mirror in the breezeless night. "Oh my, the moon's reflection on the water looks more perfect than a picture postcard," said Terry.

"Sorry, Ter, but I'm enjoying looking at the reflection in your eyes," he said.

"Oh Joe, that's so . . . ." Terry's reply was cut short as her husband took her in his arms and kissed her. After a long, passionate kiss, Joe felt Terry's body relax against his, as if she was going to melt into him. She drew a quick breath and whispered in his ear, "I think this trip was a very good idea."

"See, it pays to follow doctor's orders," he said. She kissed Joe's ear and he turned slightly, kissing her neck. Terry felt a tingle shoot through her spine. She quickly found Joe's lips and they kissed again. Their embrace was interrupted when they heard a guitar strumming an unfamiliar tune, on the deck below. They listened for a moment, looking into each other's eyes, and then turned toward the sound. They heard someone singing lyrics along with the tune.*

As the moon shines down on the Silverbank,
And the stars shine up above
There's a mystery concealed 'neath the silver veil,
a tale as old as time.
When the sun comes up at the break of day
    The whales' display begins!

> There is magic real for all to see
> The dance of the whales' delight
> The dance of the whales' delight . . . .
>
> As the sun shines down on the Silverbank
> And the clouds . . . .

Leaning against the railing, arms around each other's shoulders, they listened to the song. "Hey, pretty catchy tune. Very appropriate for the setting, don't you think?" asked Joe.

"Yes, but I was just thinking it's a shame to let one of the only queen-sized beds on this boat go to waste. Don't you agree?" whispered Terry seductively, nuzzling Joe's chest.

"I *completely* agree," replied Joe in a low, husky voice. He gently kissed Terry's forehead. They held hands walking to their cabin, and Terry thought about becoming pregnant. The advice of her doctor echoed in her mind. ". . . .take a vacation, relax and see what happens." *Maybe tonight's the night,* she hoped.

---

*From *The Whales' Delight,* music & lyrics by Deollo Johnson and Mary Whalen

Chapter 17

Reykjavik

January 30th

*T*he guests aboard the *SeaVenture* slept soundly on the gently rocking cradle of the ocean, but it was already morning in Reykjavik as Oshura Haigata entered the opulent office of Stefan Valsson, Iceland's Prime Minister. "Greetings, Oshura," said Valsson, standing, extending his hand, and offering a small customary bow in polite deference to Haigata's Japanese custom.

"Good to see you again, Stefan. How have you been?" As they exchanged pleasantries, Haigata noted that Valsson, a good friend whom he had remembered as vibrant and robust, appeared haggard, tired, and drawn. He looked older than his sixty-four years. Haigata studied his eyes. The confident look he remembered from previous meetings was missing, replaced by something else. *Anxiety, stress, what?* wondered Haigata. He decided to press on with business. "Well, Stefan, I bring good news. Japan will purchase as much whale meat as you can supply. That should remove the economic uncertainty from your whaling activities and provide a sound financial base justifying expanding your initiatives." He anticipated an enthusiastic reaction to his government's intentions, but Valsson merely responded with a wan smile. "What is troubling you, Stefan? I thought you would rejoice."

"That is indeed good news, Oshura, but I have many related issues to deal with currently. Even before this latest situation involving the *Arctic Wind,* the United States already threatened a trade embargo against Iceland. A market research study initiated in the U.S. last year reported that two-thirds of Americans would stop buying Icelandic products, including fish, if we resumed commercial whaling. The International Fund for Animal Welfare has issued numerous public statements condemning our whaling initiatives. You may recall we stopped whaling in 1989 because the international community boycotted our fish products. And in addition to external pressure, I also have internal factions opposing me. The Icelandic Tourist Industry Association opposes whaling because it estimates 40 percent of all our tourists enjoy whale watching, which now yields 10 million in U.S. dollars to our economy annually."

Haigata nodded slowly, listening intently. "And look at these," Valsson said, handing Haigata a sheaf of papers. "Official protest statements from foreign consulates."

"Hmm, Australia, Germany, New Zealand, the UK, and the United States," said, Haigata, reading the country names aloud. "I understand your concern, Stefan, but this is all the more reason to stand united and push the IWC toward adopting positions favorable to us."

"And now I have these three deaths to deal with," Valsson added, shaking his head. "I also have other issues to resolve, of which you have no knowledge."

"Such as?" probed Haigata.

"I cannot go into the details now. Trust me that it is serious. My only hope is this investigation determines the Peaceful Seas activists were at fault and caused their own deaths through their reckless actions."

"Well, Stefan, can you not apply sufficient pressure to affect the outcome of the investigation?"

"I've already taken steps in that direction, Oshura, but that is an extremely risky strategy. If my office is implicated in anything resembling obstruction of justice, my own political enemies—and believe me, I have many—will yell for my head."

"Stefan, I do not understand why you cannot simply distance yourself from this lunatic Swenson. Declare him a renegade and, as the Americans say, 'hang him out to dry'? Let the authorities deal with him severely and let this tempest die down."

"If only it were that simple," replied Valsson, wistfully. As he spoke, Haigata saw the same look in his eyes he had noticed earlier, a sad, almost fearful resignation. *About what?* wondered Haigata.

"Stefan, I stand ready to provide you with whatever assistance you require, but you must trust I can keep your confidence."

Prime Minister Valsson drew in a deep breath as he held eye contact with Haigata, realizing he had a very important decision to make. "Oshura, I am going to tell you a story that no one outside of my trusted circle knows. Many years ago . . ."

After Valsson finished, he leaned back in his chair and looked at Haigata, waiting for his reaction. Haigata smiled and said, "Stefan, you and I have more in common than you realize." Valsson looked at him quizzically, but Haigata ignored his silent request for clarification. Instead, he just pulled out a small business card and wrote a telephone number on the back. "We both have much to lose if the investigation does not conclude that the *Sea Angel* crew caused the accident. Take this card. Tell the man who answers I gave you the number. He can provide assistance and resolve any situation regarding the investigation."

Across town, Jon Andresson was concluding his meeting with Inspector Arni Hansen of the Reykjavik Police Department. Hansen, six-foot and trim thanks to a strict diet and a rigorous workout regimen at a local gym, appeared younger than his actual age, fifty-nine. His dark hair had only the slightest trace of gray, just around the temples. He still appeared remarkably similar to his photo ID, taken fifteen years earlier. He looked forward to retiring on his pension and planned on filling leisure days with his favorite activities: fishing and hiking. "Well, Jon, we will convene the preliminary hearing next week. Depending on the outcome, we will decide what further action is appropriate. I will provide you with investigative notes containing the navy's preliminary reports, victims' autopsy reports, and names of witnesses from both ships. I believe the *Sea Angel II* was too far away for her crew to have seen anything relevant. Testimony from the *Arctic Wind*'s crew who actually witnessed the incident will be more important. I think there are about seven men to interview."

"Thank you, Inspector," said Andresson, standing to leave. "I will keep the Prime Minister informed of your progress. He has taken a personal interest in this case. He is concerned the reckless actions of these activists could reflect unfavorably on our government's whaling policies. He and I both know an experienced civil servant such as yourself will present the relevant facts in the proper context. You know, I mentioned to the prime minister you are near retirement. He believes a loyal government worker should enjoy a generous pension and live comfortably after many years of dedicated service. Occasionally, some government employees use poor judgment and get caught in scandals or other unsavory business toward the end of long careers. Consequently, they never get to enjoy the rewards they earned after years of otherwise loyal service. But why am I bothering you with such digressions? As I said, the Prime Minister requested I serve as his intermediary regarding this investigation, keeping him informed of your progress. Good day, Inspector."

"And good day to you too, sir. Give my best to the prime minister," Hansen said, extending his hand. *Was that a threat or a bribe?* he wondered, watching Andresson leave.

Andresson returned to the ministry to report his conversation to Valsson, but the prime minister's secretary detained him outside Valsson's office. "He is just concluding a meeting, sir. You may see him as soon as he finishes." Andresson's jaw dropped as the door opened and Oshura Haigata exited, acknowledging him with only a perfunctory greeting. "Why hello, Jon," he said, politely nodding his head. "I believe the prime minister is looking forward to seeing you. Good day."

Andresson attempted, unsuccessfully, to hide the shock in his eyes as Haigata passed him. Andresson entered Valsson's office, wondering, *what the hell was Haigata doing here?*

Chapter 18

January 31ˢᵗ

*T*he small courtroom was uncomfortably warm, a sharp contrast to the frigid temperature outside. A tense atmosphere resulted from the close confines of the room and proximity of the participants. Jan Shalken glared at Ulf Swenson and the *Arctic Wind* crew, across the narrow aisle. The crewmembers avoided Jan's eyes, but Swenson defiantly returned Shalken's glare. The presiding district court judge, Jon Kristinsson, sensed the tension and preempted potential outbursts by firmly setting the tone.

"Remember, this is an inquest, not a trial. This is a preliminary investigation into the facts presently available surrounding the events of January 26, 2003, resulting in the deaths of Lara Shalken, Peter Wilson, and Carl Schaefer. My role is to question the witnesses, evaluate the evidence, and advise the authorities if I believe further investigation is warranted. My goal is to determine if this was an unfortunate accident or if a crime has been committed. Please answer my questions completely, accurately, and honestly. At the conclusion, I will render a decision. Now let us begin."

"Jan Shalken, please take the stand," instructed the court clerk. As Jan took his place, he seemed uncomfortable in the small witness stand. He settled his large frame in the space and looked directly at the judge.

"Captain Shalken, why was the *Sea Angel II* in the vicinity when the *Arctic Wind* was conducting activities?"

Jan began his testimony, describing his mission with as much self control as he could muster. When he began to relate the events leading to the fatal encounter, his demeanor changed. The people seated in the first row leaned back, as if they expected Jan to jump over the rail of the witness stand.

"My wife and two other crew members left the *Sea Angel* in the Zodiac to intercept the *Arctic Wind*. Those pirates murdered them because they tried to prevent them from slaughtering innocent whales! They deserve justice! Those killers had no right to do what they . . . ."

The judge quickly admonished him. "Captain Shalken, first let me extend the court's condolences regarding your wife's death. But please recall what I said earlier. This inquest will determine if the evidence warrants a criminal trial. We are not here to decide the efficacy of hunting whales. The purpose is to determine the probable cause of death of three individuals on the high seas. The court requires that you confine your answers to my specific questions."

"Yes, Your Honor, my apologies," he said, gathering himself. The judge asked several more questions.

"So, you did not witness any of the actual events leading to the deaths of the three victims?"

"No, Your Honor. I last saw the Zodiac in the vicinity of the *Arctic Wind* through

my binoculars. But they were several kilometers away. I could not see what was happening. They were barely visible, and then I lost sight of them over the horizon. When we reached the scene, the *Arctic Wind* was dead in the water. We only witnessed the recovery stage of the . . . incident," he replied, glaring at Ulf Swenson, who calmly waited to testify, seemingly indifferent to Jan's remarks.

"And what did you observe, Captain?"

"They were recovering the Zodiac's wreckage, and as we got closer, I saw three shrouded objects on the *Arctic Wind*'s aft deck. I feared they were the bodies of my wife and crew.

"What transpired next, Captain Shalken?"

"I boarded a small boat to take me over to the *Arctic Wind*. I identified the bodies of Lara, Peter and Carl," he said, recalling the dreadful experience of identifying his dead sweetheart.

Pausing for a moment, the judge continued. "And what did you observe,
        sir?"

"Peter and Carl were badly mutilated. Lara was not, but she had a deep gash through her neck, which I assumed caused her death."

"Anything else?"

"No," Jan said firmly, blinking back tears.

"Thank you, you may step down, Captain. The court calls Captain Swenson."

Ulf Swenson avoided Jan's eyes as he sat in the witness stand. The tension rose in the courtroom as the judge reached the critical part of his questioning. "What happened next, Captain Swenson?"

"My harpooner could not shoot the whales because the *Sea Angel*'s Zodiac kept maneuvering between our ship and the whales. The pilot of the Zodiac suddenly lost control and swerved directly in front of us. We could not take evasive action. They were too close. I immediately ordered the engines cut, but it was too late. Our ship crushed the Zodiac. Then the spinning propeller blades, well, I believe it is all in the autopsy report."

"So, did your harpooner ever fire the cannon?"

"No, Your Honor. The tragedy was caused by Mrs. Shalken losing control of her craft, but I do not know exactly what caused her to lose control."

Jan listened to the testimony with mounting rage. Finally, he jumped to his feet. "Swenson, you're a liar as well as a murderer! Lara would never have lost control of her craft without a reason."

"Guard! Please remove Captain Shalken immediately!" ordered the judge. A young guard took Jan's arm and led him from the courtroom. Before leaving, Jan turned and saw Swenson looking at him with a smirk. He stopped and took a step back, but a second guard grabbed his other arm and pulled him from the room.

Swenson's first mate was called to the stand next, and his testimony corroborated his captain's version. Finally, the judge asked if there were any more witnesses. "Not at this time," the court administrator said. "Three crew members from the *Arctic Wind* and Dr. Ingerson, who performed the autopsy, are scheduled to testify this afternoon."

"Then we stand adjourned until two o'clock."

Several miles across town two members of the *Arctic Wind*'s crew, brothers who lived together, and who had been on deck that fateful day, were scheduled to testify during the afternoon session. They received a phone call informing them a private taxicab would pick them up in thirty minutes and bring them to the inquest. The taxi arrived on time and the two men stepped in.

Court reconvened after lunch, and harpoon gunner Gudmund Vikinsson took the stand.

After stating his name and other preliminaries, he provided a previously agreed-upon version of the events.

"Could you please tell the court what you saw immediately prior to the incident?"

"Well, as we maneuvered close to the whales I was lining up my shot, aiming and preparing to shoot, but I could not shoot because of interference from the Zodiac's crew. They approached rapidly from the port side and began weaving between the whales and us. I was afraid someone would be seriously hurt."

"So you never fired your harpoon cannon?"

"No sir," he replied firmly, "I never did. The Zodiac suddenly went out of control and stalled right in our path. They were too close for our ship to avoid running over them."

"Do you know why their boat went out of control?"

"No sir, but they were in a difficult situation. There were many contributing factors to the accident. The water was turbulent. There might have been a disturbance from the whales. They were maneuvering through two-to-three-meter ocean swells, and the pressure wave from our bow might also have affected them. As I said, they were very close to our ship, perhaps only twenty meters."

"I see. Do you have anything else to add?"

"No, sir."

"Thank you. You are excused. I would like to call Doctor Ingerson." The doctor who had performed the autopsies took the stand next. "Doctor Ingerson, please give the court the result of your autopsies."

"My examination revealed the victims died from blunt force trauma. I believe that is consistent with the testimony we have heard, that they were crushed under the *Arctic Wind*'s hull as it passed over the Zodiac. I also found their bodies suffered additional injuries consistent with being struck by the ship's propeller blades."

"Thank you, Doctor. Is there anything else?"

"Yes sir. Unrelated to the cause of the incident, but just to complete the record, my examination of Lara Shalken indicated she was pregnant. I estimate she was a little over one month into her pregnancy." Jan was watching the testimony on closed-circuit television in a conference room down the hall from the courtroom. Doctor Ingerson's testimony about Lara's pregnancy was a shock and hit him like a body blow. He sagged in his chair as tears filled his eyes, blurring the television image.

"Is there anything else, Doctor Ingerson?"

"No, sir."

"Thank you, Doctor. You are excused." Turning to the court clerk, the judge asked if the two remaining witnesses, the brothers who lived together, were present.

"No Your Honor. They should have arrived by now. We don't know where they are. In their absence, this is all the testimony we have."

"Thank you. I believe the court has sufficient evidence to make a ruling. In the absence of further evidence, I am declaring that further testimony will not be required. We will reconvene at 9 o'clock tomorrow morning for my decision."

Chapter 19

Meeting Whales on the Silver Bank

February 1ˢᵗ

"*Y*ou don't mind doing photo duty this morning, do you?" asked Terry, as she and Joe donned their wet suits.

"Nope, I'm looking forward to testing my underwater photography skills," replied Joe.

"Great! I just want to relax and enjoy the whales today. Make sure you use the wide-angle lens, otherwise all you'll get is a picture of a hunk of flesh that could look like anything, from a whale to a horse."

"Got it. Hey, here's our Zodiac. Let's go aboard."

Leaving the *SeaVenture,* they headed east toward the rising sun. "I saw a few whales breaching and tail slapping out that way earlier," said Bob Johnson, piloting boat number one. "Figured that'd be a good place to find some whales. Plus, we'll head into calmer water there." As the small boat headed out, everyone scanned the ocean, shielding their eyes from the glare of the morning sun, each hoping to spot misty blows indicating whales. Forty minutes of cruising through the rolling waves was fruitless, as the whales proved elusive. "Must be keeping a low profile this morning," said Johnson. Suddenly Ann, one of the Australians, called out, "Whales spouting at one o'clock!" They all turned to look just right of the bow; nothing for a minute.

Then, "Yes, I see them!" exclaimed Terry. "Look, they're coming toward us!"

"That's a mother and calf. See how the distance from the head to the dorsal fin is shorter on one whale compared to the other one?" pointed out Johnson. "Okay everyone, get ready, and let's see if they hang around." They donned fins and masks as the whales swam closer. Then they just stopped, floating motionless less than fifty feet abreast of the small boat. "Looks like we have a couple of curious whales. Over you go, but quietly."

They slipped in, careful not to make any splashes, and ducked their heads beneath the surface. They saw the incredible sight of a large mother humpback and her calf, a month old but already fifteen feet long. Both whales took a breath and slowly drifted to the bottom, fifty feet below. The group watched, awed, as the baby rested on her mother's back, then glided to her side, then moved to her head and nuzzled, jaw to jaw. All the while, the whales maintained contact, brushing each other as they changed position. The baby left her mother's side, rose to surface, and took two breaths, while the mother whale, not needing to breathe as frequently, remained below.

Curious at meeting another group of small creatures dropping into her liquid world from a noisy object on the surface, the baby whale glided through the middle of the group, and then swam to the bottom. The group was mesmerized, resisting the urge to reach out, as the whale cruised past them only several feet away. She rejoined her mother, brushing against her body. Then she hung vertically in the water, appearing to stand on her tail as she looked up at the strange little creatures. Wanting to explore, she rose again, directly toward Terry. The whale came within an arm's length, turned, and made eye contact, staring at the strange little creature's two small eyes, what looked like two long, thin fins near the front and a split tail at its back. She continued to the next creature, and the next. She passed a few feet from Joe, who was pointing something unfamiliar at her. It made a clicking noise, similar to the sound her young memory associated with fish. *These must be large fish,* her whale brain told her. Her curiosity satisfied, the baby whale pumped her flukes energetically and swam away, knowing her mother would follow.

The adult whale, watching the action intently, rose toward the surface. She took a long breath and swam directly toward Joe. He froze, wondering what she would do. He knew a mother grizzly bear or a lion would attack anyone foolish enough to approach her cub. She continued closing the distance, but he had the presence to take a picture, head-on. From a distance of only about twenty feet, he had the opportunity to appreciate the immense size and power of the animal, noticing the extraordinary length of the snow-white, fifteen-foot long pectoral fins. They spread like giant wings, from which the species derived its name, *Megaptera Novaeangliae,* or *Giant Winged of New England.* Terry watched, wide-eyed, as the whale came within ten feet of Joe, turned right, then pulled her left pectoral fin against her body to avoid hitting him. She examined him with her baseball-sized eye as she passed. He was entirely absorbed in snapping pictures, and positioned himself to photograph the underside of her fluke as she accelerated to catch her rambunctious offspring.

The two whales quickly disappeared. The group—bonded by their unique experience—lifted their heads above the surface, sharing their excitement. As they floated, Johnson maneuvered the Zodiac toward them, listening to their comments.

"My God, did you ever think we would get so close?"

"What an encounter!"

"I hoped for it, but I never thought I would see it!"

"Did you see how they interacted with each other?"

"And how close they came!"

The women were especially moved, and several removed their masks, wiping tears from their eyes. Joe looked at Terry, who had crossed her arms over her heart, looking down at the water. "Hey Ter, you all right?" Terry looked up and Joe could see she was crying.

"Oh Joe, did you see the baby? She looked at me, *really* looked at me! Did you see how tender they were to each other? I could sense the caring and love."

"Yeah, quite a moment," he agreed, knowing how much having a baby would mean to Terry. He swam over and held her in his arms before climbing aboard the boat.

Bob Johnson smiled, noting the group's exuberance. He had tethered himself to the Zodiac and dropped over the side to shoot some video footage. "I got some great shots of your encounter. Climb aboard! We're heading back to the *SeaVenture* for lunch."

When they arrived, Zodiac two was already back and that group was on deck, eating. They were subdued, having spent the morning frustrated, chasing elusive whales. When they heard whooping and hollering as Zodiac one approached, they looked over and shouted questions. "How was it?" "Did you see any whales?" More cheers and whoops answered their questions, and they were caught up in the contagious enthusiasm, hopeful their luck would improve during the remainder of the week.

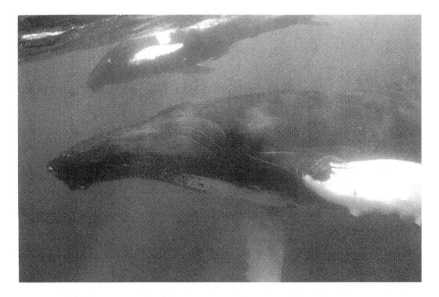

Terry watched, wide-eyed, as the whale came within ten feet of Joe, turned right, then pulled her left pectoral fin close against her body to avoid hitting him, examining him with her baseball-sized eye as she passed.

Photo by Paul J. Mila

Chapter 20

February 3rd

    *T*he *SeaVenture* departed the Silver Bank early Friday morning, cruising slowly southward toward Puerto Plata. Terry and Joe stood on the rear deck, watching the rusted cargo ship recede into the distance, remaining as a landmark for the next visitors to the Bank. "Well, wasn't it an incredible week?" Terry asked.

    "You bet, Ter. I never could have imagined the experience before we came. You know, I used to take my family whale watching off Montauk, Long Island. We saw humpbacks there too."

    "Whales from the same group we saw this week, I bet," said Terry.

    "Yeah. I used to think it was great seeing whales from a boat, spouting and all that stuff. But you only see the top of their backs, and their flukes when they dive. You don't realize how much more whale there is under water. It's just like an iceberg, where you only see about one-eighth above the surface and the rest is below. We sure had an amazing experience!"

"I hope our pictures come out. You took a lot."

"Yeah, and I got a lot of those fluke shots you wanted me to take. Why?"

"Well, the black and white pattern on the underside of each humpback's fluke is unique, just like a human's fingerprint. So, by having a catalog of whale tails, you can identify the whale if you ever see it again, either in person or in a photograph."

"I think I recall reading something about that," Joe replied. "One day, my son came home from school with some scholastic newsletter that mentioned it." Terry saw a faraway, sad look in Joe's eyes as he spoke.

"Hey," she said, squeezing his hand, "maybe you'll get the chance to go whale watching with *our* son or daughter someday."

"I hope so, I really do hope so," Joe replied, pulling Terry close and kissing her forehead as they embraced.

As their boat cruised slowly, they watched whales in the distance, breaching, tail lobbing, and pec fin slapping. After a week observing the whales' behavior, they were used to the displays, but were still awed by the giant animals' power and grace. Thirty minutes later, the *SeaVenture*'s twin engines accelerated. It soon reached top cruising speed, indicating they had cleared the Silver Bank's shallow waters and were heading across the open ocean toward Puerto Plata. Terry said, "I can't wait to show our friends our souvenir video. The crew did a great job shooting our whale encounters and got amazing footage of mothers and newborn calves. It'll be good to get home and watch it again."

"Well, the black and white pattern on the underside of each humpback's fluke is unique, just like a human's fingerprint. So, by having a catalog of whale tails, you can identify the whale if you ever see it again, either in person, or in a photograph."

Photo by Paul J. Mila

Chapter 21

Cozumel, One Week Later

February 10th

*O*ne afternoon, Joe returned home with several bags of groceries and saw Terry hunched over the kitchen table, carefully examining whale photos. "Joe, look at these pictures! You did a fabulous job. They came out great!"

"What a load off my mind," he said, wiping his brow in mock relief.

"No, really! Look at these, especially the tail shots. This close-up of the baby swimming past me is amazing!"

"Pretty good for an amateur, even if I do say so. I think the whale came out much better than you," he said, deftly sidestepping an elbow aimed at his midsection.

"Now look at these tail shots. See this one with the scratchy lines on the bottom of the fluke? I'm naming him 'Scratch.' And this one, all white except for what resembles a pattern of bubbles. I'm calling him Bubba."

"Very presidential sounding," he replied. "How do you know if they're hims or hers?"

"Well, I can't tell from these pictures, but it doesn't matter. These are for my own private scrapbook anyway. Oh look! Here's the mom and her baby. Well, at least we know *she's* a she. Now, look at the pattern on her fluke. This big splotch looks like a clover leaf."

"Hmmm, I guess so. I always failed those inkblot tests the department's shrinks gave me. I'm surprised they ever gave me a gun."

"Well, I'm naming her Clover. That fits and it's a girl's name too."

"Okay, have fun with your pictures. I'm starting supper. I'm hungry."

Terry and Joe spent the next week getting *DiveWithTerry* organized, sorting out the reservations backlog, taking new customers to explore the reefs, and settling into the daily routine of running a dive business. Returning home after a full day of morning and afternoon dives, Terry wearily sank into a padded chair next to the answering machine with a notepad. The red numerals indicated six messages were waiting. When she heard the fifth message, a familiar but somewhat shaky voice jolted her. "Hello, Terry and Joe, this is Femke van der Zee." There was a slight pause, a noticeable breath, and then her voice broke. "I need your help. Please! My sister was killed and they're trying to say it was an accident, but I know it wasn't. I don't know where to turn. Joe, I hope with your police background and international contacts, you can help me. Oh, I don't know. Please call me back. My number is . . ."

Terry could hear Femke was trying to maintain control, but by the end she was crying so much that Terry had difficulty understanding the telephone number. "Joe, listen to this call. It's from Femke!" she said, replaying the message. Joe listened and then asked Terry to play it again. "My God," she said, "what do you think could have happened?"

"I don't know, Ter, but it's too late to call her now," he said, looking at his watch and computing the time difference between Cozumel and the Netherlands. "Let's call her first thing tomorrow."

Early the next morning, Terry dialed the number Femke had left on her answering machine. She bit her lip impatiently, listening to the rings. On the fourth ring, she heard a familiar voice come through the speakerphone. "Hello, this is Femke."

"Femke, this is Terry. Joe is right here with me. We have you on speakerphone. We heard your message last night. I hope this is a good time to call. What happened?"

"Oh Terry, thank you so much for calling back. Hello, Joe."

"Hello, Femke," Joe replied. "How can we help you?"

"My sister was killed several weeks ago. I'm sure she was murdered, but they're lying, saying it was an accident. But I know . . . ."

"Femke, slow down. Tell us what happened," Joe said as Femke began to get more excited as she talked. She paused, composing herself. They heard her take a deep breath before continuing.

"Lara was a member of a conservationist organization called Peaceful Seas. They were trying to stop whalers from killing whales and were killed when . . ." All of a sudden, Terry made the connection.

"Joe, the woman we saw on TV!" she exclaimed. "Remember we thought she looked familiar? She was Femke's sister! That's why!" Joe nodded, recalling the face that he could not quite place, fitting the resemblance together in his mind.

"Go on, Femke," he said.

"We had no witnesses to what happened, only the whalers, who we believe were responsible. By the time Jan, her husband, arrived on the scene, it was all over. Three crewmembers were dead. The whalers blamed Lara, saying she lost control of her Zodiac in front of their ship, which passed over and crushed them. Last week, there was an official inquest, and the judge ruled it an accident."

"And you disagree?" Joe asked.

"An accident? No way in hell!" she exclaimed. Joe and Terry could feel the anger and indignation through the phone. "Lara was experienced and knew what she was doing on the water. It was, how do you say it, a cover-up."

"Who would be responsible for a cover-up and why?" asked Joe, trying to understand the overall situation, but treading carefully with his questions, sensitive to Femke's fragile emotional state.

"I don't know, Joe. But some witnesses who were supposed to testify are missing."

"Missing?" Joe said, his investigative instincts pricked for the first time.

"Yes. On the day they were to testify they were seen getting into a taxi, but were never seen again. The entire issue of killing whales is politically divisive in Iceland, where the investigation occurred. I think the people who favor killing whales are trying to, what is your expression, 'sweep it under the rug.' These forces are also in alliance with other countries seeking to overturn the International Whaling Commission's ban on killing whales. They cannot afford any more bad publicity. In addition, the current party in power in Iceland, headed by Prime Minister Stefan Valsson, could very well lose the next election if they are directly tied in any way to killing whales, not to mention covering up murder."

Joe listened quietly, assimilating all the information, simultaneously thinking of the potential ramifications if Femke's interpretation of the events was correct. Terry verbalized his thoughts. "Joe, Femke's talking about murder, cover-ups, obstruction of justice, international politics. This is way over our heads." Joe nodded in agreement.

"How can we help you, Femke?" he asked, genuinely puzzled as to what she expected of them.

"Joe, do you remember meeting someone named Inspector Philip Willemstad? I spoke to him and he said he met you about a year ago." Joe thought for a moment, and then recalled the connection.

"Yes, yes I do remember him. We met at an international law enforcement conference in Amsterdam. I was conducting a seminar just before leaving the NYPD. We got along very well. He's a real bright guy."

"I mentioned your name to him and he remembered you very well. He said if anyone could figure out something, you could. Since

Lara was a Dutch citizen, he was able to obtain copies of the inquest transcripts. He reviewed the information and called the judge who ruled on the case. He said the investigation seems thorough, but he has a suspicion there is more to the case. But based on the existing evidence, he has no authority to officially pursue it further. Unless we uncover definite evidence to the contrary, the judge will not reopen the inquiry. Joe, I can't let this go. Lara was my sister. I can't let her death end like this." After a long pause, Femke asked, "Joe, can you come to Holland and examine the records? I can't afford to pay you as a private investigator, but I can pay your airfare."

Joe and Terry listened and looked at each other. "Femke, please hold on a second," Joe said, pressing the mute button. "What do you think?" he asked Terry.

"I don't know what to say, Joe. She sounds so helpless. Do you really think you can do anything?"

"Off the top of my head, I don't think so. I would have to see the records and talk to Willemstad."

"Well, why don't you go? Even if you don't uncover additional evidence, maybe hearing someone she trusts say it was an accident will give her peace. If you can give me a hand here until we're all caught up with business, you can leave next week. I can hold down the fort until you return. There's no reason for me to go with you."

Joe took the phone off mute. "Femke, I can come next week. Don't worry about the airfare; we'll take care of it."

"Bless you," said Femke, crying as her tension released itself in a flood of pent-up emotion. "Bless you both."

Chapter 22

Reykjavik

February 15th

*T*hor Rodale ordered another beer. He had been drinking more heavily than usual since the *Arctic Wind*'s last voyage. The proprietor considered not serving him another beer, but relented after looking into Rodale's haunted eyes. He thought, *if ever a man needed the solace of alcohol, this man did.* Besides, the man standing next to Thor, a stranger, volunteered to take him home. Thor, a maintenance engineer on the *Arctic Wind,* had been on deck that fateful day and saw what happened to the Zodiac's crew. But he knew he could not talk about it, nor tell anyone what he had seen or how it had affected him. He was haunted by the victims' screams as they were swept under the whaling ship. As a fellow seaman, he felt a kinship with them, though their intentions were contrary to his. Being an accomplice to hiding the truth was more than his conscience could bear, at least while sober. As a result, he was almost never sober anymore.

"You've had quite a bit to drink tonight, my friend," the stranger said, sounding concerned. Thor eyed the man as best he could through his drunken haze. That he could not recognize him did not trouble Thor. When he looked into a mirror, he could not recognize the drawn face and sunken eyes staring back. He looked at his empty glass and mumbled an unintelligible reply to the stranger's comment. The proprietor looked at the stranger and shook his head.

"I think it best if you could get him home," he said. "Do you know where he lives?"

"I think we can both manage," the stranger said in a friendly manner. "Come, my friend. Let's get you safely home and into bed. You'll feel better tomorrow." Thor offered his arm without resistance, and the kindly stranger led him into the rainy night. The two men walked about three blocks, until they came to a poorly lit street with few pedestrians but heavy vehicular traffic. A bus approached. The driver was tired. It was his last run of a boring, uneventful night. He noticed two men starting to cross the street. As he applied the brakes, he saw one of the men retreat to the curb while the other one stumbled, *or was he pushed,* the driver would reflect later, into the bus's path. The wheels skidded on the rain-slick pavement and the driver heard, and felt, a sickening "thump" as Thor fell under the front wheels.

Stopping the bus as quickly as he could, the driver jumped out and saw Thor's crumpled body. He grimaced when he saw blood mixing with puddles in the street, running into the storm sewer. Then he looked for the unfortunate victim's companion, but he had vanished into the night. When police questioned the bus driver, he testified the man seemed to stumble as he crossed the street. But still he questioned himself, playing over in his mind what he had seen looking through his rain-spattered windshield on the dark street. Did the other man's hand push Thor Rodale in front of the bus, or were the fingers trying to grasp his raincoat and pull him back? He was not sure.

Chapter 23

Amsterdam, Holland

February 18th

    *J*oe reflected on his last two days in Cozumel, hoping he hadn't forgotten to resolve any important issues before leaving. He noticed the "fasten seat belt" sign illuminate, indicating the plane was on final approach into Amsterdam's Schiphol Airport after the long, nonstop flight from New York's JFK. His thoughts drifted to the upcoming investigation, but were interrupted when the plane's tires screeched hitting the runway. He cleared immigration and customs in only thirty minutes, and then scanned the crowd for a familiar face. Finally, he recognized Femke van der Zee's tall, athletic form in the crowd. "Good to see you, Femke," he said, embracing her.

    "Yes it is, but I wish under different circumstances," she replied. "How is your dear wife, Terry?"

"Oh, she's fine. She'll have her hands full running the dive operation. But then again, she was doing a good job before I met her, so I'm sure she'll be all right."

Femke turned and introduced a tall, robust man. "Joe, this is my brother-in-law, Jan Shalken, Lara's husband."

"How do you do," Joe said extending his hand. "I'm very sorry for your loss."

"Thank you, Joe. It's difficult describing it to someone who has not had the experience. The sudden loss, feeling part of you has been ripped out," Jan said.

Joe held Jan's handshake and maintained eye contact. "Believe me, Jan, I know what you're going through because it happened to me many years ago." Jan did not know what to say, but felt a kinship to Joe, bonded through terrible, mutual tragedies.

"Jan, Joe's wife and children were killed in a tragic automobile accident several years ago," Femke informed Jan.

"Then I extend my condolences to you, Joe. Sometimes one is so consumed by his own personal loss, he forgets horrible things also happen to others."

"Thank you, Jan. Yes, you're right, but I think it's all part of the grieving process." Joe observed that the skin on Jan's face seemed loose, as if the underlying fat layer had been consumed, and that his clothes fit as though they were a size too large. He made a mental note. *Looks like he's lost weight, probably a combination of tension, stress, and depression.*

"I thought with your long flight and seven-hour time difference, you'd be jet-lagged, so I planned a relaxing dinner at my house. Is that all right?" asked Femke.

"You bet. I feel okay right now, but I'll probably crash a few hours later."

After a short walk, they arrived at Femke's car, a silver Corolla. Jan let Joe sit in the front seat, as a courtesy. As Joe sat down he looked over his shoulder at Jan, whose knees were under his chin. *For such tall people, the Dutch certainly buy small cars,* thought Joe.

The ride to Femke's house took forty-five minutes. As they drove, Joe noted Dutch architecture featured homes constructed of stone, as opposed to wood-frame construction in most United States suburban areas.

"I've arranged a meeting with Inspector Willemstad tomorrow, but not until late morning. I thought you might need some additional time to get acclimated," she said.

"Thanks, I appreciate that," Joe replied. "As I recall, Philip Willemstad is a sharp, no-nonsense guy. He doesn't appreciate people wasting his time. I would really like to have all my wits about me when I meet him."

"We're here," said Femke, slowing as she pulled into a parking spot in front of a modest, two-story white stone building. Jan assisted Joe with his luggage while Femke went inside and prepared dinner.

When they sat down to eat, Joe called into the kitchen where Femke was putting the finishing touches to dinner. "Femke, please don't fuss over me. Can I help you at all?"

"No, Joe, I'm just about done."

"Hmm, smells real good. What are you making?"

Femke entered the dining room carrying a large, steaming pot. "It's a Dutch specialty called *boerenkool mettwurst*."

"What's in it?" asked Joe.

"Sausage, mashed potatoes, and kale," replied Femke.

"Hmm, this is really good," remarked Joe, as he sampled a healthy portion.

"Glad you like it." Femke looked over at Jan and was going to ask him if he was also enjoying the meal. Seeing him take a large second helping provided the answer, and she just smiled.

After dinner, Jan educated Joe about the activities, goals, and methods of the Peaceful Seas organization. "So, Peaceful Seas is not one of those eco-terrorist organizations that you read about every so often," concluded Joe.

"Not at all," replied Jan. "We advocate nonviolence, avoid confrontation, and work through the courts and legal systems of various countries. Confrontation is the last resort. But even then, we use peaceful means. As I said, we are strictly nonviolent."

"So, there is no way the crew aboard the *Arctic Wind* would have been defending themselves from any threats from your group?" Joe asked.

"Not a chance," Jan replied vehemently. "In fact, they never claimed they were defending themselves. They justified their actions saying our Zodiac crew precipitated the confrontation and Lara caused the accident by her reckless actions."

"And you disagree?" said Joe, asking a rhetorical question, projecting what he assumed were Jan's thoughts.

"Of course! We confronted them, but only because they persisted illegally killing whales. And Lara's seamanship was first-rate. She knew what she was doing. No way on God's earth could she have lost control of her boat!" Jan's eyes blazed. His voice rose and Joe could see the veins in his neck bulging with a surge of blood as he fought to control his temper.

"But you didn't see what actually transpired."

"No, we were too late getting to the scene," Jan said, looking at the table with frustrated resignation over the fact that he could not have saved Lara. Joe watched the change in body language sympathetically. It appeared Jan was deflating like a pricked balloon, right before his eyes. He heard a stifled sob and realized Femke had joined them at the table, probably several minutes earlier.

"Well, I hope I can help, but I won't know until we meet Willemstad tomorrow. Thank you for a delicious meal, Femke. I'm going to turn in, if you'll show me where I'm sleeping." As they all rose to leave the table, he kissed her cheek and then shook hands with Jan. He followed Femke upstairs to his bedroom, and within ten minutes was soundly asleep.

Chapter 24

February 19th

*"W*e have an 11 o'clock appointment to see Inspector Willemstad," Femke told the receptionist at police headquarters.

"I'll tell the inspector you're here," she replied, curtly but courteously.

Joe, Femke, and Jan made small talk passing the minutes, when Philip Willemstad's booming voice startled them. "Detective Manetta, how good to see you again!" he exclaimed, enthusiastically shaking Joe's hand. Joe, a well-built six-footer, felt small next to Willemstad's six-foot-four frame.

"Good to see you too, Philip," Joe said, extricating his hand from Willemstad's beefy mitt, "but since I gave up the *detective* title, it's just 'Joe' Manetta now."

"Ah yes, I do recall the story your friends in New York told me, about how you lost your heart to a mermaid in Cozumel, or something like that," he laughed.

"Yes, something like that," Joe replied, smiling. "I'll tell you all about it sometime."

Willemstad turned to Femke and Jan, and apologized for not addressing them immediately. "That's all right, Philip," Femke replied graciously. "We're just glad you two have a good relationship so we could review the records concerning my sister's death without the usual protocols and formal delays." The reference to the business at hand quickly removed the initial levity.

"Yes, Femke. I have not forgotten what brought you and Jan here today," Willemstad replied in a somber tone. "Come into my office and make yourselves comfortable."

As they sat around a small table in Willemstad's office, he brought in a large cardboard box filled with files. "My counterparts in Iceland have generously provided copies of all their files. Court transcripts, the complete autopsy report, and other investigative information," he announced.

"What kind of other information?" Joe asked.

"Well, for instance, the results of the harpoon gunner's polygraph tests. They asked him directly if he fired his harpoon at the crew of the Zodiac. He said he did not and the polygraph interpretation indicates he was telling the truth."

"Interesting that they would release so much information without court orders and other required documents," replied Joe.

"Yes, I'm quite surprised too. They seem extremely cooperative, I suppose to prove they have nothing to hide and this was just an unfortunate accident."

"Or to convince us they are not really murderers!" replied Jan vehemently.

"Well," continued Willemstad, "having reviewed this material thoroughly, I have to agree the evidence supports their official position that this was an unfortunate accident. I wish I could come to another conclusion, but in good conscience, I cannot. You may inspect the material, but you must do it here. I cannot permit this information to leave my office."

"We understand," said Joe. "Do you have a conference room we can use? Maybe we can reconvene in a couple of hours and review our conclusions."

"Yes, come with me. There's a room down the hall. I have some meetings, but I'll stop in later this afternoon. If you want to order lunch, just call my secretary. Good luck."

"Well, we have a lot of work ahead of us," said Joe. "Let's get started."

Three hours and several cups of strong coffee later, Joe rubbed his eyes from the mental fatigue of examining numerous files. "Well, here's where I'm coming out on this. My initial impression was the investigation was conducted very thoroughly and professionally, building to a logical conclusion that this was an accident precipitated by the Zodiac crew."

"Impossible!" interrupted Jan, pounding his massive fist on the table with such force that Joe waited a moment before continuing, in case the thick wooden table collapsed.

Joe glanced at Femke briefly. "Jan, I know how you feel, but without witnesses to the contrary, we can't challenge the court's ruling."

Jan looked down and clenched his powerful hands in frustration, feeling powerless to affect the outcome of the situation. Joe continued. "But I also found some unresolved issues. First, the mention of two witnesses mysteriously vanishing is a loose thread that bothers me, although there could be an innocent explanation. More important was the report about the condition of Lara's body. Did either of you read that section of the autopsy report?"

"Yes," said Femke. "I have it right here, why?"

"Well, it says all three were killed when the *Arctic Wind*'s hull crushed them. Then their bodies suffered additional trauma from the ship's propeller. But Jan, didn't you testify that Lara's body was not battered or broken?"

"Yes." He hesitated, composing himself before continuing. "Lara only had a severe neck wound. Even that was gruesome, horrible to see. But I was so relieved her body did not suffer more damage, I gave it no more thought."

"Well, why didn't she suffer the same wounds as the others?" Joe persisted. "Have either of you seen these autopsy photos?"

"No, I could not bear to look," said Femke, closing her eyes as she spoke. Joe looked at Jan, who just avoided his eyes and shook his head.

"Well, there's a big difference in the appearance of the bodies. The other two are pretty well battered and also suffered slicing wounds from the propeller blades. But Lara looks as though she's asleep, except for this deep gash in her neck. I'm not a forensic pathologist, but I think something else caused her fatal injury." He reached for the telephone and asked the operator to contact Willemstad. Several minutes later, he joined them in the conference room.

"Well, have you reached any conclusions?" he asked.

Femke and Jan let Joe speak for them. "On the face of it, it seems we have no strong basis to challenge the findings, but I have one question, Philip. When Lara's body was returned for burial, did you request another autopsy?"

"Why, no. The original autopsy was sufficient and seems to have been competently performed. We saw no need."

"Well, Philip, I think we've found some inconsistencies. We need a second autopsy to resolve some questions regarding Lara's death."

"I see," said Willemstad, looking at Jan and Femke. "That will require an exhumation order, which the family must request." Jan and Femke looked at each other and then nodded.

Chapter 25

Tokyo, Japan

February 21st

*O*shura Haigata stared at the speakerphone intently, as if attempting to project his will through the phone lines. "Good day, everyone, or good evening, depending on your location. Please identify yourselves for the record."

"Jon Andresson, Iceland."

"Stig Carlson, Norway."

"Eric Braunnel, Finland."

"Thank you. As you know, we have less than four more months until the IWC meeting. I trust we can hold everything together until then," he said sharply. Everyone knew he was directing this comment toward Jon Andresson, who felt his neck hairs bristle, waiting for Haigata to press him on the status of the investigation. He was relieved when Haigata began with his own report instead.

"I will provide my update first." Haigata's enthusiasm annoyed Andresson. *He can't wait to impress us with his diplomatic puffery,* he thought. "Japan has now spent in excess of 340 million in US dollars to successfully encourage the following Caribbean nations to vote with us at the next IWC session: Antigua, Barbuda, Dominica, Guinea, Grenada, St. Vincent and the Grenadines, St. Lucia, St. Kitts and Nevis, and Panama. Also supporting us in other regions are the Solomon Islands and Morocco."

"A very impressive list," commented Stig Carlson.

"Thank you, but I have more good news," gushed Haigata. *Isn't he an effervescent son of a bitch today?* thought Andresson, happy no one could see his eyes reflecting contempt for Haigata. "We know we can count on China, Korea, Russia, Iceland, and Finland, so we are only a few votes away from gaining a majority voting bloc at the IWC. I have now convinced my government to focus our financial and economic incentive initiatives on West Africa. That should give us the three-quarters majority required for voting control. Nothing can stop us now," he concluded triumphantly.

"Congratulations, Oshura," commented Eric Braunnel. "We all applaud your government's efforts." *When do the trumpets blare?* wondered Andresson.

"How is work proceeding on the Revised Management Scheme?" prodded Haigata. Andresson let Eric Braunnel give their report.

"Well, Jon and I have laid solid groundwork," began Braunnel. "Although we have not been assigned to any working groups, we have managed to move several proposals along for consideration. Of course, we are ensuring our proposal to abolish the commercial whaling moratorium remains on the agenda. We are also proposing that the committees recommend abolishing whale sanctuaries in the Antarctic Ocean and Indian Ocean. Anything else, Jon?"

"No, Eric, that sums up our progress."

"Excellent, gentlemen," said Haigata. "Stig, how about you?"

"Well, unfortunately, I cannot report the same degree of success. The DNA registry is moving ahead, but I am attempting to weaken the non-compliance penalties. In addition, I'm trying to confuse the issue by providing conflicting scientific evidence regarding the validity of the DNA approach. Consequently, there's a possibility I may succeed in postponing the program's implementation."

"Well, keep up the good fight and do not be discouraged," said Haigata. "We all support your efforts." *Condescending bastard,* thought Andresson.

"Thank you, Oshura," replied Carlson.

"I think we can conclude the call, unless anyone has anything else to add," prompted Haigata. After several seconds of empty air, he said, "Thank you, everyone. My secretary will contact you to schedule our next call." He watched his speakerphone intently, until he heard three clicks, indicating all participants had terminated their connections.

When he was sure the line was clear, Haigata buzzed his secretary. "Place the call to Mexico now," he ordered curtly. He stood, stretching his legs, and looked out the window toward Tokyo Bay, which was unusually placid. He reflected on the potential impact of learning from Andresson that the renegade whaling cowboy disrupting his plans was Ulf Swenson. *Amazing how connections made earlier in life can affect your life years later,* he thought. He sat down at his desk, impatiently shuffling papers until his secretary had contacted Mexico. He turned as the intercom came to life.

"I have President Juarez on the line, sir," she said.

"Mr. President, thank you for taking time to speak with me today."

"My pleasure, Oshura. It is always good to talk with you, especially when you have favorable news."

"Well, as a matter of fact, I have very good news, Hector," Haigata said, knowing he could slip into conversational informality after the president had addressed him by first name. "Japan has authorized me to inform you we are proceeding with financing and construction of the $600 million salt works plant, near San Ignacio Lagoon."

"Well, that is indeed good news, except for the location. The San Ignacio Lagoon is a popular and financially lucrative tourist destination. Tourists come from all over the world to experience contact with friendly grey whales. It provides a very strong economic benefit to the region. Can't you build the plant elsewhere on the coast, as we originally discussed?"

"I'm afraid not, Hector. We need direct ocean access at that location to make the project economically viable. I know you are concerned that dredging the lagoon will disrupt the grey whale sanctuary. I am sending a team of scientists to assist your government in producing reports validating our position that the whales will find suitable sanctuaries several miles north of the lagoon. That should keep the pain-in-the-ass Americans off your back."

"Well, I'm not sure of that, Oshura, but hopefully, a detailed scientific study should help blunt unfavorable media coverage."

"Rest assured, these men are highly regarded in their field. I am confident we can proceed on schedule. Furthermore, I am positive the project will provide even greater long-term economic benefits to the region than whale watching. I know you are very busy, Mr. President, but I just wanted to personally give you the good news."

"Thank you, Oshura. I appreciate your courtesy," he replied, sensing Haigata's intention to terminate the call. "Have a good day. Good-bye."

"Good-bye, Mr. President." Haigata turned and looked at a large wall calendar. His next call to President Juarez would precede the IWC meeting by several days, just prior to the salt works plant groundbreaking. It was perfectly timed to pull the string on his economic proposal. In exchange for his country's investment, he would request that Mexico shift its voting position and support his group's pro-whaling proposals. He relaxed in his plush, leather executive chair, satisfied about gathering additional support. Haigata smiled, enjoying the omnipotent feeling that only money could buy.

Chapter 26

Reykjavik

February 24th

"*V*alsson here," answered the prime minister, looking at his mantle clock. Few people knew his private number and he wondered who would call so early in the morning,

"There are still two people on that list I gave to you. Why are they still alive?" asked the voice in a low, menacing tone.

"You've always been impatient, and it has always gotten you into trouble," Valsson replied wearily. "We are working as rapidly as possible, but it must be done with caution. Does this really need to be done?" he asked, hoping for a reprieve from the dirty business in which he had become entwined.

"Enough with your sermons and your stupid questions," the other voice replied coldly. "Just take care of it. You have the power."

Stefan Valsson put the handset down, terminating the call. *Yes, I have the power, but* he *has control,* he thought, ruefully, as he picked up the telephone and made another call.

Later that day, Alfred Haggar, the cook from the *Arctic Wind,* gave no thought to the two men he observed casually walking away from his car. An hour later, driving along a narrow, winding road on the outskirts of the city, he depressed the brake pedal of his old 1985 Volkswagen Beetle as he eased into a downhill curve, slightly faster than the posted speed limit of thirty kilometers per hour. Coming out of the curve, the incline steepened as it led into a sharp "S" curve, posted at a reduced speed of twenty kilometers per hour. As Alfred applied more brake pressure, the pedal sank to the floorboard with a sickening, mushy thump. Alfred frantically pounded the pedal as he negotiated the first part of the "S," briefly stealing a glimpse at the needle on the speedometer, which was now passing forty-five kilometers per hour. As the little Beetle entered the next part of the "S," the weight of the rear-mounted engine caused the rear wheels to slide out into space. The car skidded off the road and the rear end pitched down. Alfred found himself staring up at the sky, still gripping the steering wheel. The car slid backward, tumbling and rolling down a 500-foot embankment. Mercifully, Alfred was already dead when the ruptured fuel line sprayed gasoline over the hot engine and the mangled wreck erupted in a ball of flame.

In another part of town, Gudmund Vikinsson, the *Arctic Wind*'s harpoon gunner, hid in a temporary apartment, staring at articles he had torn from the newspaper. He reread the story about two crewmen who never arrived at the inquest. They were still missing. Then he reread the account of the bus accident that had claimed Thor Rodale's life. Unrelated events? Coincidence? Vikinsson did not believe in coincidence. Why wasn't anyone making a connection? He decided to remain hidden, venturing out alone only for short periods and only when absolutely necessary. He did not yet know that tomorrow morning, he would be adding the story of Alfred Haggar's automobile accident to his grisly newspaper collection.

Chapter 27

Amsterdam, Holland

March 21st

*I*t had taken a month to process legal documents authorizing the exhumation of Lara Shalken's body. Joe met Inspector Willemstad at the morgue for the autopsy. "Good morning, Joe. You're alone today?" asked Willemstad.

"Hello, Philip. Yes, Femke and Jan just didn't feel they could face this ordeal. I told them I'd give them a full report as soon as we finish."

"A wise decision. Let's go inside. Doctor Visser is already waiting for us."

As they entered the autopsy room, the strong, antiseptic chemical smell struck Joe, triggering a flood of vivid memories. He recalled the harsh lighting in the cold autopsy rooms in New York when he had been an NYPD detective. He remembered witnessing autopsies of numerous young men and women, after violence, drugs, and other mayhem had cut their lives short. "Doctor Visser, Joe Manetta," said Willemstad, making introductions as the two men shook hands. "Mr. Manetta is a former police detective and is assisting us with our investigation."

"I see. Nice to meet you, Mr. Manetta."

"Good to meet you, Doctor. And thank you for fitting us into your busy schedule."

"That's quite all right. Philip and I go back a long way. I'm sure I owe him more favors than I've done for him. The body is over here." As they stepped over to a metal table, Doctor Visser pulled on latex gloves and removed the shroud from Lara Shalken's body. The odor of decay and visible deterioration of the body, having been buried for over a month, assaulted Joe's senses. He studied her face, recalling how attractive she had appeared in the CNN television picture.

Doctor Visser's voice broke his concentration. "I performed a cursory examination before you arrived. As you can see, there are very few external wounds or injuries, except for this deep gash on the side of her neck. That was likely the fatal wound, but we will examine that last. First, I want to examine the rest of the body and see if we can find other injuries that will help us determine exactly how this unfortunate woman died."

"Did you review the notes from her previous autopsy, Doctor?" Joe asked.

"No, I deliberately did not. I did not want to prejudice my conclusions before I performed my own examination. That's a common mistake, often resulting in critical evidence being overlooked." Joe nodded as he glanced at Willemstad. Even though surgical masks covered their facial expressions, Willemstad could see that Doctor Visser's thoroughness impressed Joe.

Doctor Visser talked his way through the examination, as an overhead microphone captured his comments for transcription. "I do not see any bruises, scrapes, or abrasions on the front of the body. Turning her over, there are no visible wounds to her dorsal area, no apparent broken bones." He gently turned her on her back again and continued. "I am cutting through the stitches from the previous autopsy, forming the Y-shaped incision over the sternum. The organs have already been measured, weighed, and replaced during that autopsy, but I will examine them again. I do not see any evidence of blunt-force trauma to the vital organs, no evidence of piercing or cutting."

The detailed examination continued for an hour. Joe and Philip watched Dr. Visser intently as he methodically probed the body.

"I am now examining the neck wound. I see a deep cut on the left side of her neck, exposing the cervical vertebrae. The tissue on either side of the wound is severely abraded. The damage resembles a friction burn. The carotid artery is completely severed and the spinal cord is severely damaged. Death would have come instantaneously from a broken neck. If she had lived through the initial injury, she would have died quickly, within a few minutes, from substantial blood loss due to the severed carotid artery. I am probing deeper and examining the damage to the spinal column. A single blow of substantial force has damaged cervical vertebrae numbers C-3, C-4, and C-5. I am going to remove C-4, which appears to have sustained the most damage. I see a reddish brown discoloration in a deep groove in the bone. It may be residue deposited from whatever caused the damage. In my opinion, the neck wound caused her death. The lungs were clear of seawater, indicating she did not drown. I see no significant trauma to the rest of the body."

Doctor Visser stepped back from the autopsy table, removed the microphone from his neck, and peeled off his latex gloves as he spoke to Philip and Joe. "In my opinion, a single blow broke Lara's neck, killing her."

"By the ship's propeller?" Joe asked, wincing as if he felt the pain Lara had endured.

"No, I don't believe by the ship's propeller. In those cases we usually see multiple wounds as the turning propellers slice repeatedly through the victim's flesh. From the photos I saw in the files, the other two crewmen suffered those kinds of wounds, in addition to the trauma of being crushed by the ship's hull. Lara suffered none of that. I think the fatal blow knocked her out of the

Zodiac, away from the *Arctic Wind*'s path. She was probably dead when she hit the water."

"Killed by what?" asked Willemstad. "The files indicate harpooner Gudmund Vikinsson testified that he did not fire his harpoon, and he passed a polygraph test. And you are telling us she was not crushed by the ship or struck by the propeller blades."

"Well, right now I cannot tell you. I am also puzzled by the abrasion damage to the tissues around the neck wound. I'll have our forensic lab analyze the C-4 vertebra bone specimen I removed. Perhaps we will find a clue there," he said as they left the examination room.

Joe was immensely relieved to leave the morgue. The smell, the sights, the sounds, all brought back memories he wished to leave buried. He savored a deep breath of fresh air and then asked, "Well, what do you think, Philip?"

"I do not think about anything until I have all the facts. I will have an opinion when we have the laboratory results. Strange, there was no mention of the abrasion around Lara's neck wound in the original autopsy report. Did I miss it?"

"I don't recall seeing it either," remarked Joe.

"Well, I hope Doctor Visser's analysis will provide some definitive answers. So far, we just raised more questions."

"True," Joe replied, "But it doesn't seem like an open-and-shut case anymore, does it?" The two law enforcement professionals locked eyes, each wondering where the investigation would lead.

Chapter 28

Reykjavik

April 3rd

"**M**inister Andresson, everyone is on the conference line now."

"Thank you, Sara," he said, taking a deep breath as he joined the call, knowing he had to share some sensitive developments with the group. "Jon Andresson here."

"Hello Jon, we didn't think you were going to make our call," said Stig Carlson, in a congenial tone.

"Sorry I'm late. I was unable to leave a meeting with Prime Minister Valsson regarding some important issues."

Haigata abruptly interrupted the conversation. "Well, let us proceed with our updates. The IWC meeting is only two and a half months away. I want to make sure we have consolidated our positions. Eric, how are you and Jon coming on your projects?"

"We made headway getting at least one of us assigned to a committee working on non-compliance penalties with IWC rules. Before the general meeting, we will both join a committee responsible for recommending the continuance or abolishment of several whale sanctuaries. In any case, we will be able to influence votes."

"The credit here belongs to Eric," said Andresson. "I had to spend a significant amount of time managing developments concerning the deaths of the three anti-whaling activists."

"What *developments?*" shouted Haigata, in such a shrill tone that Andresson recoiled from his speakerphone. "I thought the judge concluded the investigation, ruling their deaths were accidental and caused by the activists. What are you talking about?"

"Well, it seems Lara Shalken's family, in Holland, has requested the investigation files, including transcripts of the inquest, autopsy reports, etc."

"And you just *handed* them the files? You could have stalled for months!"

"Prime Minister Valsson felt holding back information would have raised suspicion. The files were complete and consistent, pointing to the conclusion that the activists were responsible for their deaths. We believed there was no risk sharing the files."

"Well, I hope not," commented Stig Carlson. "Additional unfavorable publicity is the last thing we need going into the IWC meeting." *Idiots!* thought Haigata, as he listened. *One more thing to worry about, just when victory is within our grasp.*

Andresson cleared his throat and continued his update. "My sources have informed me that Dutch authorities are now examining the records, and someone from Mexico is helping them with their investigation."

Haigata had buried his head in his hands as he listened, but at the mention of Mexico, he lifted his head and stared at the small speaker. "Who from Mexico? Do you have a name?"

"No, but I can find out."

"Yes, please do," he sighed. "Let us move on. Stig, do you have an update on the whale DNA project?" he asked.

"I have arranged for our own scientists to testify to the committee that DNA testing would be unreliable, but I believe the committee will eventually implement the proposal."

126

"I see. Well, keep up your efforts. It will help if we can delay it, even for a few months."

"I'll do my best, Oshura."

"I have a brief but very positive update," said Haigata. "We have held high-level discussions with Mexico, and I am confident we have sufficient leverage to persuade them to vote with us, and also to eliminate a grey whale sanctuary on the Baja Peninsula. If no one has anything else to report, we will adjourn and reschedule for next week. I want to meet more frequently as the IWC meeting date approaches. Thank you, everyone. Jon, please call my private line immediately."

Jon Andresson listened to the clicks as the callers terminated their connections, and drew a deep breath. He knew Haigata was waiting impatiently, probably staring at his telephone, willing it to ring. *I might as well get this over with now. No point procrastinating.* He dialed Haigata's number. He answered on the first ring.

"Yes, Jon, I'm here. What is going on with this new investigation?"

"Well, Oshura, we do not know very much yet. At the request of a Deputy Inspector Philip Willemstad, we have sent the investigation files, court transcripts, and autopsy reports to Amsterdam. Evidently, he is working with Lara Shalken's family."

"And who is the Mexican? How did a Mexican get involved?"

"This person is not Mexican. He's a former New York City police detective who relocated to Cozumel."

"Do we know anything else about him?"

"Not at this time, Oshura."

"Then find out all you can," Haigata ordered. Andresson could visualize him speaking through clenched teeth and was extremely relieved several thousand miles separated them. "I still can't believe you were stupid enough to release all that information."

"Oshura, I already explained that . . . ."

"I remember your pathetic explanation," snapped Haigata, cutting him off. "Just find out all you can about this New York detective, or whatever he is. Fast!"

"I already have people looking into it," Andresson replied as Haigata slammed the receiver down.

Chapter 29

The Atlantic, Southeast of Bermuda

April 4th

By April, the Caribbean was getting warmer. The sun was stronger and the whales sensed an increase in the ocean temperature. Responding to the inner voice of instinct, or perhaps to a decision based on a rational thought process, the whales began departing the Silver Bank for their summer feeding grounds in the Northern Hemisphere. The mother humpback wanted to remain as long as possible, until her calf was strong enough to make the long three-month journey. Still, the adult whale knew she could not wait much longer. She had not eaten for several months, living off her own fat reserves, and she had to provide her calf with nourishment. It was time to leave.

One morning, the mother whale headed north and her calf followed. At first, the steady direction confused the calf. They were not swimming in a great circle through the Silver Bank or back and forth between familiar areas as usual. This was different. Her mother was showing her something new, and she must learn this new lesson to survive and preserve their species. They continued north and several days later, a male escort joined them. The mother whale recognized him as the male who had accompanied them to the Bank several months earlier. Had he been successful mating? She did not know, but his company provided social comfort. The mother whale could not move faster than her calf's pace, so she welcomed additional protection against ocean predators during their migration northward.

The mother humpback and her calf followed the male escort as he veered northeast, instead of the familiar northwesterly direction, which would have taken them closer to the coastline of the United States. Evolution had imprinted the memory of a route followed by generations of whales that would take them between the Carolinas and Bermuda, and eventually to their summer feeding grounds in New England waters. But, after a winter living off their stored fat, both the bull whale and mother humpback were hungry. She knew she must eat to maintain her milk supply and sustain her calf for several more months. The bull knew a generous food supply existed further out in the Atlantic, east of Bermuda, after which they could resume a northwesterly course.

Whalers from the Basque region of Spain were heading west, far from their homeland, searching for whales. Venturing far across the Atlantic was a risk they would not have normally taken, but they were desperate. Their boat was old, slow, and relatively small compared to the more modern whaling vessels of other nations. Dwindling profits had driven most countries to abandon whaling. But these were pirate whalers—rogues. They would take from the ocean what they could, legally or otherwise. The meager revenues did not permit them to maintain their ship properly, and it had become a rusted hulk, belching dark, oily smoke from worn-out diesel engines as it pitched through the waves. Their catch since leaving port thirty-five days ago was dismal. They had taken only three sperm whales, two of them juveniles. Economic desperation had driven them westward, toward Bermuda. The crew conducted the boring routine of maintaining a ship at sea, when the lookout spotted activity off the port side, near the horizon.

The mother humpback had just finished nursing her calf when the bull noticed a large school of tiny fish just ahead. He accelerated, pumping his huge flukes to propel his massive, fifty-ton bulk through the water. When he reached the school, he did not lunge-feed but descended below the prey, driving them toward the surface. The female humpback recognized from experience that today's hunting strategy would be cooperative feeding. She joined the bull, descending below the school, forcing the remaining stragglers toward the surface. Then the two whales circled the immense school, releasing air from their blowholes, surrounding the confused fish with a curtain of bubbles. As the school became more frightened, their instinct caused them to swim closer together for protection. The whales tightened the radius of their circling pattern, "bubble-netting" the hapless fish into a compacted living mass called a "bait-ball." Using a communication method unknown to humans, they synchronized their movements. The two whales simultaneously turned toward the surface, rising through the middle of their bubble net. Their cavernous mouths engulfed hundreds of pounds of fish as they broke the surface in a cacophony of foam and noise. The baby whale remained a short distance away, observing the proceedings with an intelligent realization she was learning new hunting behavior.

This surface commotion caught the lookout's attention on the Basque whaler. "Whales off the port bow!" he cried. The captain spun the wheel hard to port. Several minutes later, they were within killing range. The baby whale's only experience with boats had been the encounters in the Silver Bank. Expecting to meet friendly little creatures with strange little fins, she swam toward the whaler. The first mate pointed to the calf, less than one hundred feet from the bow, and shouted to the harpoon gunner. "That one first." He knew harpooning the baby would draw the adults near the boat. *Why burn precious fuel chasing whales?* he reasoned. Then, he gave the gunner another order. "Use a cold harpoon. No sense wasting an expensive penthrite grenade on a small whale. It'll die easily enough without an explosive charge." The harpoon cannon roared and the metal spike, attached to the boat with a heavy line, buried itself into the calf's back. As the mortally wounded whale thrashed wildly in pain, the two adult whales turned toward the ship, responding to the small whale's distress.

The mother whale swam to her baby while the bull headed straight toward the ship, a strange foreign beast that had brought violence into their peaceful world. Reaching the ship, the bull descended and then turned upward, breaching the surface only feet from the bow. Surging from the water to deck height, the enraged whale made eye contact with the gunner for a brief second before crashing back into the water. In that brief second, the gunner saw not only intelligence in the whale's eye, but also other human emotions: anger and hate. He was startled. *The damn whale knows I did it; it wants to kill me!* The momentary realization that he was dealing with an intelligent being did not stop the gunner from pivoting the harpoon cannon down toward the bull whale and firing a harpoon into its skull, killing him instantly. He quickly reloaded, this time using an explosive harpoon, and aimed at the female, swimming close to her dead baby. The harpooner calmly took aim and fired. The last conscious thoughts the female humpback had as she looked at her baby were confusion and sorrow. Her grief quickly ended in a final explosion of iron and steel.

. . . . the bull noticed a large school of tiny fish just ahead. He accelerated, pumping his huge flukes to propel his massive, fifty-ton bulk through the water.

Photo by Paul J. Mila

Chapter 30

Cozumel

April 5th

*F*ive divers neared the end of the day's second dive, swimming near the sea floor at about fifty feet, along a reef called Tormentos. The group had hoped to find spotted eagle rays and had not been disappointed, even though it was late in the season for the rays to be in the area. Early in the dive, they had surprised a large, six-foot ray resting on the sand. The divers were mesmerized as the beautiful animal rose slowly from the sea floor, surrounded in a veil of sand, and majestically flew like the eagle for which it was named, but through the water, not air. Although it appeared to be swimming in slow motion, it quickly disappeared into the blue. Terry had gotten the attention of a novice diver and was pointing to her own air gauge, a signal for the diver to check how much air remained in his tank. The diver flashed five fingers, closed his hand into a fist, and then flashed three fingers, indicating he had eight hundred pounds of air pressure in his tank. Terry nodded in recognition and was responding with the three-finger circle "OK" sign when a shadow passed over them. They looked up and saw another huge eagle ray, more than eight feet from wingtip to wingtip, blot out the sunlight momentarily. A curious barracuda followed close behind. They gazed toward the surface in wonderment as the ray continued on its way, ending their brief eclipse. Unfortunately, the moment passed too swiftly to signal the other three divers. Several grey angelfish were entertaining them, swimming in tight circles through their rising bubble column. Finally, Terry used her tank-banger to get their attention and signaled them to slowly ascend to fifteen feet for their three-minute safety stop before surfacing.

On the boat, conversation was animated, as always after such an exciting dive. *Seeing the big animals really turns 'em on,* mused Terry, as she joined the conversation. After dropping the divers at the Reef Club pier, Manuel headed back to port. "Give it all you've got, Manuel. I'm bushed!"

Later that evening, Terry was busy preparing dinner, losing herself in her thoughts. She missed Joe, and wondered how he was doing in Amsterdam. She vaguely heard the beginning of CNN's news broadcast. " . . . . and yesterday, Bermuda authorities detained pirate whalers from Spain who had wandered into Bermuda's territorial waters. They impounded their ship pending an investigation about the dead whales." The words "dead whales" caught Terry's attention and she looked up just in time to see the end of the video clip. It showed a ship towing two dead whales by their flukes and a smaller one, obviously a calf, on the whaler's deck. She was staring at the flukes, which were turned so their distinctive pattern was visible on camera. She was still staring at the screen when the announcer concluded, "For more details, log on to our Web site, at www.cnn.com."

Terry immediately turned on her computer, anxiously tapping her foot, waiting for it to power up and log on to the Internet. *Come on, come on, damn it! Log on!* Finally, her home page appeared and she entered CNN's Web site. She scrolled to the story and clicked on the photo that accompanied the text. Her hand trembled as she recognized a familiar cloverleaf pattern on one of the dead whale's flukes.

. . . . a shadow passed over them. They looked up and saw another huge eagle ray, more than eight feet from wingtip to wingtip, blot out the sunlight momentarily. A curious barracuda followed close behind.

Photo by Paul J. Mila

Chapter 31

Amsterdam, Holland

April 6th

*J*oe, Femke, and Jan were eating breakfast when the phone rang. Femke stopped pouring coffee and anxiously grabbed the phone before the second ring. "Hello."

"Good morning, Femke. This is Inspector Willemstad."

The sound of his voice triggered a wave of apprehension. "Good morning Inspector, do you have any information?" she asked, her voice wavering. She was uncertain which would be worse: discovering new evidence indicating her sister had been murdered or having to accept Lara's death as a horrible accident. Her hand tightened on the receiver as Willemstad continued.

"Well, yes. Our analysis has turned up some interesting information, but I would rather discuss it with you in person. I am available later this afternoon, if that is convenient."

"One moment, please, Inspector," she said, covering the phone with her hand. She turned to Jan and Joe, who were watching her intently, attempting to decipher what Willemstad had been telling her. Her voice broke under the strain. "He says they have found new information, but he wants to see us in person, this afternoon."

"Tell him yes! We'll be there whenever he wants to see us," replied Jan, trying to contain his anticipation.

"This afternoon will be fine, Inspector. What time should we come?"

"I have a two-hour lunch meeting beginning at noon, and then I'm free. Why don't you come anytime after that? I'll be in my office. Just tell my secretary I am expecting you."

"Thank you, Inspector. We'll be there. Good bye."

"Did he give you any indication about their findings?" asked Joe.

"No. I don't know how to interpret that."

"Well," said Jan, "either they found nothing and he did not want to disappoint you, or they found new evidence that Lara's death was no accident and he did not want to upset you over the telephone."

"In other words, it doesn't pay to try and figure it out now," concluded Joe. "I know it will be difficult, but I suggest we finish breakfast and try to relax until this afternoon." They ate, but more to occupy their minds than to satisfy their appetites.

After breakfast, they kept busy reading newspapers, watching television. Every few minutes, each stole a peek at a clock resting on a carved stone mantle, framing a beautiful fireplace. Each felt the clock was moving too slowly. At about 10 AM, the phone rang, jarring them out of their individual time-killing routines. Femke answered the call and Joe watched her expression change from anxiety to surprise. "Terry! How good to hear your . . . why yes, Joe is right here. You sound upset. Is everything all right?"

Joe jumped up from his chair and was at instantly at Femke's side. When she handed him the receiver, he heard Terry crying.

"Hi, Terry, it must be about four in the morning there. What's wrong, hon?"

"They killed them Joe. They're both dead!" she said, sobbing into the phone.

"Who's dead? What are you talking about?"

"Clover and her baby, the whales we saw in the Silver Bank. They're both dead, Joe. It was on the news last night. I couldn't wait any longer to call you."

"The whales? The mother and calf we saw in the Dominican Republic?" he replied, trying to fit the pieces together.

"Yes. Pirate whalers killed them near Bermuda," she sobbed.

"Are you sure it was the same whales we saw?"

"Yes, yes, I'm sure. Even on TV, I could clearly see the cloverleaf pattern on the fluke. There was a third whale, too. Oh, goddamn, I can't believe it."

"Terry, I'm so sorry, I don't know what to. . . ."

"I'm taking the next plane out and I'll be there as soon as I can."

"Here? What about our dive business? Why are you coming?"

"Because I can't sit here and do nothing, damn it! Maybe I can help your investigation. Maybe I'll contact that Peaceful Seas group. I have to do *something,* Joe! I'll get someone to cover our business while I'm away. I can refer customers to at least two other dive operators." Joe did not even attempt to convince Terry not to come. He knew from experience not to try dissuading Terry once she had made up her mind.

"Well, okay, just let me know your travel plans as soon as you can. We have an appointment with Inspector Willemstad this afternoon. He called to say they've found some new information, but we don't know what it is yet. If I'm not here, just leave a message on Femke's answering machine."

"Okay, Joe. Love you."

"Love you too, hon. Try to relax. Bye." As Joe hung up, he turned and found Jan and Femke standing next to him.

"What happened?" asked Femke. "Terry was speaking so loudly, I heard something about someone killing whales."

"Yes. When we were swimming with the humpbacks in the Dominican Republic, we took photos of a mother and calf, along with other whales. The mother had a cloverleaf pattern on the underside of her fluke, so Terry named her Clover. Well, it appears some whalers came upon the mother, calf, and a third whale near Bermuda and killed them. They must have wandered into Bermudan territorial waters, because authorities intercepted and boarded them and took them to Bermuda. The media picked up the story and Terry saw the news photos on CNN and recognized Clover and her calf."

"Oh how terrible!" responded Femke.

"Barbarians," said Jan bitterly. "These whalers talk about regulating whaling so they can institute a policy they call *sustained* whaling. But they still kill females and calves. How is that supposed to sustain the whale population? You can't trust these bastards to regulate themselves."

"Well, Terry is fired up and she needs to do something. I know her and she won't let go of this until she feels she's made some effort or contribution to the cause. I expect she'll arrive in a day or so."

"Almost time to go," said Femke. "We should leave now if we want to meet Philip after his meeting."

Chapter 32

April 6th

"Good afternoon," said Inspector Willemstad, rising to greet Femke, Jan, and Joe. "Please sit, make yourselves comfortable," he said, noticing Femke and Jan's tense expressions. "I know this is difficult for you and you're anxious to find out what we've learned, so I will get right to the point. I have invited Dr. Hans Devroot to join us, because some findings are technical. He conducted most of the tests and can explain the results much better than I."

"What kind of doctor is he?" asked Joe.

"He is a prominent physicist with a Ph.D. in some branch of physics I cannot spell, let alone understand," replied Willemstad, smiling. Just then, the intercom on Willemstad's desk buzzed.

"Dr. Devroot has arrived, sir."

"Thank you. Please show him in."

A tall, thin man, about forty-five years old, entered. After introductions, they sat around a large conference table while Devroot set up a slide projector. He removed a pair of thin, wire frame glasses from his breast pocket, slipped them on, and began his presentation. "Before I start, let me first express my sincere condolences to your family."

"Thank you, Doctor," replied Femke and Jan, almost simultaneously. Devroot sensed the tension in the room, so he began immediately.

"This slide shows the cervical vertebra, C-4, which Doctor Visser removed during the autopsy and sent to me. As you can see, there is a groove in the bone with a reddish-brown discoloration. The official findings of the first autopsy concluded that the victim died from being struck by a ship's propeller. I looked for evidence to support that finding, but I did not find any evidence." Jan and Femke glanced at each other and leaned closer, on the edge of their chairs. Joe remained motionless, but intensified his concentration. His investigative senses heightened as Devroot continued.

"This slide is a magnification of the groove in the bone, C-4. The viewing angle is not from above but seen along its axis, looking on end, so to speak. As you can see, the groove is symmetrically V-shaped, at an angle directly into the bone. If the blade of a ship's propeller had struck the bone, you would expect to see an *asymmetrical* V-shaped cut, because a propeller blade is set at an angle and slightly curved. Consequently, it would cut through the bone at an angle. This next slide is magnified, looking down, directly above the cut. You can see a reddish-brown discoloration. At first, we thought it might be dried blood, but closer examination revealed something different. We extracted a sample and found the substance was granular in nature. We analyzed it using a spectrometer and determined it was metal, ferrous in nature, and had been through an oxidation process."

"Oxidation?" asked Femke.

"Yes, in layman's terms, rust. This metal would not have been used to manufacture a ship's propeller. The metals used to manufacture ships' propellers are very hard non-ferrous metals, for two reasons. First, because of the obvious oxidation, rust, problem. Second, to minimize the effects of cavitation, which causes . . . ."

"Excuse me, Doctor," interrupted Joe. "Cavi-what?"

"Cavitation. You see, the high rotational speed of propeller blades cutting through the water causes vapor cavities in the water flowing over the blade. When the vapor cavity re-liquefies, the resulting pressure changes in the water flowing over the blade causes structural damage to the propeller. The problem came to light when ocean liners began operating at higher speeds. After many hours of operation, the crew would notice increased noise, vibration, and less efficiency. When they examined the propellers, it looked as though someone had taken a sledgehammer to the blades. Research intensified when the U.S. Navy got involved. They couldn't have their super-quiet submarines vibrating and sounding like washing machines as they cruised the oceans."

"So, what are these vapor cavities?" Joe asked.

"Well, in layman's terms, bubbles."

"*Bubbles?* So you're saying that unless you have very hard metal, *bubbles* can damage a ship's propeller blades?"

"Yes, but think of the bubbles bursting as mini-explosions. Even with hard metals, some damage will still occur. The degree of damage depends on water conditions, speed, and type of metal. Most ships use bronze, zinc anodes, alloys of manganese and bronze, or a nickel, aluminum, and bronze alloy called nibral. That's a metal alloy containing extra-high nickel content relative to the bronze, increasing the tensile strength of the blade. The U.S. Navy has even been incorporating exotic materials such as titanium on some submarines." Joe noticed that Jan's eyes were glazing over and Femke looked bewildered.

"And I suppose your point is none of these metals showed up in the sample you took from Lara's neck vertebra," Joe interrupted, jumping ahead to Devroot's conclusion.

"Correct, Mr. Manetta. Instead we found metal of a softer substance, relatively speaking, with a higher degree of iron content. There is no way this sample came from a ship's propeller."

"But could it have come from a harpoon?" asked Jan, who had been silent.

"Yes, Mr. Shalken, it could have come from a harpoon. Depending on the hunting location, some harpoons are cast iron, and harpoons used in cold climates contain alloys, so they are less brittle. But in general, they have a ferrous content consistent with this sample. That would also account for the symmetrically straight V cut in the bone. The front blade or a stabilizing fin of a harpoon traveling on a relatively straight trajectory would make such a wound."

"And," added Willemstad, "That kind of a weapon would also cause the abrasion damage we noticed in the soft tissue surrounding the neck wound." The room fell silent as the group pondered the significance of Devroot's analysis. Muffled sobs broke the quiet as Femke thought of her sister's final moments. The anger welling up in Jan exploded in violence and he pounded his massive fist on Willemstad's conference table. Devroot's slide projector went dark as the sudden vibration snapped the hot filament inside the bulb. "Thank you, Doctor Devroot," Said Joe, rising from his chair. He looked at Willemstad. "Looks like we'll be taking a trip to Iceland," he said.

"I'll contact my Iceland counterparts and make the necessary arrangements," said Willemstad.

"I was glad to have been of assistance."

"Thank you, Doctor," said Willemstad, extending his hand.

"Good luck to all of you," said Devroot, as he packed his damaged slide projector and left the room.

Chapter 33

April 6th

No one spoke during the ride from the police station to Femke's house. Listening to Dr. Hans Devroot's analysis had been emotionally draining. Each silently pondered the implications of his conclusions. Entering the house, Femke noticed there were messages on her answering machine. She pressed the play button and listened.

"Hi, Joe, it's Terry. I can get a late flight Friday and arrive in Amsterdam Saturday morning. Call me back. Bye. Love you."

"Well, I knew she'd be coming soon," said Joe. "I'm surprised it took her this long to make travel plans."

"I was thinking, maybe she should wait to see what Inspector Willemstad has in mind. We may be in Iceland in a couple of days, and it might make more sense for her to meet us there."

"Good idea, Femke. Let's call her back now and give her an update." Terry answered on the first ring. "Hi, hon. How are things in sunny Cozumel?"

"Hi, Joe! Everything is okay here. Business is good and I found someone to cover our customers. By the way, we did receive a strange notice in the mail from Mexican immigration about irregularities concerning your immigration papers."

"Hmmm. That's strange. Well, everything should be in order. I'll take a look when I get back. Listen, it appears something other than a simple accident caused Lara's death. We'll be traveling to Iceland in a few days. Why don't you sit tight, and as soon as I know our plans, I'll call you. It might make more sense to meet us in Reykjavik."

"Joe, I really want to get over there, meet some of the people from Peaceful Seas, and see if I can help in some way."

"Terry, I understand. I really do. But just wait a day or so. We should know what we're doing by then, okay?"

"Well, all right. Now I'll have to unpack and pack again. Call me soon."

"I will. Take care. Love you."

"Love you too. Bye."

The rest of the day and evening was tense. Femke cried whenever she thought about her sister. Jan barely contained his emotions, like a smoldering volcano waiting to erupt. Joe was busy planning an investigative strategy. Later that evening, the phone rang. "Hello, Femke here. Oh, hello, Inspector. Yes, Joe is right here."

Joe listened carefully and took notes while Willemstad spoke. "Okay, Philip, we'll see you tomorrow afternoon." Turning to Jan and Femke, he updated them. "Philip booked us on a KLM flight to Leifur Eriksson Airport in Keflavik tomorrow night. Then we take a forty-minute shuttle bus ride to Reykjavik. On Monday morning, we meet three people: Inspector Hansen, who is Willemstad's counterpart, Doctor Ingerson, who performed the original autopsy, and the judge who presided over the original inquest."

"What happens at this meeting?" asked Jan somberly.

"We give it our best shot. We present our findings and hope they reopen the inquest. If they change their findings as a result of this new evidence, it will go to trial."

"I want to see that bastard Swenson hang," said Jan.

"I don't think Iceland has capital punishment, Jan."

"Well, one way or the other, justice will be done," he insisted with determination.

Joe looked into Jan's eyes as he spoke, and thought, *this is not a man I would ever want to cross.*

"I better call Terry and have her meet us in Iceland this weekend. We can pick her up at Keflavik airport and save her the bus ride to Reykjavik."

Chapter 34

Reykjavik

April 8th

"**M**r. Andresson, I have Inspector Hansen on the line for you. He says it is urgent."

"Thank you. Put him through, please. Hello, Inspector, how can I help you today?"

"You can't. I'm calling you as a favor. I just received a call from Philip Willemstad, my counterpart in Amsterdam. He has been investigating Lara Shalken's death, at her family's request."

"Yes, I think I had heard about that."

"Well, what you have not heard, until now, is that authorities in Holland performed another autopsy and determined she was not, I repeat, *not,* killed by the *Arctic Wind*'s propeller."

"Killed by what, then?"

"He claims they can prove a harpoon fired from the *Arctic Wind* caused her death. They are flying to Reykjavik later this week to present their findings. They have requested the doctor who performed the first autopsy attend the meeting, a Doctor Ingerson, I believe. I strongly advise that you to be there also."

"Yes, of course, I agree." His mind started to race ahead. *What the hell is Prime Minister Valsson going to say about this?* Andresson thought. Then, he buried his head in his hands, anticipating the conversation he would soon have with Oshura Haigata.

"Well, Jon, you do what you need to do. I'm just a simple policeman. I don't understand everything going on here. I don't ordinarily get involved in your political world, and I do not like getting dragged into it at this late point of my career. Quite frankly, I do not understand how one doctor could be so totally mistaken." *You would understand if you knew he was told before the autopsy what his conclusion had to be,* Andresson thought.

"Yes, well, what needs to get done will get done. As I said earlier, the prime minister appreciates your cooperation. Thank you very much for the advance information, Inspector."

"Okay, Jon, call me if you need anything else." *But I hope you won't,* thought Hansen. Andresson called Prime Minister Valsson, informing him about the latest developments. He decided to take a walk before calling Haigata. Later that day, with no more excuses to postpone the call, he dialed Haigata's number and told him the news.

"So! Neither you nor Valsson saw any problem in giving them the documents! Now look at the mess you've put us in. The IWC meeting is in June, and now we have to stop this scandal from blowing up in our faces!" Even with the door closed, Andresson feared his secretary might hear Haigata's piercing voice screeching through the speakerphone. He picked up the receiver, taking the call off speakerphone. "What do you propose to do, Jon?"

"I will attend the meeting and learn what they have uncovered. Then I will deal with it."

"It will be too late by then, you fool!" Andresson sat up in his chair. As a senior diplomat, he was offended by Haigata's undiplomatic language.

"Oshura, there is no need to talk like that!" Ignoring him, Haigata continued.

"What do you expect this Doctor Ingerson to say? Can he defend his conclusions?"

"I don't know, Oshura, he is not a strong man. As you may recall, we forced him to arrive at certain conclusions."

"Then you cannot allow him to attend the meeting!"

"It will not look good if he is not there, and I don't know what I can do at this point to. . ." Andresson was relieved to hear the line go dead, indicating Haigata had terminated the call. He felt unsettled, not knowing Haigata's next move.

Chapter 35

Keflavik International Airport

April 13th

*T*erry had just cleared immigration and customs at Leifur Eriksson Airport and was pushing a heavily laden luggage cart when she saw Femke and Joe in the crowd. "Joe!" she exclaimed, waving her hand above her head. He saw her and ran to greet her.

"Great to see you," he said, lifting her and swinging her in a half turn, kissing her as he set her down. "I missed you!"

"I missed you too," she said, kissing him back.

"Hi, Terry," Femke said, sensing she was intruding on a private moment.

"Hello, Femke. It's good to see you too, except for the circumstances, of course. How have you been?"

"I'm fine, but, as you may have heard, we've learned unsettling information regarding the case. But, at least I feel we're getting closer to finding the truth about Lara's death."

"Well, I just hope we can help."

"Yes, Joe has already helped. Now that you are here too, I feel very confident."

"By the way, dear, are you just visiting or relocating?" said Joe, looking at the numerous bags piled on Terry's luggage cart.

"Well, a girl has to be prepared for any eventuality," replied Terry, with mock defensiveness. "Who knows what the weather will be, or what I'll be doing, or who I'll be doing it with?"

"Whatever you'll be doing, it better be with me," said Joe, as Femke laughed. She had never witnessed Terry and Joe's interplay before, and found it amusing. As they struggled to squeeze the luggage into the small trunk of Femke's rented car, Joe asked, "Really, Ter, what is all this stuff?"

"Well, like I said, clothes for different kinds of weather, and my scuba gear."

"Scuba gear? For what?"

"Who knows? But I'm prepared for anything. I also want to meet the Peaceful Seas group. Who knows how I might get involved? If I have to do any diving, I don't want to use unfamiliar equipment in difficult diving conditions."

"Did you bring my stuff too?"

"Nope. This water's too cold for wet-suit diving and you aren't certified to use a dry suit yet."

"Hey, I can handle it!"

"Don't go getting ego-bruised on me, dear. You have to learn and practice dry-suit diving in good conditions. Otherwise, you can't control your buoyancy and you might float around feet-up or, even worse, shoot to the surface and get a severe case of the bends."

"Well, I hear you're the best teacher around," Joe said, hoping to combine humor and flattery to convince Terry to teach him.

"Nice try, hon," she said, kissing him lightly on the lips, "but I don't do dry-suit lessons in unfamiliar, cold, turbid water and strong currents. Now jump into Femke's car or you'll be taking the bus back to Reykjavik."

"Oh, now I see who's the *real* boss in this relationship," Femke said, laughing, as she started driving.

"Yes, Femke, it's a tough life," sighed Joe.

"Oh now, you know I make it worth your while," said Terry, snuggling next to Joe in the back seat. Joe saw Femke smiling at them in the rearview mirror, and he just grinned back.

"Hurry home, driver," he ordered.

It was 10 PM when they arrived at their hotel suite. Jan came out to help unload the car, and Femke introduced Terry. After some conversation and a glass of wine, Terry said, "Well, I'm wiped. Long trips really drain me, and this was a long day. Femke, where's the bedroom? I really need some sleep."

"I'll show you," said Joe. "I'm kind of tired myself. I think we'll call it a night."

"Good night, Jan. It was good to meet you. Good night, Femke."

"Good night, you two," said Femke, throwing Joe a knowing smile. Terry caught it and mentioned it to Joe when they went to their room.

"What was Femke's Cheshire-cat smile all about?"

"I guess she can read people, and she read my mind," said Joe, putting his arms around Terry, kissing her neck, then gently nibbling her ear lobe. She smiled, shivered, and threw her head back. Joe ran his fingers through her long hair and kissed her lips. "Terry, I've really missed you," he said pressing against her.

"Hmmm, yes, I can feel just how much you've missed me," she said, smiling into his dark brown eyes. She kissed him back and fell onto the bed, pulling Joe down on top of her.

"So, how tired are you?" he whispered as he kissed her more urgently.

He felt her quiver as she said, "Tired. But not too tired." She returned his kiss. "I've missed you too."

Chapter 36

April 14th

    *S*unlight streaming through the window Sunday morning woke Joe. He realized he and Terry had been sleeping entwined in each other's arms, probably most of the night. *Man, have I missed my wife,* he reflected. He gently shook her awake, and Joe's deep brown eyes were the first things Terry saw. "Hi, sailor. Do you have a girl in every port?"

    "Nope, just the *same* girl in every port, I hope," Joe said, brushing Terry's auburn bangs from her eyes. "That's better. Looking into your fabulous green eyes is a great way to start my day. You know, this has been the longest we've been apart since we've been married."

    "No wonder I've missed you so much," Terry replied, pulling herself closer, snuggling into Joe's embrace. Joe took a deep breath as he felt his body responding to Terry's touch, when they heard Jan's booming voice through the door.

"Hey, wake up, everyone! I called room service and ordered a wonderful breakfast for us. It should be here soon!" Joe let out a deep sigh, as Terry laughed.

"Don't worry, dear. We'll have our alone time later," she said, kissing him briefly.

"Yeah, timing *is* everything. Well, let's get up before they come looking for us." During breakfast, Jan offered to show Terry and Joe the *Sea Angel II,* moored at the Old Town dock, and introduce them to the crew and other Peaceful Seas members. Femke declined, having seen the ship before and not wanting to see the *Arctic Wind,* also moored nearby. "I just need to relax and prepare myself for Monday," she said solemnly.

Across town, Doctor Ingerson had just completed his daily three-kilometer morning power walk. He always used the early-morning brisk walk to clear his mind and to enjoy thinking only about his exercise. But today was different. Tomorrow he would testify about his findings in Lara Shalken's autopsy. He originally testified she had been accidentally killed when the *Arctic Wind* had crushed her Zodiac and the ship's propeller had sliced through her neck. He was already aware that a Dutch forensic team had reached different conclusions. Defending his conclusions was a familiar task. He had successfully defended his findings in court many times against challenging cross-examination. He was confident in his ability as a combative and persuasive expert witness. But that was when he had reached valid conclusions from honest analysis. This time, he had been pressured to state a false conclusion. *Can I project confidence defending a lie?* he wondered. The fact that his deception entailed criminal implications caused him further anxiety.

Ingerson was still thinking how he would navigate the testimonial minefield of possible arguments and counter-arguments, when he arrived back at his apartment building. He considered extending his walk to continue planning how he would deliver his testimony, but he was hungry. So, he decided to return to his apartment and eat breakfast.

He rode the elevator to the eighth floor and was surprised to see his apartment door ajar. "Hello? Anyone there?" he asked, cautiously pushing the door open.

"In here. Building maintenance," came a reply from the apartment. He walked through the foyer and saw a maintenance man adjusting a living room window. He walked quickly across the room, not noticing his computer had been turned on. Consequently, he did not see the short letter on the monitor. He did notice the maintenance worker was wearing thin rubber gloves, similar to the kind medical personnel wore. He thought it odd, but dismissed the thought.

"What's wrong with the window?"

The maintenance worker turned to face him and smiled as he replied. "We've had complaints about some windows being difficult to open and close, so we are checking the tracks on all windows in the building to see if they are warped and need replacement."

"I've not reported problems with my windows."

"Well, this one is beginning to warp. I adjusted it and it works fine now, but see if you can move it easily. Try sliding this upper window, like this." The maintenance worker leaned out the open bottom window, pulled the top window down, then pushed it up. "Now, Doctor, you try it."

Ingerson stepped to the window and leaned out. As he grasped the outside window frame with both hands, the maintenance worker shifted his position and said, "Let me steady you." He put his hands around Ingerson's midsection. When he felt the doctor relax, he quickly pushed him. Ingerson lost his balance and his hold on the window frame. It happened so quickly, he had no time to scream as he plummeted, hitting the pavement in front of his building with a sickening, wet thud. Horrified pedestrians looked up to see only an empty window, eight floors up. The maintenance man calmly stepped to Ingerson's computer, moved the mouse, and clicked the "print" command. After the printer ejected the note, he proofread it. Satisfied, he placed the note on the keyboard, where he knew someone would find it. He looked around the room one last time and then left, removing the rubber gloves after closing the door.

Chapter 37

April 15th

    *J*an drove Joe and Terry to the harbor, located in the Old Town area of Reykjavik, where the *Sea Angel II* was moored. As they exited the cramped vehicle, Jan stood still for a moment, looking at the *Sea Angel II,* misty-eyed, remembering the many voyages he and Lara had taken. Terry walked to the bow and looked at the ship's name. "What happened to the *Sea Angel I?*" she asked.

    "It was blown up and sunk while saving whales in the Pacific, just over three years ago," Jan answered matter-of-factly. Terry wheeled, looking at Jan, not saying a word, but questioning him with her eyes. "There was a lengthy investigation. Another ship was nearby when it happened, a whaler called the *Hakudo Maru.* We suspected someone from that ship didn't want anyone else on the high seas with them and blew the *Sea Angel,* but we couldn't prove anything. Whoever did it knew how to handle underwater demolition. The survivors found parts of a detonating device from a magnetic mine floating in the wreckage. We assume divers attached the device to the hull below the water line. She sank in minutes."

"Was anyone killed?" asked Joe.

"Yes. Twenty-two crewmembers, including my older brother, Karel, the first mate on the ship. Most were not yet thirty years old. They were sleeping in their bunks and never had a chance. A passing cruise ship from Alaska bound for Hawaii rescued four survivors. Without that good fortune, we never would have known what happened.

"I had admired Karel all my life. He was my hero. His death inspired me to continue this effort. I vowed one day I would find his killers. I have tried but with no success."

"Good God!" exclaimed Terry. "I had no idea that . . . ." her voice trailed off as Jan finished her sentence.

"That the whale wars sometimes resulted in casualties and death? Lara was not the first to die. We are committed to saving the whales, being their guardian angels. But we are engaged in a dangerous business."

"I had no idea," Terry said, still shaking her head in disbelief.

"I know you both want to help us, but please be aware of the risks you're taking by your involvement." Joe and Terry looked at each other. Each knew what the other was thinking. Each had lost a loved one and they were grateful fate had granted them a second chance. It was not a gift they took lightly. "And there is the *Arctic Wind,*" Jan said, interrupting their thoughts. They looked where he was pointing. Anchored in the bay a quarter mile from the dock they saw a low-slung black ship, about 150 feet long. An ominous-looking piece of equipment, shrouded, was attached at the bow.

"Is the harpoon cannon under that tarp?" asked Joe.

"Aye, it is," replied Jan.

"I imagined a smaller ship," remarked Terry.

"That's a combination killer-factory ship," explained Jan. "It can accomplish the dual jobs of killing the whales and then rendering them. Larger than a conventional killer boat but smaller than a factory ship, it presents an economical approach for smaller whaling operators, especially pirate whalers. It also enables them to pursue whales into shallow areas where the large factory ships can't go. For the whales, it has been a deadly development. Countries that can afford to invest in large-scale whaling operations use different hunting methods. They send a fleet of several small killer boats accompanied by a large factory ship, which processes the dead whales. That's the preferred method the Japanese use now, and the method the old Soviet whaling fleets of the past used."

Standing next to the *Sea Angel II,* Jan said, "Come aboard and let me introduce you to the Peaceful Seas crew." They climbed the gangplank, which rose steeply on the high tide, and walked toward the bow, where thirty young men and women greeted them. They embraced Jan enthusiastically and he introduced Terry and Joe. Terry was struck by their youthful exuberance and international diversity. They hailed from Canada, the United Kingdom, Sweden, the United States, the Netherlands, and Denmark. "Seems like a large crew for a ship this size," remarked Joe.

"Oh they're not all crewmembers," replied Jan. "Several are visiting and using the ship as a hotel. They flew in because of the publicity surrounding the investigation. They're also here to organize protests due to the recent announcements that Iceland has already resumed limited whaling." After introductions, the conversation quickly turned to whales. Terry and Joe impressed the Peaceful Seas group with their stories about swimming with humpback whales. They asked numerous questions about Terry and Joe's adventure and their impressions of the whales. Joe noticed how much Terry enjoyed talking about meeting the humpbacks. He had not seen her so animated in many months. Turning to Joe, Terry said, "Maybe I could stay with them tomorrow. You, Femke and Jan will be busy at the inquest tomorrow. There isn't much that I could do to help there."

"That makes sense," replied Joe. "But try not to get yourself arrested," he said, grinning. "Don't forget, I'm retired and I don't have any official clout with the local gendarmes over here."

"So much for my knight in shining armor," Terry replied as they shared a laugh.

After an interesting and enjoyable meeting with Peaceful Seas, they headed back to their hotel to meet Inspector Willemstad and Doctor Visser, who had flown into Reykjavik that morning. They spent the remainder reviewing their material and evidence to prepare their presentation. They knew tomorrow would be pivotal.

Chapter 38

April 16th

    Several Peaceful Seas members arrived at the hotel lobby to pick up Terry. They were organizing an anti-whaling rally in the Old Town area of Reykjavik. "Good luck at your meeting today," she said, leaving.

    "Take care," shouted Joe, still shaving in the bathroom. Several minutes later, as they were leaving for their meeting at the coroner's office, Jan heard the telephone ring. "I'll be right back. Let me see who's calling." Joe and Femke were waiting impatiently when Jan appeared at the front door and waved them back into the house.

    "What's wrong?" asked Femke, as Jan motioned to be quiet.

    "Yes, I understand. We'll be there later this afternoon."

    "What happened? Was our meeting cancelled?"

"No, just postponed a few hours. It seems Doctor Ingerson will not be attending."

"What? That's outrageous!" exclaimed Femke. "He cannot just avoid . . ."

"Apparently he committed suicide yesterday morning," Jan interjected.

"How?" asked Joe.

"It seems he jumped from his eighth-floor apartment window."

"How did they determine it was suicide?" asked Joe.

"Well, evidently he wrote a note just before he jumped. They found it on his computer keyboard. They scheduled Ingerson's autopsy for this morning. His assistant will be conducting it, and he is the only other forensic expert qualified to comment about Ingerson's findings on Lara's autopsy."

"It's déjà vu, all over again," Joe said out loud, but just to himself. He recalled the last time he had dealt with several untimely deaths, supposedly accidental, but in reality very intentional, during his investigation in Cozumel two years ago.

"Pardon?" asked Femke.

"Oh, nothing. Just a funny feeling I get sometimes. Have there been any other strange deaths of people related to this case?" he asked.

"Not that I'm aware, but we can certainly ask at the meeting," replied Jan.

Later that afternoon, they were ushered into a small conference room. Inspector Hansen, Judge Jon Kristinsson, who had presided over the original inquest, and Doctor Bors Kronegard, the late Doctor Ingerson's assistant, soon joined them.

"Thank you for coming all this way, Mr. Shalken," Hansen said. "It is good to see you again, but unfortunately still under difficult circumstances. Ms. Van der Zee, my condolences on your sister's unfortunate death." Femke and Jan acknowledged Hansen's welcoming remarks with a polite smile and a slight nod. He continued. "I understand you have conducted your own autopsy in the Netherlands and arrived at different conclusions."

"Correct," declared Willemstad. "Doctor Visser will present his findings to you."

"Fine. Doctor Visser, will you proceed?"

"Thank you. Now here you see . . . ."

Thirty minutes later, Dr. Visser concluded his presentation and all eyes turned to Dr. Kronegard. *He's got that deer-in-the headlights look,* thought Joe. *This should be interesting,* "Well, Dr. Visser's examination and presentation were outstandingly meticulous and conducted with the utmost care and thoroughness." *Is this guy a politician or a medical examiner?* wondered Joe. "I cannot comment why Dr. Ingerson did not look at the available evidence in the same manner. As you know, he cannot be here to defend his analysis, and I was not part of the original autopsy." *Conveniently so, and probably why you're still alive, Doc,* thought Joe, listening to his inner NYPD voice. "After considering Doctor Visser's presentation, I would agree there is now considerable doubt concerning the original findings."

"Well, there may be another explanation," interjected Inspector Hansen. All eyes turned toward Hansen. "But as far as placing blame or criminal intent on someone, I don't think you have sufficient evidence yet to bring this matter to trial."

Jan leapt to his feet, leaning ominously across the table toward Hansen. "What the hell do you need? A signed confession and a live video of their murders to prove it to you?" Hansen reflexively shrank back as Femke put her hand on Jan's shoulder and restrained him.

"Mr. Shalken, you are out of order!" said Judge Kristinsson angrily. "This is not a courtroom, but I will summon the guards to remove you if you cannot control yourself."

"I, I'm sorry, Your Honor. It will not happen again," apologized Jan, as he sat down.

"Mister Shalken, I understand your frustration," Hansen continued in a condescending tone. "But we need more evidence. For example, we don't know what metals were used to manufacture the *Arctic Wind*'s harpoons and propeller. At this point, it is all conjecture and guesswork. Very good guesswork, I might add. And possibly sufficient to reopen the inquiry, but not definitive proof that will hold up in a criminal court."

"Well, aren't there records indicating where the *Arctic Wind* was built?" asked Femke. "Wouldn't those records tell you how they constructed the ship?"

"Not really," countered Hansen. "The ship has probably been in for maintenance and repairs several times during her lifetime, and most likely, her propeller has been replaced more than once, probably in foreign ports. And this is not like an airliner, with requirements to maintain an unbroken chain of detailed records indicating what parts have been changed and by whom."

"Well, doesn't the manufacturer usually stamp the propeller, indicating its metal composition, weight, date of manufacture, things like that?" inquired Willemstad.

"Yes, but you would probably have to inspect her underwater. I don't think Captain Ulf Swenson will be accommodating and put her into dry dock for you. In any case, she is scheduled to depart in two days. As of now, we do not have the authority to hold her in port," replied Hansen. *I think I know where I can find a diver on short notice,* thought Joe. Hansen was watching Joe carefully, and saw a flicker of thought in his eyes, the look investigators are trained to recognize when they strike a nerve or if someone is concealing information. He decided to probe. "Detective Manetta, you were about to say something?"

"Correction," replied Joe. "It's *Mister* Manetta now. I've been retired from the New York police force for almost two years."

"Ah yes. I'm sorry, I forgot." *Forgot? How could you have forgotten anything about my background when we've never met before?* thought Joe. *Looks like somebody's been feeding you little tidbits of info.* Joe tried to seem uninterested, and threw Hansen a vacuous stare, but he continued to probe. "You haven't said much today, *Mister* Manetta. Do you wish to share any theories or observations?"

"Not really, Inspector. There are times when you can learn more just listening, and for me, this is one of those times." *Take that bullshit to the bank, bub.*

Hansen just stared at Joe, not knowing what to make of him. *I assumed a New York detective would be much sharper,* he thought.

After an hour of discussion, Judge Kristinsson made a ruling. "I have heard enough today to convince me this inquiry should be reopened. Inspector Hansen, I authorize you to impound the *Arctic Wind* in port until I officially close the inquest. I am scheduling a final hearing thirty days from today, May 16. That should give everyone sufficient time to gather additional evidence and to further analyze existing information. At the conclusion, I plan to make a final ruling whether or not there will be a criminal trial. Are there any questions?"

"Your Honor, why don't you just eliminate all this 'guesswork,' as Inspector Hansen calls it, and simply issue a search warrant for the *Arctic Wind*'s harpoons and prop?" asked Joe.

"Inspector Hansen would have to make that request to me, Mr. Manetta," replied the judge, turning to Hansen.

"At this time," interjected Hansen, "I am not prepared to make such a request to the court. The information presented today is still opinion, as far as I am concerned. Furthermore, numerous witnesses provided a significant amount of testimonial evidence at the original inquest, leading to the conclusion that the deaths were an unfortunate accident."

Before Joe could reply, the judge cut him off. "In view of the inspector's position, you are all free to supplement his investigation by gathering additional evidence and information yourselves, and present it on May 16. Are there any other questions?"

"Just one, Your Honor," replied Femke. "In addition to Doctor Ingerson's death, have there been any other deaths, suspicious or otherwise, of people connected with the case?"

"Inspector?"

Hansen blinked, then cleared his throat, stalling for time to compose his answer. "Well, there have been some related accidents," admitted Hansen. "Shortly after the original inquest, a bus struck and killed Thor Rodale, a maintenance engineer on the *Arctic Wind*. But it was a rainy night and the road was slippery. Alfred Haggar, the ship's cook, died when he drove his car off the road on a winding curve. But these appear to have been random accidents."

"And as I recall," added Judge Kristinsson, "didn't two crewmembers who were supposed to testify during my original inquest fail to appear, and aren't they still missing?"

"I'm afraid so," replied Hansen, looking around the table. He noticed Joe staring directly at him. *Time to start connecting the dots, pal,* thought Joe, looking straight into Hansen's eyes, unsettling him with an expression which was definitely no longer vacuous.

Across town, Terry and the Peaceful Seas demonstrators were on the dock where another whaling ship had moored several hours earlier. The whalers had killed two minke whales, thirty-footers, as part of Iceland's "scientific whaling" program. As the crew disembarked, the demonstrators waved placards expressing anti-whaling sentiments. Local television reporters jockeyed for good positions, shooting footage for the evening news and interviewing the demonstrators. Because a cold, steady drizzle fell, the crowd was small but very animated. The confrontation invigorated Terry, who ignored the rain.

Ulf Swenson and the *Arctic Wind* crew were drinking in a dockside bar that catered to seaman and heard the commotion across the street. Stepping outside to investigate, Swenson said, "Let's have some fun, men." They heckled the anti-whaling demonstrators, much to the news media's delight. They would now have entertaining video for the evening's news broadcasts. Swenson saw Terry in the crowd, noticed the red highlights in her auburn hair, and decided to harass her. He walked over and stood behind her. "Excuse me, Miss," he said politely. She turned and was surprised to see a huge man standing next to her. "Now what's a pretty little thing like you doing carrying a heavy sign like that?" At just over five feet nine, and very athletic, Terry was not used to being called "little," and the remark caught her attention.

"I can handle this sign and anything else I need to," she shot back. "Aren't you with them?" she asked, nodding toward the whalers exiting their ship.

"Well, let's just say they and I are kindred spirits. My ship's over there," he said, pointing toward a low-slung black whaling ship, anchored in the middle of the bay. "And I'm her captain."

Terry turned to look where Swenson was pointing and was stunned when she recognized the *Arctic Wind*. Realizing she was face-to-face with the captain responsible for the deaths of the Jan's wife and crewmembers of the *Sea Angel II,* plus countless whales, Terry's temper boiled over.

"Do you realize the harm you've done?" she shouted. "I'd like to see you skewered on the business end of one of your harpoons," she said sharply.

"Now, I'm just trying to make a living, the only way I know how. Little girls shouldn't go around wishing people harm."

"And little boys shouldn't play with such dangerous toys," she retorted. "Why did you approach me anyway?"

"I saw your hair and thought we might be related," he replied, grinning, pointing to his own red hair, several shades darker in the rain.

"I don't think so. I'd know if I had an obnoxious brother." Swenson's grin quickly faded, replaced by a sinister leer.

"No, I was thinking you're probably one of my bastard children. God knows I've had so many women in so many ports. Your mother could have been one."

"You son of a bitch," Terry yelled, throwing down her sign. It clattered to the pavement, attracting the attention of several cameramen. They wheeled around just in time to video Terry throwing a roundhouse right at Swenson's jaw. He blocked the punch, holding her wrist in his massive hand. They were frozen for a moment, eyes glaring at each other, inches apart. Flashbulbs popped as news photographers captured the bizarre tableau.

"My, you're a feisty bitch! I believe you really could be one of my daughters," said Swenson, flashing a malevolent grin. The remark incensed Terry, prompting her to let loose with a left hook. Swenson deflected the blow with his arm as several Peaceful Seas demonstrators ran over and stepped between them, pushing Swenson back and pulling Terry away. She watched, infuriated, as Swenson turned and walked away, laughing as his crew cheered. The Peaceful Seas group clapped Terry on the back and congratulated her for garnering more publicity than they had hoped for. She was excited, finally meeting the enemy up close, in the flesh, not an abstraction or a sterile image on a television screen. She felt good playing a role, though small, in bringing attention to the needless killing of whales. Terry thoroughly enjoyed the action, and the Peaceful Seas group enjoyed her contagious enthusiasm.

Chapter 39

*B*ack at their hotel suite, Femke, Willemstad, Jan, and Joe assessed their options. "Well, we still have thirty days to prove Lara was murdered and get justice," said Jan.

"Not much time," added Femke.

"Yes," said Joe, "but even though Hansen was trying to discourage us, he unintentionally gave us some good direction."

"How so?" asked Femke.

"The first thing we need to do is determine the metal composition of the ship's prop and harpoons. That will indicate if we are even on the right track."

"Well," countered Willemstad, "even determining if the harpoon's metal matches the sample from Lara's body would not be conclusive."

"Why not?" asked Jan, visibly agitated. Femke placed her hand on his shoulder to calm him.

167

"Well," replied Joe, "it won't be as accurate as a ballistics match, where you can conclusively prove a particular gun fired a particular bullet." Jan looked at Willemstad, frustrated.

"I'm afraid he's correct," said Willemstad. "We only have trace amounts of metal to compare."

"Still, it's an important start," said Joe, restoring an upbeat tone. "Even though all we have so far is circumstantial evidence, you never know where it will lead."

"How do you propose we examine the *Arctic Wind*'s propeller?" asked Femke. Before Joe could reply, they were interrupted by a loud knock at the door. She opened it and Terry entered. The steady drizzle had soaked her clothes and matted her long hair. Wet bangs stuck to her forehead.

"Well, right on cue. You couldn't have timed your entrance any better," said Joe, laughing at Terry's confused expression. "By the way, how was your day, dear?"

Though exhausted and shivering from the damp cold, Terry was still exuberant. "It was great, Joe! It really felt good finally confronting whalers in person. On the other hand, several hours of marching around with placards on a chilly, rainy afternoon isn't exactly my idea of fun. But we got good television coverage, and I suppose it helps getting as much publicity as possible. All in all, I guess I'd rather be underwater when it's raining," said Terry, still shivering. "I sure could use a cup of tea, coffee, anything hot."

"Coming right up," said Femke. "Terry, are you just shivering from the cold? You seem upset," said Femke as she prepared some hot tea.

"Well, I had a run-in with the captain of the *Arctic Wind*."

"You met Ulf Swenson?" exclaimed Jan.

"Yes. I can assure you it was not a pleasant experience. It got a little heated."

"He's a dangerous man," said Jan. "You could have been hurt."

"Well, the Peaceful Seas folks were there to protect me, so I felt safe. They got between Swenson and me and made sure I didn't hurt him," laughed Terry. "I'm getting to know them. They're a dedicated group and I really like them. You know, they even asked me to talk to some school groups about my experience swimming with humpbacks. I guess our adventure with the whales really impressed them. So, what happened at your meeting today?"

After Joe told Terry about their meeting, she looked at Femke and Jan, and then again at Joe. "Well," she said, "sounds like you need a diver to check out the props on the *Arctic Wind*."

As they all nodded, Joe jumped in. "Right! My thoughts exactly. If we can get under the stern, we can . . ."

"Hold on, sailor! It'll be *me,* not *we.* I told you before that you're not trained in dry-suit diving. This is the North Atlantic, not the warm Caribbean with the 100-foot visibility you're used to. It's going to be cold, murky, and I'll probably be diving at night."

"Well, I could learn to . . . ."

"Sorry, dear. This isn't the time for on-the-job training. I told you before, if you can't handle the air trapped inside a dry-suit, you could pop to the surface like an upside-down cork and get hurt."

Joe pursed his lips, knowing he could not persuade Terry. He also realized she was correct. "Okay," he said quietly. "We have thirty days before the *Arctic Wind* leaves port. When do you want to dive?"

"How about as soon as this run of bad weather breaks?"

"Not only is the weather stormy, Terry," said Jan, "but we've had a harsh winter and the water is still extremely cold. Even with your special equipment, I don't know if you could dive in these waters right now. I'd recommend waiting a couple of weeks."

"Do they have some kind of a weather channel here?" asked Joe. Femke turned on the television, midway through the nightly news broadcast. They were shocked to see Terry's image suddenly appear on the screen, just as the camera captured her throwing a roundhouse punch blocked by Ulf Swenson.

"My God!" yelled Jan.

"Well, dear," laughed Joe, "you certainly know how to get publicity."

169

Chapter 40

April 17th

"*W*hat do you mean they're reopening the inquest?" Swenson screamed into the telephone. "They've kept me tied up in this goddamned port too long! I need to be on the ocean, earning a living! You assured me you would take care of everything!"

"Yes, I know I did, but that was before the Shalken family obtained sufficient evidence convincing the authorities to reopen the investigation, and . . ."

"Enough bullshit. Just fix the problem!"

"What do you mean?"

"You know damn well, just like the others."

"No! I will not be involved in more killings, not even to protect you for your mother's sake!"

"You spineless, phony weakling! You'll . . ."

"I will do no more for you!"

"You did what you did to protect your own ass and your own political career, not because you cared about my mother."

"Yes, I admit it was for me, but also for my country."

"Ah, ever the true patriot," said Swenson, sarcasm dripping from his tongue. "Save your political bullshit for your ass-kissing cronies. Just remember, if I go down, I'm taking you down with me. Your role obstructing this investigation, your involvement in the additional deaths, your relationship with my mother, it will *all* come out. You'll be finished, your political party will be finished, and your . . ."

"You would throw this country into turmoil, just to . . ."

"Just to save my skin? You can count on it! And as long as you mentioned my mother, I wonder how the present Mrs. Valsson would feel about meeting your ex-lover, whom she doesn't know even exists? Maybe they could compare notes, since they have so much in common. Now that would be an interesting meeting wouldn't it?"

"You wouldn't . . . ."

"And let's not forget about your two very successful and respected children. I wonder how they would like to get to know their half-brother? Do you think they'd approve of me, being so refined as they are? Perhaps I should arrange a nice big family gathering, so everyone can get to know each other."

"Why you bastard, I'll. . . ."

"Now that's the first accurate thing you've said during this entire conversation. But don't blame *me* for that title. *You* bestowed that distinction on me forty-two years ago." Prime Minister Stefan Valsson buried his head in his hands contemplating what had brought him to this point in his life. He had achieved everything a man could desire: power, wealth, fame, a loving wife, and successful adult children. But a mistake, a weak moment years ago, had finally come back to haunt him. "There's still one more name on that list. Now do what you need to do!" He heard the line go dead as Swenson slammed the receiver down. Several minutes later Valsson stood, walked slowly to his desk, and flipped through his Rolodex until he found the business card he was looking for. Then he dialed a number he had hoped he would never have to call again.

Chapter 41

May 8th

    *T*hree weeks of cool rainy weather and high winds prevented Terry from diving. The group passed the time following other avenues of investigation. They researched construction and maintenance records of the *Arctic Wind,* and contacted manufacturers of harpoons and ship propellers. Despite their combined efforts, they found nothing conclusive.

    By the second week in May, the weather had improved sufficiently for Terry to attempt a night dive in the cold waters where the *Arctic Wind* was anchored. Joe watched Terry assembling strobe lights on a camera he had never seen before. "Hey, where's your trusty old Sea-and-Sea MX10?"

    "I'd rather use this new digital camera. Call me paranoid, but I don't trust anyone here handling and developing film. Help me load this stuff into the car."

"Aye aye, Captain!" said Joe as he loaded Terry's dive equipment for the short drive to the dock.

The dock was deserted, so Jan, Joe, and Terry transferred the equipment unobserved into a small motorboat Jan had rented. Because the sun does not set until after 10 PM during May in Iceland, Terry planned to dive after midnight. The bay was mirror calm, but Terry decided to suit up before leaving the dock, rather than trying to don the bulky dry-suit over warm clothing while the boat was moving. When she was ready, Joe threw off the mooring lines while Jan expertly guided the boat through the crowded harbor, threading his way past a variety of watercraft until he reached the open bay. The moon was partially obscured by clouds but still threw sufficient light so they could see the *Arctic Wind* silhouetted against the horizon. Jan steered an indirect path toward the ship. He made a wide, sweeping arc, in the event Swenson posted lookouts. The ship was moored with a single bow anchor, causing it to swing into the current bow-first. At Terry's direction, Jan proceeded until they were about one mile ahead of the ship, directly in front of the bow. He cut the engines, letting the boat drift so he could gauge the current's speed and direction. Terry reviewed her dive plan. In the cold night air, her breath was visible as she spoke.

"Okay, it looks like we're perfectly positioned to drift toward the *Arctic Wind.* When we get a little closer, I'll slip over the side, drift, and let the current take me toward the ship. When I get about several hundred yards in front of the ship, I'll descend just deep enough to clear the hull when I reach it. I'm guessing no more than twenty feet deep. Jan, what's the draft on a ship that size?"

"It depends on several factors, not just the length, but I would estimate five to seven meters."

"Then I'll plan for a depth of thirty feet. That's almost ten meters. That should give me more than enough margin for error. I'll let the current take me toward the stern. I have to avoid using any underwater lights. In this little boat, you wouldn't be able to see them, but someone looking down into the water at a steeper angle, like a lookout on that ship, would notice them."

Jan asked, "Without lights, how are you going to know how deep you are? You won't be able to see your gauges."

"No problem. Instead of using the depth gauge attached to my regulator, I'll use my wrist computer. It tells me my depth and it's also got backlighting. See?" she said, pressing a small button, illuminating the small screen in a soft green glow.

"But underwater in the dark, how are you going to know you're headed toward the ship? Without lights, you might miss it."

"Simple. I have an underwater compass." Jan looked slightly confused. As a ship's captain, he was familiar with compass navigation, but he was not a diver and had never used an underwater compass. "I just strap it on my wrist and before I go under, I hold the compass and point this line here, called a lubber line, toward the *Arctic Wind*. Then I hold the compass level, so the needle points true north. Next, I turn the bezel so this notch here lines up with the needle. While I'm underwater, as long I keep the needle lined up with this notch, I'll know the lubber line is pointing toward my target. So I just follow it. See? Simple. For light, I have this glow-stick. When I crack it, it'll give me just enough light to read the compass, but not enough to be seen above the surface. So, I don't have to use any lights."

"Just what the well-dressed gadget girl should always wear when she goes out," said Joe.

"Well, another gadget I wish I had is a re-breather."

"A *what?*" asked Jan.

"A re-breather. It enables you to breathe underwater without emitting any bubbles," said Terry. "I don't like the idea of working close to this ship and risk having a lookout see my bubbles. It's like a flashing sign that says, 'Hey, there's a diver under your boat!'"

"Ah, yes, I can understand that."

"Yeah, too bad you didn't think of that earlier," said Joe.

"Well, actually I did but I couldn't get one on such short notice. Jan, as soon as I'm in the water, start the engine and steer in a large arc to the *Arctic Wind*'s stern. Hold your position against the current about a half mile away and wait for me. After I take pictures of the prop, I'll let myself drift toward you. Joe, when the boat's in position, drop this homing beacon and let it hang at about twenty feet. I have a directional range finder that will zero in on the signal, and I'll follow the signal to the boat. That's it. Any questions?"

"Nope, that's pretty clear," said Joe as Jan shook his head. "Just be careful. No chances, okay?"

"Yep. Got it. Looks like we're here. Help me get my tank on." When Terry was ready, she inflated her buoyancy vest and slipped over the side, making as little splash as possible. As she floated away from the boat, Jan started the motor and quietly headed away from the *Arctic Wind,* steering in a sweeping arc from the bow and heading to a position a half mile behind the stern. Terry kept a low profile, drifting face down, breathing through her snorkel to conserve air. She looked up every few minutes to check that she was drifting toward her intended target, and aligned her compass.

On board the *Arctic Wind,* Captain Swenson had stationed a watch on the bow, but the young seaman was preoccupied selecting a tune on his new MP3 player instead of watching the water around his ship. Several hundred yards away, Terry noticed the glow of a cigarette up on the bow. *Time to disappear,* she thought, pressing the deflation button on her buoyancy vest. As the air escaped, she slipped below the surface just as the sailor on the bow noticed a slight disturbance. He looked out over the water, but saw nothing.

Inky blackness enveloped Terry as she descended. *Okay, time to orient myself.* She cracked the glow-stick and checked her wrist compass. She turned her body until the needle indicating true north lined up with the notch on the bezel. Then she swam in the direction the lubber line indicated, which she knew pointed straight toward her intended target, the *Arctic Wind.* After several minutes, she pressed the backlight button on her wrist computer, which indicated a depth of eighteen feet. *Okay, gotta go a little deeper and I'll check it again when I'm near the ship.* Several minutes later, Terry saw the *Arctic Wind*'s anchor chain, descending on an angle through the murky water. *I must be near the bow, so I can chuck the glow-stick.* She watched it sink slowly toward the bottom. *Let's see how deep I am.* She pressed the backlight button on her computer. Nothing. She pushed it again; still no light. *Shit! The batteries must have died in the cold water.* Terry didn't risk using her underwater flashlight to check her back-up depth gauge. *Should've kept the glow-stick.* She assumed she had descended sufficiently to clear the ship, when the sound of her tank scraping the underside of the hull startled her. *Damn!* She quickly jackknifed and finned deeper.

The sound traveled through the ship and Captain Swenson looked up from his logbook and listened. But there was only silence. Terry looked up at the hull as she drifted toward the stern. Finally, she saw the vague outline of the ship's rudder and oriented herself so she could kick against the current, slowing her drift. She passed several feet below the propeller and finned harder to stop and hold her position. Then she moved within three feet of the propeller. Terry could not risk using her underwater light to examine the prop, so she aimed her camera and took the shot. The strobe illuminated the prop for a brief second, allowing her to see writing stamped on the blade, but not long enough to read it. The lookout was standing along the port rail at mid-ship, but looking away from the ship, toward a barely visible horizon. He noticed a brief flash in the water under the stern and looked into the water. Terry took two additional photos. Two more flashes. *Okay, I'm outta here!* The lookout ran toward the stern, but there was nothing, just . . . *bubbles?* Captain Swenson, alerted by the sound of running footsteps, came up on deck.

"What's going on? Did you see something?"

"I'm not sure, sir," stammered the young seaman. "I thought I saw a flash of light underwater, near the stern." They ran to the stern and looked at the water. A slight disturbance suddenly broke the smooth black surface. Swenson blinked and looked with more attention. *Did I see bubbles or just ripples from the current sweeping past the hull?* Swenson's mind raced, considering the possibilities. *But still, my lookout reported a light flash under the ship. Then, bubbles?* "Get me several grenades from the harpoons," he ordered.

"Aye, sir!" Swenson watched the young man running toward the bow and then he looked into the water again. A minute later, the seaman handed Swenson a grenade. He armed the grenade by tying a line to a hook that dislodges the pin from the grenade when fired into a whale's body, causing it to detonate. He dropped it over the side where he had seen bubbles. Terry had just started swimming away from the ship. Enveloped in total blackness, she never saw the grenade descending. When the grenade descended twenty feet,

Swenson yanked the line. The explosion caught Terry off guard. The shockwave slammed into her body. She dropped the camera and held her head from the concussive pain in her ears. Terry felt cold water rushing into her left ear. She spun around in the water, totally disoriented. Only her training and experience prevented a fatal panic attack as she recognized the symptoms. *Cold water entering my inner ear, dizziness and vertigo—my eardrum's ruptured!*

"Holy shit!" exclaimed Joe, as he saw a geyser of foam erupt from the water and then heard the explosion. "Did you see that?"

"My God," said Jan. "They must have seen her. We have to help her!" Before he could accelerate toward the ship, a second explosion erupted from the other side of the *Arctic Wind.*

"Wait a minute," said Joe. "They're bracketing the ship. They don't really know where she is. Just wait. We can't move now. If they see us, we're all dead." The second grenade exploded farther from Terry than the first one, but she was already disoriented and in pain from the first blast. She winced as the impact of the shockwave from the second explosion hit her. Her head throbbed as if a brick had hit her, and then she felt water seeping into her facemask. She tried to orient herself, *which way is up, which way is down?* But the loss of equilibrium in the weightless, black void made it impossible. She decided to fin harder, hoping to distance herself from the *Arctic Wind.* She feared losing consciousness from another explosion and then drowning if the regulator slipped from her mouth. Terry purged the water from her mask, but it soon began to fill again. It reached her nose and she sniffed. She fought the gag reflex as the liquid hit the back of her throat. But when she felt the sticky warmth she realized it was not water but blood, oozing from ruptured vessels in her ears and nose. Terry knew she was battling for her life. *I can't die like this!*

"I don't see a damn thing, do you?" yelled Swenson, running from port side to starboard, hoping to see the floating body of a diver emerge. "Give me another grenade!" He stared at the water as if he could see through it, looking for some indication of a diver's presence. Just as he was about to throw it, he looked out, away from his ship. In the distance, he saw a vague outline. *Is that a small boat off the stern?* "Give me your binoculars," he ordered. The seaman froze. Swenson put the grenade in his jacket pocket and reached for the instrument hanging from a cord around the seaman's neck. Without taking his eyes off the distant object, he grabbed for the binoculars. Only then did he realize they were not the regulation binoculars the seaman should have had, but his digital music player. "You stupid bastard! Get your binoculars and return to your station! I'm fining you a week's pay!"

"Yes, sir. I'm sorry, sir," stammered the seaman. But Joe had *his* binoculars and was watching the *Arctic Wind*. He saw the two men on deck looking down at the water and then outward in their direction. He told Jan to cut the motor and drift with the current, farther away from the *Arctic Wind*. It would mean a longer swim for Terry, but they could not risk being seen. After dismissing the seaman, Captain Swenson looked out into the blackness, but the shape he thought he had seen had melted into the night. He took the grenade from his pocket and held it out over the railing. He checked the water again, preparing to drop it. *Nothing there.* Shaking his head in disgust, Swenson went back to his cabin.

Fighting the pain, Terry still remembered to activate her directional range finder. She watched the glowing bars indicate which direction to travel. Sweeping it left showed one bar; to the right, three bars, a stronger signal. *Okay, swim right.* She knew as she got closer to Jan's boat the number of bars should increase, but they stayed at three. She swept her hand left and then right, but the strongest signal was still dead ahead. *I'm going in the right direction. But why isn't the signal getting stronger? I should be getting closer but I'm not.* She guessed Jan's boat was also drifting, so she finned harder. Fighting to maintain consciousness, Terry purged her mask each time the seeping blood reached her nose. *Why the hell isn't Jan holding his position?*

Terry had been underwater for more than forty minutes and knew she was low on air. She had been kicking hard, first against the current taking pictures, then escaping from the explosions, and then swimming to reach Jan's boat. She glanced at the directional range finder again. The reading indicated she should be very close to Jan's boat, but her vision was blurring as another attack of vertigo swept over her. The physical exertion, the cold water, and the blood loss had taken their toll. Terry sensed she was passing out. Her last thought was, *Get to the surface!* She pressed the inflation button on her BC and, as the vest inflated, she began to rise.

Joe saw through his binoculars that the deck of the *Arctic Wind* was clear. "All right, Jan, start the motor. Give it enough power to get a little closer. Terry should surface soon." Peering at the black water apprehensively, Joe was relieved to finally see air bubbles near the boat. "Over there," he pointed. Several seconds later, he saw Terry surface. He yelled to her, but when she didn't respond, he sensed something was wrong. "Jan, get over to her quick. She's hurt!" As Jan pulled alongside, Joe saw Terry was unconscious and jumped into the water to keep her head above water. As pulled her toward the boat, he noticed Terry was not holding the camera. *Damn, all this for nothing,* he thought. But as he and Jan lifted her into the boat, Joe saw the camera emerge from the water, dangling from a lanyard Terry had secured to a D-ring on her BC before her dive. They placed her in the boat, but when Joe removed her facemask and hood, he was startled to see her face covered with blood. "Terry!" he yelled, shaking her and trying to rouse her. After a few seconds, she coughed and opened her eyes. "Terry! Talk to me!"

"I think I got the shots we needed," she replied weakly, "but I won't know until we get back and take a look. Damn, I'm cold! Oh, my head's killing me!"

"We have to get you to a hospital! Here, let me hold these towels over your ears and nose to stop the bleeding!"

"What happened, you guys? I had to swim almost half a mile more than I planned and I was low on air. What the hell were they dropping on me, depth charges?"

"We saw activity on deck and thought they spotted us, so Jan backed away out of visual range. It looked like they dropped underwater grenades. Jan, let's get the hell out of here!"

"Don't go too fast, Jan," mumbled Terry. "The bay is dead calm tonight. After all this, I don't want to throw up a wake and let them spot us now."

Jan had the small outboard at the dock in ten minutes. They quickly unloaded their gear and raced to a nearby hospital, where they were directed to the emergency room. After the nurses stopped Terry's bleeding and applied warm towels to raise her body temperature, the doctor examined her. "Well, you have a ruptured left eardrum and ruptured blood vessels in your nose and sinuses. You may also have suffered a concussion. What exactly happened to cause these injuries, Mrs. Manetta?"

"Just a dive accident, doctor. I had difficulty equalizing during the descent and I felt my eardrum pop. I must have panicked and surfaced too fast, and that caused other problems." The doctor listened to her explanation with raised eyebrows.

"I see. Well, I'm no expert in dive medicine, but I am surprised you would have sustained all these injuries, from the actions you described."

"Oh it happens to divers all the time, Doctor."

"Well, in that case, I think I will stick to something safer, like downhill skiing. Here's an instruction sheet I want you to follow for the next few days. And no diving until a doctor clears you, understand?"

"Yes, thank you, Doctor."

While Jan drove back to their hotel, Terry said, "I don't think the doctor believed my story."

"Well, I think he did, up until when your eyes started turning black and blue," said Joe.

"Oh my God, are they? Give me a mirror."

"Okay, but remember, you asked for it."

Blood vessels and capillaries had hemorrhaged from the concussive force of the underwater explosions and blood was pooling under her skin.

"Oh no! I look like a raccoon!"

"Or someone who just lost a tough ten-rounder," replied Joe. When they arrived at the hotel Femke was shocked at Terry's appearance.

"Terry, what happened? Are you all right?"

"Yes, I think so. It's a long story, and I won't be diving for a few months. But *please* get me something hot to drink," pleaded Terry. She attached her camera to her laptop computer's USB port, fumbling momentarily as she worked out the numbness in her fingers. She switched on her digital camera and accessed its software. "C'mon, c'mon," Terry urged, drumming her fingers on the table while the computer booted up. The hard drive clicked for what seemed an eternity. Finally, the desktop menu appeared. Terry clicked the mouse on her photo-imaging program's icon. Seconds later, it accessed the correct program and another menu appeared. She clicked the choice for *Get Photos*. Another menu appeared. She selected *From Camera*. Everyone stared anxiously at the monitor. The *Arctic Wind*'s propeller suddenly appeared.

"Oh my!" gasped Femke. Terry zoomed in on one of the prop blades. A name came into view: *Helseth*. She blinked at the unfamiliar name.

"What does that mean?" asked Terry.

"That's the manufacturer. Yes! I know the company," replied Jan. "They're based in Norway." Next, the letters indicating the blade's metal composition appeared: *NiAl-Bronse*. "That's nibral!" exclaimed Jan.

"That proves it!" said Terry. "It's different from the composition of the trace metal found at Lara's autopsy." Femke stared at the screen in silence. Jan's eyes narrowed and his lips tightened. The impact of what they saw on the screen hit them. The spinning blades of the *Arctic Wind*'s propeller had not killed Lara Shalken.

"So now we go to the authorities," said Jan firmly.

"Not yet." said Joe. "This proves what did *not* kill Lara. We need evidence indicating what *did* kill her. We need a metal sample from the *Arctic Wind*'s harpoons. If we go to the authorities now, someone could leak the information. There are still six days before the next scheduled hearing. We have to board that ship somehow and get our hands on a harpoon."

Chapter 42

May 10th

Harpooner Gudmund Vikinsson sat on the floor of his small basement apartment, staring at newspaper clippings pasted to his bedroom wall. He was disheveled; hair long and uncombed, shirt unbuttoned, pants stained, his face rough with three days' stubble. An empty vodka bottle lay next to a shoe. He blinked, trying to focus on the stories arranged in date order regarding his shipmates' untimely deaths. He glanced at the first story. It was just a short piece about two brothers who had failed to appear at the inquest and were still missing. Then his eyes moved to a longer article, about a bus accidentally striking and killing a pedestrian named Thor Rodale. His glassy eyes moved right and stared at a bold headline. *Man Dies in Flaming Auto Accident*. He shook his head, reading the grisly account of Alfred Haggar's death. Bus accidents? Car accidents? "Accidents my ass," he said out loud to no one but himself. He leaned over and picked up another news article he had clipped out two weeks ago. It was about a prominent doctor who had recently committed suicide. The story mentioned the doctor had performed the autopsies on the three victims killed in the whaling ship accident. *Suicide?* He chuckled as he taped the article to the wall. Vikinsson was no trained investigator, but he could certainly connect the dots. And he feared becoming the next dot. He shook his head again, trying to clear the alcoholic haze providing temporary relief from guilt and from feeling like a cornered animal. He tried to think, evaluate his options, and decide on a course of action. But the grip of a liter of 80-proof Absolut was too strong. He fought for several minutes and then surrendered, letting sleep overtake his troubled brain. His last conscious thought before passing out was hoping not to have the nightmare again. It always began with the explosion of the *Arctic Wind*'s harpoon cannon and ended only when the vision of mangled bodies jolted him awake screaming, drenched in sweat.

The next morning, Gudmund Vikinsson awoke with his usual hangover. His head pounded, but he was grateful the nightmare did not come last night. At least not that he could recall. He stumbled into the shower, his first in several days. Afterward, he felt somewhat refreshed and clearheaded. He stepped to the sink, splashed cold water on his face, shaved, and felt even better. Then he sat in the kitchen, reasoning out his problem. *Yes, if I approach the authorities, tell them what I know, they will protect me as an official witness.* Holding his head in his hands, his mind raced. *If I also tell my story to the newspapers, there will be too much publicity for anyone to harm me. I'll be safe.* His tortured mind kept racing, playing out other options. *But if I go straight to the police, they may charge me with a crime. Perhaps I should first contact the family. They could convince the police to offer me a deal in exchange for my cooperation. Yes! I need to contact the family first.* His empty stomach reminded him it was time for lunch. Gudmund prepared a light repast of bread, ham, cheese, and milk. As he ate, he rethought his strategy. *I know they are staying somewhere in town, probably in a hotel.* Convincing himself this was the best course of action, he decided to find a public telephone and a directory.

Vikinsson had no way of knowing efforts to connect the last dot, him, to the other victims had already been set in motion. Two gentlemen had been methodically stopping at every waterfront bar, showing local patrons Vikinsson's picture. He was smiling in the photo, much younger but still recognizable. "Could you help us find this man? His wife is gravely ill and he doesn't know." Who could refuse such a plea for assistance? If nothing turned up in the most promising establishments—seedy dives catering to the inexpensive needs of wretched souls drowning their demons with cheap liquor— they would expand their search further from the waterfront. They would continually widen their net until they caught their fish. But these fishermen were luckier than most. As they were leaving the fourth bar, they tapped the shoulder of a man whom they had initially overlooked. They held the photo as steadily as possible in front of the man's glazed eyes, without expecting success. As they turned to leave, the soggy synapses in the old man's brain fired in delayed recognition. "Oh, tha's Gudmund," he slurred. The two gentlemen wheeled around and sat down. They generously offered to fund the old man's drinking for the entire day if he could just provide an address, a recent sighting, *anything*. "Oh yeah, he was here lash week. Went to his place for a drink, apartment number fifty-three, I think. Two streets and make a right. Downstairs. Yesh, number fifty-three."

The two left the bar quickly. The owner, a friend of Vikinsson who had been eavesdropping, telephoned his friend to warn him about two surprise visitors. He worried about his friend. He knew he did not have a sick wife. After several rings, a recording came on informing him the number had been disconnected and was no longer in service. *I suppose poor Gudmund couldn't afford to pay both his phone bill and his bar tab,* mused the owner. The two gentlemen quickly reached the corner where the old man had instructed them to turn right. Proceeding down the street, they quickly realized the numbers were going in the wrong direction and they should have turned left. "The old man was probably too drunk to know right from left," said the short stocky one to his partner. They laughed as they backtracked.

Vikinsson closed the door of his basement apartment, walked up four steps to street level, and headed where he knew he would find a public phone. He had only walked a block when two men, one short and stocky, the other a little taller and lean, rudely brushed past him, almost knocking him off balance. "So sorry," the short one said without looking back, scanning the front doors for building numbers, not even making eye contact. Vikinsson continued walking. The taller gentleman pointed. "There! Number 53!" The two men stopped momentarily and then slowly passed the door, to avoid being noticed. They proceeded another block, then casually doubled back and went down the four steps and knocked on the door. After receiving no answer, the shorter one pulled a lock-pick from his jacket pocket, while the taller one stood behind him, obscuring the view of any curious pedestrians. In less than a minute, he heard the lock click. He put his weight against the door, springing the lock. They quickly entered and closed the door behind them. The apartment was dark but the taller one found a lamp and turned the switch. The light illuminated the wall in front of them. They gazed at the news clippings and pictures featuring their gruesome handiwork. They smiled when they realized they had indeed found their quarry's home. "I think we should sit and make ourselves comfortable," said the taller gentlemen.

Vikinsson walked several blocks until he found a public telephone booth with a telephone directory. He recalled from the official inquest that Lara's last name was Shalken, and her husband's name was Jan. *They would be staying in a hotel, but which one?* He tried to reason out the problem logically, but his alcohol-numbed brain could not process logical thoughts. He had just enough cognition to recall that one hotel catered to international tourists. This one, The Grand Hotel. He looked up the number and called. He asked for Jan Shalken but did not hear the operator say, "Just one moment please." Consequently, a woman's voice startled him.

"Hello, this is Femke."

Gathering himself, Vikinsson replied, "I'm sorry. I was trying to reach Jan Shalken. Do I have the wrong number?"

"No, this is the correct number but he is not here right now. May I help you?"

185

"It is very important that I speak to him. When will he return?"

"I expect him soon. May I help you or can he return your call?"

"No. He cannot call me. But I have information about Lara Shalken that . . . ."

"Lara was my sister!" Femke exclaimed, so loudly that Vikinsson almost dropped the phone. "What information do you have?" Femke was frantic, on the verge of losing her composure. "Please tell me!"

Vikinsson's fuzzy mind raced, trying to think. *What do I say? How much do I tell this woman?* "I was there that day. I saw everything. I can help you, but I need your help."

"Yes, yes, anything! Do you want money, what do you want?"

"No, no money, but I need . . . ."

"Jan, Jan, quickly, speak to this man. Just wait one moment please. Lara's husband, Jan, just came in. He will speak to you."

"What's wrong, Femke?"

"Jan, talk to this man. He was there when Lara was killed. He can . . . ." Jan ripped the receiver from Femke's hand while Vikinsson listened.

"What is it? Who are you?" he shouted into the phone.

"My name is Gudmund Vikinsson. I was the harpoon gunner on the *Arctic Wind* the day your wife was killed, but I swear I did not do it. You must believe me. I need your help to stay alive!"

"Yes, yes, we will help you. When can we meet? Where can we meet?" Jan's mind raced with questions for this mysterious caller.

"Tomorrow. We'll meet in a public place. You know the clock tower in Old Town?"

"Yes, we know where that is. What time?"

"Twelve noon. I will wear a blue coat, a black wide-brim hat, and sunglasses. I must not be recognized. But I need to identify you. Stand under the clock tower with a newspaper in your right hand. When you see me, wave the paper and then slip it under your left arm. If I wave back, then approach me."

"I will have some friends with me."

"No! First come alone. Then I will meet your friends."

"Okay, okay," Jan quickly agreed. "Who killed Lara?" he suddenly shouted into the phone.

"I cannot say more now. Just meet me. Please! I have much to tell you. There is also videotape in a safe on board the *Arctic Wind* that you must see. I have to go now. Meet me tomorrow."

"No! Don't go yet. I have more ques . . . ." CLICK. The line went dead and Jan and Femke just stared at each other.

Vikinsson hung up the phone and headed back to his apartment. He was shaken by the emotional intensity of the conversation. It had not gone exactly as he had planned, but at least he had arranged to meet Lara Shalken's family and they had agreed to help him. But he needed a drink, badly. Before returning to his apartment, he went to the tavern. *Just one drink, to steady my nerves.* He looked through the tavern's window and saw his friend, the owner, beckoning him to come inside. Vikinsson opened the door a crack, then looked at his watch. It was later than he thought and he decided he was more hungry than thirsty. He waved to his friend, closed the door, and moved on. "Gudmund! Two men were looking for you earlier today. They . . . ." *He can't hear me now. I'll tell him tomorrow.*

Vikinsson inserted the key into the lock but the door opened. *I was sure I locked the door. But maybe I didn't.* He entered, turned on the light, and was startled to see a short, stocky Asian gentleman standing in front of his wall of news clippings. "Who are you? What are you doing in my . . . ." He realized the man looked familiar. *Wasn't this the man who bumped into* . . . . Vikinsson never saw or heard the taller gentleman behind him.

He woke and found himself tied to a chair. He shook his head, but the pain was intense. He focused and saw two men standing in front of him. Vikinsson regained enough sense to realize he was in danger. He tried to scream, but the gag in his mouth permitted only an inaudible whimper. The two men calmly watched his eyes grow wide, scanning the room, looking for something, anything. Then his eyes stopped on a bottle of Absolut vodka on a small table next to the chair. "Are you thirsty, Mister Vikinsson?" asked the taller gentleman. Gudmund nodded enthusiastically. "Well, if you agree not to yell or shout, perhaps we could share a drink together." He nodded again, more enthusiastically this time. *Maybe these fellows aren't so bad. Maybe this isn't what I thought it was,* his soggy mind rationalized. The short, stocky man poured vodka into a shot glass, gently removed the gag, and held the glass to Vikinsson's lips. He drank enthusiastically. *God, I feel better. I really needed that drink. I wish they would untie my hands, though.*

"Is that better?" asked the taller, man. "How about another?"

"Sure. Can you untie my hands? What do you want with me?"

"Sorry, we cannot untie your hands, yet. But we would like to drink with you." The shorter, stocky one lifted the glass to Vikinsson's lips and he drained it. He felt a little woozy.

"Aren't you going to join me?" he asked.

"Sure," replied the shorter one, filling two glasses with water for himself and his partner. "How about another drink, my friend?"

"I think I've had enough for a while. Who are you?"

"Our names are not important to you," said the taller man. "But we think you need more to drink. Here." He held the glass to Vikinsson's lips. He took a sip and refused to drink more. The shorter gentleman grabbed his hair and yanked his head back while his partner poured the vodka into his mouth. He coughed and spit it out. "Look, you wasted it. But we have more for you. Lots more." Vikinsson shook his head in a vain attempt to clear the growing fog. But it cleared just enough for him to realize he was going to die. *But they can't make me drink!* As if reading his mind, the shorter one looked at his partner and said, "We can't waste any more time." He pulled Vikinsson's head back again and pinched his nose shut. His partner took the half empty bottle of vodka and tried to push it into Vikinsson's mouth. But he clenched his teeth and tried to breathe, drinking some, spilling the rest. Then the taller one took a short piece of hose and jammed it past Vikinsson's teeth into his throat, making sure it went into his esophagus and not the trachea.

He took a full bottle of Absolut and poured the contents into the hose, directly into Vikinsson's stomach. In a few moments he began to feel sick. Then his vision blurred. And just before he passed out, Vikinsson no longer cared that he was going to die.

Chapter 43

May 11th

    *J*an stood under the clock tower in Old Town, holding a newspaper in his right hand as instructed. He looked at his watch again. *11:50. Ten more minutes and I'll find out what really happened to Lara.* Trying to control his anxiety, he leaned against a building to look casual. He started hyperventilating and took a deep breath to control his breathing. He pretended reading the newspaper, but the words appeared as a meaningless jumble of letters to his brain. He was about to check his watch again when the clock tower struck. After the twelfth chime he scanned the passers-by, but saw no sign of a man wearing a blue coat, black wide-brimmed hat, and sunglasses. At 12:15, he grew more anxious. By 12:30, he was despondent, his hopes dashed yet again. His mind raced. Where was Vikinsson? What could have happened? Several minutes later, he looked at Terry, Joe, and Femke sitting anxiously in a car across the street. He noticed Femke seemed particularly agitated, biting her lower lip. Finally, he checked his watch one last time — 12:45. He threw the newspaper into a garbage can and crossed the street to the car. "Let's go. Vikinsson isn't showing," he said, slipping into the driver's seat.

"What could have happened?" asked Femke. "He sounded so genuine, so sincere."

She looked at Joe, who remained uncharacteristically quiet. They pulled away and drove past the dock area, where they noticed a commotion.

"Let's pull over there. I have a feeling. A *cop* feeling," said Joe. A large crowd gathered at the water's edge, held back by police tape. Joe walked over, and when a policeman held up his hand, signaling to halt, Joe flashed his old detective shield. The policeman just stared, confused by the unfamiliar badge, so Joe simply said, "New York." The cop smiled and let Joe through. He proceeded to the edge of the dock cordoned off by police and looked into the water. A body floated face down, dressed in a blue coat. A wide-brimmed black hat was wedged between two pilings. Joe returned to the car.

"Well?" inquired Terry.

"I'm afraid we won't be getting any more information from Mister Vikinsson."

"Oh no!" said Femke. "You mean he's . . . ."

"Yep. I'm afraid our best hope has departed the earth and is shooting his harpoons on some other plane of existence."

"When do you think it happened, Joe?" asked Terry.

"Who knows? Hey, Jan, the tide's going out now, right?"

"Yes, that's correct."

"About how fast does it go out around here?"

"Pretty quickly. I suppose the level of the harbor would fall almost one meter per hour. Why?"

"Well, I saw a wide-brimmed black hat wedged between two pilings, about two feet above the water line. So that would mean someone dumped the body within the last hour, probably while you were waiting for him to show. Pretty gutsy move in broad daylight."

"Goodness, do you think his killers saw Jan or us?" asked Femke.

"I don't know, but I don't think it's wise to hang around. Let's get out of here fast. I don't get it. Who has that kind of pull, to make so many people connected with this case just disappear or die so conveniently?"

"Do you think the government's involved?" asked Terry.

"Well, it's certainly not random and it's also not the work of amateurs. It's too clean. No loose ends. This is cloak-and-dagger stuff."

"Pardon?" asked Femke.

"Oh, just American slang for dirty work done by spies, government agents, that sort of thing," explained Terry. "You know, if I were a witness, I'd be long gone by now."

"Maybe that's what Swenson is counting on," concluded Jan.

"Well, the authorities only have another week to keep the *Arctic Wind* in the harbor," said Terry. "After that, they're free to sail to wherever with another crew."

"To escape justice and continue killing more whales, or anyone else who tries to stop them," said Jan.

"That reminds me," said Terry. "I meet with the Peaceful Seas group tomorrow. We're planning our response to the pro-whaling initiatives we expect at the International Whaling Conference next month."

Chapter 44

May 12th

Back in the hotel, Terry, Joe, Femke, and Jan were planning their next move. Femke and Jan were extremely quiet and pensive. "You two all right?" inquired Terry.

"It's frustrating. We were so close to breaking this case open. Now, I don't know," said Femke.

Jan continued. "I've lost my wife, my best friend, and the love of my life. Femke has lost her sister. We know who did it but we cannot prove it conclusively. After all this, look where we are. Nowhere."

Joe said nothing, but listened, as Terry tried to restore the group's confidence. "Well, think about it. I believe we are indeed somewhere. We have the photos of the *Arctic Wind*'s prop blades, so we know the official cause of Lara's death is wrong. And thanks to the late Mr. Vikinsson, we know he didn't kill her, but that someone else definitely did, even though we still cannot prove who. Not yet, anyway. Then, he mentioned a mysterious videotape, Jan. What do you suppose that's all about?"

"I don't know, Terry. Maybe it shows how Lara was killed, but now we'll never know."

"Not unless we recover it," said Joe. "Didn't Vikinsson tell you it was located in a safe on board the *Arctic Wind*?"

"Yes, but we don't know where," said Femke.

"A ship's safe is usually kept inside or near the captain's cabin," said Jan.

"Well, now it looks like we have two targets on that ship. Those harpoons and the contents of that safe," Joe said.

"We need a plan," commented Terry. "I have to leave for the Peaceful Seas meeting now. I'll join you later tonight and we can discuss it over dinner."

"See you later. Be safe," Joe said, as Terry left quickly, slamming the door behind her.

"Well, we can't just sit here and do nothing!" exclaimed Jan.

"I agree," said Joe, scanning the photos of the *Arctic Wind*'s prop blades. "Look, we need to make sure that ship doesn't go anywhere. It would be easier to keep an eye on it if it was moored at the dock, not out in the harbor. I don't trust Swenson to stay put much longer, and we need to get our hands on those harpoons. But I don't see how we can, with the ship in the harbor, a half mile from shore. Swenson could easily dump them."

Their conversation was suddenly interrupted when the telephone rang. "Hello?" answered Femke.

"Hello, is this Ms. Van der Zee?"

"Yes, who is this?"

"This is Inspector Hansen. I'm calling to schedule a meeting tomorrow."

"But the judge's hearing is four days from now. He gave us until the sixteenth of the month."

"Yes, I know, but I just wanted to review any new information you have so I can inform the judge before your meeting on the sixteenth. Are you, Mr. Shalken, and Mr. Manetta available at nine in the morning?"

"Yes, I suppose so. I think we can . . . ."

"Fine. I'll see you in my office tomorrow morning. Good day, Ms. Van der Zee."

"What was that all about?" asked Joe.

"Inspector Hansen wants to see us at nine tomorrow morning in his office, supposedly to review what we've learned since the last meeting."

"I don't like it. I think he's fishing for information," interjected Jan. "Joe, do you trust him?"

"No, not at all. But we can't just avoid him. We're playing in his ballpark and he makes the rules. Until now, he has definitely not been very helpful. I get the feeling he's under pressure to find out what we know, put obstacles in our way, that sort of stuff. I have an idea. Give me the phone, please."

Terry returned to the hotel early in the evening, and Joe filled her in on the developments. "Hansen has scheduled a meeting for tomorrow morning at 9:00 in his office. He said it's to give the judge an idea of where we are before the meeting on the sixteenth."

"Do you trust him, Joe? The clock is ticking on holding the *Arctic Wind* in port. Last time we met, I got the impression he was trying to squash the whole investigation, or at least delay it until authorities allowed the ship to leave."

"Good point. No, I don't really trust him. We were talking about that earlier, trying to figure out what motives drive the inspector. Well, I can be a sneaky guy too, you know. By the way, how was your meeting with Peaceful Seas?"

"It went well, I guess. They're trying to assemble as much data as possible to counteract the proposals the whaling proponents will raise at the conference. Frankly, Peaceful Seas has said it all before, so I don't know how good our chances are. The buzz is that many members who voted with us last time are either switching positions or are sitting on the fence to see how the meeting goes before committing. And get this, Joe: Because of our experiences swimming with the humpbacks a few months ago, they really want me to speak!"

195

"Great!" said Joe supportively, slapping Terry on the back. "Didn't Lord Raleigh, or Sir Raleigh, whatever his title is, already ask you about speaking?"

"Yes, but I'm no scientist. I don't have any background supporting this cause. I feel like excess baggage. What am I going to say that matters to these people?"

"Knowing you, dear, you'll find something interesting to say," said Joe, as Jan and Femke shared a tension-breaking laugh.

"Easy for you guys to say. I'm the one who has to speak in front of an international assembly without making a fool of myself."

"Well, let's forget that for now and focus on our presentation. If we don't convince Hansen tomorrow, and then the judge, that the case warrants further investigation, it's all over."

"And then Lara's death goes unpunished," added Jan, grimly.

Chapter 45

May 13th

*T*he next morning, they arrived at Inspector Hansen's office, but his secretary ushered them into a larger conference room. They were surprised to find Judge Kristinsson sitting next to Hansen.

"Please make yourselves comfortable and sit down," Hansen beckoned. He noticed Terry but could not recall meeting her before. "Excuse me, but have we ever met regarding this situation?" Before Terry could answer, Joe jumped in.

"Sorry, Inspector. Forgive my manners. This is my wife, Terry. She has been helping us with the investigation.

"Oh, I see. Yes, well, pleased to meet you, Mrs. Manetta." Shaking hands, he noticed the black-and-blue marks around her eyes, which were just beginning to fade. "Are you feeling all right, Mrs. Manetta?"

"Oh yes. Thank you for your concern, Inspector," Terry laughed. "Just a little diving accident."

"I see. Well, in the interest of time, I took the liberty of inviting Judge Kristinsson so he can make an immediate ruling whether or not to continue the investigation."

"Why how efficient of you, Inspector," remarked Joe as he sat down, glancing at his watch and noticing the smirk on Hansen's face. *We'll see who's the sneakier bastard in a few minutes, pal.*

"Thank you," replied Hansen, completely missing Joe's sarcasm. "I would like to conclude the proceedings as quickly as possible. Now, as regarding your evidence, I don't think that . . . ."

"Well," Joe interrupted, "I was just thinking about the history of this case, the strange chain of events, and how much this case reminded me of some old cases I investigated in New York. Why, I recall one investigation that . . . ." Hansen was caught off guard and didn't know how to halt Joe's monologue. He listened impatiently, drumming his fingers on the table, annoyed while Terry, Femke, and Jan just watched Joe quizzically. After fifteen minutes of Joe's raconteuring, Hansen broke in sharply.

"Detective Manetta, I'm sure we . . . ."

"That's *Mister,* now. I guess you forgot again, that I haven't been *Detective* Manetta for quite a while. In fact, did you know that's how I met Terry? Well, there I was, a New York City detective all the way down in Cozumel, and . . . ."

"*Mister* Manetta, then! That will be quite enough. I am sure we would all enjoy hearing your exciting crime-fighting exploits some other time, but right now, the business at hand is . . . ."

Suddenly, the conference room door burst open. Inspector Willemstad rushed in, accompanied by Doctor Kronegard, the forensic specialist who performed Lara's second autopsy. Hansen, flustered, looked at Judge Kristinsson in confusion and then at Joe.

"Inspector Hansen, I took the liberty, *also* in the interest of time, of inviting Inspector Willemstad and Doctor Kronegard, since the importance of our new evidence really depends on the good doctor's judgment." This time, the sarcasm was not lost on Hansen, who replied appropriately.

"Why, how efficient of *you,* Mister Manetta."

"Thank you, Inspector, anything I can do to help the cause," said Joe, smiling pleasantly as he and Hansen exchanged dagger-stares. *Never try to bullshit a bullshitter, pal.*

Finally, Judge Kristinsson put the meeting back on course.

"Ladies and gentlemen, I do have other meetings later today, so please present your evidence for evaluation."

"Yes, Your Honor," Terry began. "If you would please each take a set of these photos I took of the *Arctic Wind*'s propeller." She opened a large manila envelope and passed one set to the judge and Hansen, a second set to Willemstad and Kronegard, and kept the third set. "Sorry you have to share, but I didn't realize we would have so many people here today. Your Honor, this is very straightforward. A ship's propellers are stamped with the manufacturer's name and metal composition. If you examine photo one, it clearly shows all that information. The metal composition of the blade is in the top right corner of the photo." They all rotated the photo so the words, *NiAl-Bronse* appeared at the top. "That's an alloy called nibral. These other two photos are just different angles I shot, to make sure I captured the information I wanted. You can see they also contain the same information."

"Doctor Kronegard, what is your opinion?" asked Judge Kristinsson.

"Your Honor, since the metal sample found in Ms. Shalken's cervical vertebra was composed of different metal, these photographs confirm it did not come from these propeller blades. In my expert opinion, some other object caused the fatal wound."

"Are we sure beyond a doubt these photos are actually the *Arctic Wind*'s propeller?" asked Hansen, attempting to raise doubt.

"I took them myself from underneath her hull!" exclaimed Terry, her anger rising. "That's how I got these!" she said sharply, pointing to her black and blue eyes. "Someone on that goddamned ship tried to blow me out of the water!"

"And I also was there, along with *Mister* Manetta," said Jan, glowering at Hansen, who averted his piercing stare.

"There is really no other logical conclusion, Your Honor," interjected Willemstad. "A lethal object from the *Arctic Wind,* most likely a harpoon, caused Mrs. Shalken's death. In addition, Mrs.

Manetta's recent near-death experience while taking these photos confirms this matter requires further investigation."

"Very well. I am satisfied," said the judge. "Inspector Hansen, please contact Captain Swenson immediately and inform him that I am ordering him to moor his ship to the Old Town pier, where it will remain until further notice. Secondly, I am issuing a search warrant for a complete inspection of the ship, to be carried out within two days."

"Your Honor," said Terry. She was about to object to the delay executing the search warrant, when Willemstad caught her eye and imperceptibly shook his head.

"Yes, Mrs. Manetta?"

Terry caught Willemstad's signal and retreated. "Nothing, Your Honor. Sorry for interrupting. It can wait."

Turning to Hansen, the judge continued. "Finally, please inform Captain Swenson I want to meet him, his officers, and crew early tomorrow morning in my office for an official interview. Is there any other business?"

"No, Your Honor. I will carry out your instructions immediately," replied Hansen, quietly.

Gee, why so glum, pal? thought Joe.

"Thank you and good day," said Judge Kristinsson, leaving the room, followed by Hansen, who turned and threw a withering glare at Joe as he left.

Once alone, the group broke into animated conversation. Terry asked Willemstad, "Why did you send me that signal? I wanted to ask the judge to execute the inspection sooner."

"I knew where you were going, Terry. But the wheels of justice don't turn as fast here. I was concerned you might annoy the judge just when he decided to rule in our favor."

"Got it. When in Rome . . . ."

"Exactly!"

Femke turned to Willemstad. "I was surprised when you arrived. Were you invited?"

"Well," Willemstad said, "Joe was concerned Hansen would try to quash the investigation and end it today. He called me, and when I found out no one invited Doctor Kronegard, I decided to bring him along. Sorry we were late. We got caught in traffic."

"No problem," said Joe. "It was just like the cavalry arriving in the nick of time." Femke and Jan shook their heads, puzzled at the unfamiliar reference.

"So telling all those stories was . . . ."

"Good old American filibustering, stalling for time," said Joe, laughing. Terry could see Femke and Jan were still bewildered.

"I'll explain the concept to you later," said Terry. "Let's get some lunch. I'm famished."

Chapter 46

May 13th

    *L*eaving the courthouse, Terry spotted a small, quaint restaurant overlooking the bay. "Hey, that place looks interesting. Let's duck in there and get a bite while we plan our next moves." They ordered lunch and a bottle of wine to toast their success keeping the investigation alive. Waiting for their food to arrive, Willemstad said, "I'm concerned that if we wait for them to execute the search warrant, evidence may be lost. Two days is a long time."

    "My thoughts exactly," agreed Joe. "The minute Swenson finds out what information we have, which will happen at tomorrow's meeting if not sooner, he'll send the harpoons or any other incriminating evidence on board to the bottom of the ocean."

    "And then if you recover anything, you won't be able to prove it came from the *Arctic Wind*," said Willemstad, as the waiter served their salads.

"So we have to get on that boat and get the evidence first!" said Jan.

Femke looked up from her salad. "So how do you propose to do that, Jan? Are you going to ask him for an invitation?"

"Well, you might not have to," interjected Terry. "Listen, I have a plan."

"A plan? Already? Fast work," said Joe.

"Now look, this involves all of us. Oh good! Our main course is here. Let's eat while I explain."

"I should have warned you, my wife loves a captive audience," Joe said, turning to Willemstad as Terry flashed a look of mock annoyance. "Proceed, dear."

"Okay. Now first we . . . ."

Terry described her plan while Femke, Jan, and Joe listened attentively. They were still discussing it an hour later over coffee and dessert. "If we all play our roles correctly, it just might work," agreed Femke.

"As long as Swenson doesn't decide to cut anchor and run," remarked Jan.

"I don't think he'll do that," said Joe, pointing to the window facing the harbor. They turned and saw the *Arctic Wind* slowly proceeding toward the Old Town dock, as the judge had ordered.

After lunch, they headed toward the main shopping district to start implementing Terry's plan. They drove past the pier, where the *Arctic Wind*'s crew was busy securing the ship. Terry noticed a large man on deck barking orders. "Look, there's Swenson."

"I see him," replied Jan, in a flat, cold tone. Terry saw Jan's knuckles turn white as his fingers tightened, holding the steering wheel in a death grip. Their first stop was a clothing store specializing in various types of commercial uniforms. Next they drove to the airport, where they rented another automobile, selecting the model and color her plan required. Finally, they returned to their hotel to unwind and review tomorrow's plans.

Chapter 47

May 14th

*T*he next morning after breakfast, they prepared for the day's action. Terry adjusted her uniform and asked, "Well, Joe, how do we look?" He assessed Femke, Jan, and Terry with a professional eye. He felt the familiar sensation of adrenaline pumping, just before a police operation commenced. Not yet a rush, but heightening his senses to combat readiness. They all noticed Joe's demeanor change. Terry recognized it immediately. She had seen it before, in Cozumel, when Joe had led the operation that ultimately brought down an international drug cartel. But this was the first time Jan and Femke had ever seen Joe in "police mode." His jaw was set firmer; his eyes were cold, analytical, all business. The friendliness in his face had vanished. *Mister* Manetta had transformed back into *Detective* Manetta. Joe felt the change too, as if he had slipped into familiar, comfortable old clothes. He realized he enjoyed the feeling. He looked at Jan, Terry, and Femke, dressed in police-type uniforms.

Not identical to the local police, since they were supposed to be from a different police agency, but close enough to look official and intimidate any civilians they might encounter.

"Jan, change those damn patterned socks. No uniformed cop would wear those. They should be plain black, blue or a dark grey, to match your uniform."

"Joe," Femke said, "who would notice such a small detail?"

"I've seen smaller mistakes kill guys," he replied sharply. "You two," he said turning to Terry and Femke, "make sure you wear your hats forward over your eyes, not back on your heads. That way it looks more official, not like you're out for a walk in the park. Remember, to effectively order civilians around, you must look official and act with authority. Establish that *you* are in charge. Impose your will. You're not *asking* them to do something. You're *telling* them, *ordering* them, in a tone that says *you* are unmistakably, unquestionably in control. When you say something, they have to know it's a firm order, not a debate or a request. They have to believe there is an *or-else* behind your order so you don't have to start making empty threats. Got it?" All three nodded in assent. "And make sure you carry yourselves erect. Use sharp, crisp movements, no casual body language. One more thing: Any seamen you encounter will probably be European, right Jan?"

"Yes. Most likely Icelandic, Finnish, Norwegian, or maybe German."

"Right. Then Terry, I'd recommend you let Jan and Femke do all the talking. If they pick up an American accent, they might get suspicious, maybe challenge you or start asking for credentials."

"Sure. Sounds logical," agreed Terry.

"Good. Everyone understand the plan?"

"Got it," replied Femke, still off balance by the change she had observed in Joe during the last ninety seconds.

"Good. You've just been taught what we teach new recruits during several weeks of academy training. And that's *after* they've already been pre-screened and selected as the personality types who are comfortable projecting authority."

"Don't you mean to say you *used* to teach, in the *past* tense, dear?" said Terry with a wink that brought Joe back to the present and lightened the mood.

"What? Oh yeah," he said grinning which told them he was back. But he knew they had gotten the message. And the old clothes still felt good.

"By the way," asked Femke, "are you sure *you* should be the one going to the courthouse to stall their meeting, rather than boarding the ship? After all, you've actually been a policeman, and have experience ordering people around."

"Well, I know it's a bit risky doing it this way, but Jan needs to get aboard the *Arctic Wind*. He knows what he's looking for. And, I really think I have a better chance of delaying them at the meeting than either of you ladies, no offense."

"None taken, but . . . ."

"I agree with Joe," said Jan. "The meeting could get pretty confrontational. And Joe has the best credentials to get access to the judge."

"Besides, you need someone there as devious as Hansen," said Terry, smiling at Joe.

"Thanks, hon, I love you too," he said as Terry blew him a kiss. "Right. It's settled. I'll attend their meeting, try convincing the judge to expedite the search warrant and also delay everyone as long as possible. You three do your thing on the boat and let's keep our cell phones on. You don't want to be on board when Swenson gets back. I'll let you know when they're heading back to the *Arctic Wind*. Terry, are your arrangements with the Peaceful Seas folks all set?"

"Yep. The *Sea Angel II* will be in position when we get to the dock. How much time do you think we'll have?"

"Well, to make a 9:30 meeting, they'll leave no later than 9:00. The meeting should last no more than fifteen or twenty minutes. Just long enough for the judge to present our evidence to Swenson and inform him about the search warrant. I'll try to make things longer and buy you some more time. It should take them at most thirty minutes to get back, twenty probably."

"So that means we have to be out of there by 10:30 at the latest."

"I'd shoot for 10:15 to be safe. It's 8:15 now, so let's roll! I need to leave so I'm there before their meeting starts, and you three need to be in position to board ship as soon as Swenson and his crew leave." Joe hugged Terry, kissing her cheek gently. "Be safe, hon," he whispered.

"You too," she said, hugging him back. Joe took Femke's car and drove to the courthouse, while Terry, Jan, and Femke drove their rented faux-police car to the Old Town piers. They parked two blocks away from the pier where the *Arctic Wind* was moored. At 9:05, a large van arrived at the dock. The crew, led by the unmistakable figure of Ulf Swenson, got in and drove off. "Good. At least they're not early," commented Femke as Jan pulled out and drove to the pier. Jan pulled up to the *Arctic Wind,* screeching to a halt, feigning urgency. Jan, Terry, and Femke rushed up to a startled young seaman standing at the foot of the ship's gangplank. "Everyone must evacuate the ship immediately!" Jan declared in an authoritative tone, made more commanding by his massive six-foot-six frame.

"Why? My captain left orders that no one boards or leaves the ship," countered the young man, six inches shorter, staring up defiantly into Jan's face.

From his immediate right, Femke said, "We have information a bomb is on or underneath your ship. It may explode at any moment." They watched the young man's eyes grow wide with shock. He opened his mouth as if to say something, but no sound came out.

Jan firmly asked, "Who else is on the ship? We need to evacuate them immediately!"

Bombarded by commands, the young seaman was momentarily disoriented. He stammered, "Just two mechanics in the engine room beside myself. What bomb?"

"We don't know," barked Jan in an annoyed tone. "But haven't you noticed the *Sea Angel II* has docked very close to your vessel? The anti-whaling organization Peaceful Seas owns her. They certainly have no love for your ship and its mission, do they?" He paused momentarily, letting the young man answer the rhetorical question in his own mind. Terry pointed toward the *Sea Angel II* for effect. Understanding the implication, he wheeled and ran up the gangplank.

"Follow me!" he yelled to the three uniformed officers, whose credentials he had never challenged. They quickly found the two mechanics busy working below deck in the *Arctic Wind's* hot engine room. "You must leave immediately!" the seaman ordered. The two men, wearing only sweat-stained undershirts and grimy coveralls, looked at each other and then at their shipmate, confused. "The police suspect there may be a bomb on the ship! Get out now!" The two mechanics needed no further clarification as they pushed everyone aside in their haste to evacuate the ship.

"Is anyone else aboard?" Jan asked.

"No. I don't believe so, sir."

"Good. But you must leave also. We will start searching the ship before our bomb squad arrives with a dive team. Hurry!"

At the courthouse, Joe waited until 9:15, then entered the building. "I'd like to see Judge Kristinsson," he said politely to the receptionist.

"I'm sorry, but the judge is busy preparing for a 9:30 meeting."

Time to turn on the old cop personality, Joe old boy, his familiar internal voice instructed. "Yes, I know. I'm here on international police business concerning the judge's meeting," said *Detective* Manetta, flashing his gold NYPD shield. "He is expecting me." She hesitated, then looked at the gold shield again.

"Oh, of course. This way please," the receptionist replied, escorting Joe down a long, drearily painted hallway to a large conference room. *Guess they got a sale on the same institutional-green paint that we did in New York,* mused Joe. She opened the door for Joe, but before entering, he turned to her and said quietly, "A group of men will arrive shortly for the 9:30 meeting. I know the judge would appreciate it if you detained them until my meeting is over, okay?"

"Yes sir," the astonished woman said, turning to walk back to her station. Joe entered the conference room and Judge Kristinsson looked up, startled by the intrusion. Inspector Hansen, eyes bulging, appeared shocked, then annoyed, then angry, all in less than three seconds. Joe was amused, observing Hansen's range of negative emotions. He maintained eye contact with Hansen and smiled, projecting a mental greeting that he wished he could say out loud, *you're worst nightmare is back, buddy!*

"What are you doing here?" was the extent of Hansen's challenge.

"I'm sorry, Mr. Manetta," said the judge, "but I am expecting some guests shortly."

"Yes, I know Your Honor, the *Arctic Wind*'s remaining crew. That's why I came early. I didn't want to interrupt your meeting. I just had some quick follow-up questions about our meeting yesterday."

"Yes, about what?" said the judge impatiently.

"Well, it's about the search warrant."

"I expect to have a team of officers inspecting the ship tomorrow morning," interjected Hansen. *Yeah, conveniently late,* thought Joe.

"Well, that's the problem, Your Honor," continued Joe, directly addressing the judge and pointedly ignoring Hansen, who was busy checking his watch. "It's the timing. You see, we — I mean Inspector Willumstad, Miss Van der Zee and Mr. Shalken, specifically — have concerns about the safety of the evidence on board the ship."

9:30. Where are they? wondered Hansen, looking at his watch again.

"Please explain your concern, Mr. Manetta."

"Well, considering the incredible chain of events that has led us to this point, your Honor, starting with . . . ." Joe recapped the case history, while Hansen fumed.

9:40, where the hell are those idiots?

"What do you mean the judge cannot see us!" growled Ulf Swenson, unaccustomed to anyone, especially a small woman, detaining him.

"I'm sorry, sir, but as soon as he is ready. . . ."

"My men and I have to get back to our ship! This is unacceptable! I swear I will see that . . . ."

209

"Excuse me, Your Honor, I want to see if our guests have arrived," said Hansen. As he opened the door, they all heard Swenson's bellowing voice down the corridor.

"I *demand* to see . . . ."

"Captain Swenson, this way please," said Hansen, running down the hall to the reception desk, wiping perspiration from his brow. "What do you mean keeping these people out here all this time!" he shouted at the receptionist.

"I'm sorry, Inspector. I was told I could not disturb the judge."

"By whom?" As soon as he asked the question, his jaw muscles tightened as he realized who had given the spurious order. "Never mind," he said through clenched teeth, glaring at the receptionist. "Please follow me, gentlemen. My apologies for keeping you waiting." Hansen burst into the conference room, interrupting Joe, who was still talking to the judge. "I'm sorry Mr. Manetta, but you must leave now! These people have a scheduled meeting."

"Inspector Hansen, Mr. Manetta has shared some interesting aspects of the case with me," said Judge Kristinsson. "I want the search warrant for the *Arctic Wind* issued and executed today, as quickly as possible. Please see to it immediately."

"What search warrant!?" exclaimed Swenson.

"Please sit down, Captain. I have some questions for you and your crew and then you will have your answers. Thank you for coming, Mr. Manetta." Joe patted Hansen on the back as he stepped past him, going out the door.

"Hey, buddy, glad I could help. See you later." He maintained eye contact just long enough to see Hansen glowering at him. As he walked down the hall, he checked the time: 9:45. *Well, I bought them an extra fifteen minutes.* Passing the receptionist, he nodded and smiled. She returned an angry glance, aware he was the reason Hansen had publicly scolded her. *Not your day for making friends, Joe old boy,* said his familiar internal voice. He returned to his car and waited for Swenson and his crew to leave so he could warn the team how much time they had left.

Chapter 48

May 14th

*W*ith the entire crew off the *Arctic Wind,* Terry, Femke, and Jan had the run of the ship. "Okay, I'll search the bow," said Jan. "The harpoons should be stowed up front near the harpoon cannon."

"We'll search Swenson's cabin for the safe where this videotape is supposedly kept," said Terry.

"His cabin should be down that stairway near the stern," said Jan, pointing.

"C'mon, Femke. Let's get below and find that tape!"

Swenson was digesting the information he was getting from Judge Kristinsson when his cell phone rang. Seeing the call was from the seaman to whom he had entrusted his ship, he immediately answered, even though the judge was speaking to him. "What? A *bomb?* On *my* ship?" There was stunned silence in the conference room as the crew exchanged confused glances. Terminating the call, Swenson announced, "This meeting is over. Authorities

211

are inspecting my ship because those supposedly *peaceful* whale enthusiasts have made a bomb threat. Let's go, men!" He ran out of the conference room, followed by his crew.

The judge turned to Hansen and asked, "What authorities?" Hansen shrugged in confusion. Kristinsson said, "I suggest you get down there and find out what the hell is going on, Inspector!"

Outside the courthouse, Joe was surprised to see Swenson and his crew leaving the building early. They jumped into their van and raced away, tires screeching.

"Holy shit!" he exclaimed, looking at his watch. Only 9:55. The meeting had ended earlier than planned, and Swenson was rushing back to his ship. He immediately called Femke's cell phone.

"Hello, Joe?"

"Listen, the meeting broke up early. Swenson and his crew just left."

"What?" she exclaimed.

"They'll be there in half the time we planned. Are you almost finished?"

"No. Jan found the harpoons, but we haven't located the safe. He's coming below to help us."

"Well, hurry the hell up! You only have fifteen, maybe twenty minutes max!"

"Okay, I'll tell Terry and Jan," she said, checking the time — 10:00. Joe broke the connection, started the car, and raced toward the pier, cutting off Hansen pulling out from his reserved parking space.

On the ship, the trio had ransacked Swenson's cabin looking for the safe, to no avail. "Where the hell would it be?" asked Terry in frustration.

"Bolted to the floor, probably under his desk. But it could also be free-standing or maybe built into the cabin wall," replied Jan. Femke looked at her watch: 10:05.

"We only have five, maybe ten minutes."

"We've looked under every desk and table in this cabin, the walls are clean. I don't get it," Terry said. "Jan, where else could it be?"

"I don't know and we don't have any more time."

"Well, at least you found the harpoons."

"But I want that damned tape!" exclaimed Jan. Frustrated, he kicked a wooden model of a sperm whale, placed as an end table next to a leather arm chair. "Ow!" Jan yelled in pain as his foot struck the immovable whale. Terry went over to examine the whale, and rapped it with her knuckles.

"Jan, this isn't wood. It's metal, carved to resemble wood grain. And it's bolted to the floor."

Femke came over and examined the whale. The blowhole was open as if the whale was taking a breath. Looking more carefully, she exclaimed, "Oh my God! Look closer, *into* the blowhole!"

Terry peered into the recess. "It's a dial, like a combination lock. This is the safe!" Femke looked at her watch; 10:12.

"They'll be here any minute! How do we open it?"

Jan looked around the cabin, searching for something he knew should be nearby. He found it, fastened to the outside of the cabin wall. He returned with a metal fire ax. "I'll smash the safe open. I left three harpoons lying by the gangplank. You two get at least one of them off the ship. Hurry!" Terry and Femke raced toward the gangplank where Jan had laid the harpoons. Together they carried one off the ship as they heard metal smashing against metal inside the cabin. No sooner had they placed the harpoon in the trunk of their car than the van carrying Swenson and his crew pulled up. Swenson jumped out, racing past the faux-police car, completely ignoring the two uniformed women, and ran up the gangplank. The remainder of the crew, fearing a bomb might really be aboard, was more cautious and went across the street where the young seaman was standing with the two mechanics.

Swenson heard the sound of metal smashing metal below deck and ran to investigate. The sound was coming from his cabin. He stepped inside and was shocked to see a man rummaging through the contents of his safe. "Who the hell are you?" he demanded. Jan turned and was momentarily stunned to find himself standing face-to-face with his hated enemy. Swenson saw the uniformed officer was holding a videotape cassette in one hand and a woman's gold bracelet in the other. "What do you think you're going to do with

. . . .*you!*" he exclaimed, finally recognizing Jan. He lunged at Jan, grabbing him by the throat, but Jan broke free and delivered a fist to Swenson's jaw, knocking him back against the cabin wall. Both men were so large, the cabin could barely contain them. Swenson shook his head to clear the effects of the blow, reached up and pulled a nineteenth-century wood-handled lance from the wall. New England whalers had used lances to kill whales they had harpooned. He hurled it at Jan, who raised his hand in a defensive reflex as he turned and ducked. The sharp, rusty point smashed the tape cassette, grazed Jan's forehead and pierced the far wall. Jan scrambled to his feet, dropping the bracelet, not realizing the lance had struck him until blood trickled into his eye. He grabbed for the lance but Swenson had already pulled it from the wall and was, jabbing at Jan. The two adversaries circled in the cramped cabin. Both realized only one would leave the ship alive. Swenson slowly advanced at Jan, jabbing, trying to strike a mortal blow. Jan backed out of the cabin, constantly facing Swenson. He knew he needed more room to maneuver away from the deadly tip of the lance. He slowly backed up the stairway toward the main deck as Swenson advanced. The two men continued their macabre dance of death, Swenson jabbing and lunging, Jan backing up, shifting side to side, avoiding the thrusting, menacing, rusty point, while blood ran into his eye obscuring his vision.

Joe arrived at the pier, followed by Hansen and a police contingent. They stared, frozen in momentary disbelief at the scene on the ship's deck. Terry and Femke ran up the gangplank, followed by several policemen. Swenson had Jan backed against the ship's railing. He grinned malevolently, realizing the irony of the moment. His had finally cornered his prey, and now he was going to kill Jan with the same type of weapon that had once killed so many whales. Ignoring the policemen's shouts to drop his weapon, Swenson lunged, aiming for Jan's chest. Jan was deceptively agile for such a large man and he quickly sidestepped Swenson's thrust, grabbing the long metal shaft of the lance as the tip grazed his midsection. The momentum carried both men over the rail into the water on the seaward side of the ship, out of sight of the spectators gathered on the pier.

The impact of landing in the water jarred the lance from their grip, and it sank. As the two men rolled, grappling for an advantage, Jan maneuvered behind Swenson and tried to push him under. Swenson slipped out of his grasp, but Jan got behind him again and then found his hand tangled in the gold chain around Swenson's neck. He pulled the chain hard, choking him. Swenson gasped for breath and grabbed the chain with both hands, working his fingers under the chain, trying to loosen the garrote. But as he forced his fingers between his neck and the chain, he rolled it so the shark teeth were pointing upward, pressing into his neck. He felt the razor sharp teeth digging into his flesh, so he pulled the chain harder to ease the pain. In desperation, he reached behind his head with his left hand, trying to break Jan's grip. His hand found Jan's wrist and he gripped it, pulling with all his strength. But Jan kept the pressure on. Swenson's mind raced, searching for some way to distract Jan. Finally, his twisted mind provided an answer. Gasping for breath, he rasped, "Too bad Lara was already dead when I found her. I always wanted to fuck her." The remark stunned Jan and he loosened his grip on the chain. Swenson took a breath, felt momentary relief, and sensed the opportunity to seize the advantage. *Two or three more seconds and I'll be able to drown this bastard once and for all.* But Jan suddenly recalled seeing Lara's bare wrist without her wedding bracelet. Realizing Swenson had robbed her most treasured possession from her dead body jolted Jan from his shock.

"You killed my Lara," Jan cried out. Hate and rage surged through him. Gritting his teeth and tensing every muscle, he dug his knee into Swenson's spine, gaining leverage. He pulled the chain with almost superhuman strength, slicing Swenson's fingers to the bone. "You murdering son of a bitch!" he roared, pulling the chain even tighter. Swenson's eyes bulged as the chain cut his air off and the upturned shark's teeth pierced his neck, turning the water around the thrashing men into crimson foam. Swenson felt stinging pain and threw his head from side to side, vainly attempting to dislodge the teeth. But that only caused the serrated teeth, as sharp as Hoffritz steak knives, to saw through his windpipe. Every breath became a sickening wheeze. Gasping for air, he continued thrashing, as the teeth sliced his jugular vein and carotid artery. Arterial blood

215

under pressure shot several feet into the air, covering both men and temporarily blinding Jan as it sprayed into his face. Several wheezy gasps later, Swenson lost consciousness, bled out into the sea, and died. Joe and two policemen dove into the frigid water and pulled Jan away from Swenson's body, which was floating face-down in a sea of red. "My Lara. He killed my Lara," he kept repeating, as they pulled him from the water.

Minutes later, police divers pulled Swenson's lifeless body from the water as his shocked crew watched. Inspector Hansen called Doctor Kronegard, notifying him there had been a violent death. He arrived at the dock several minutes later, along with two ambulances. A policeman led the doctor to Swenson's body, lying facedown. He knelt and turned the body over. He recoiled, startled to see the bloody shark teeth protruding from Swenson's neck. He stared at Swenson's face, still contorted in rage, fierce blue eyes staring sightlessly skyward. "What? What happened here? who killed this man?" he asked, looking around for anyone to say something, to make sense of what he saw. Finally, Joe, wrapped in a blanket and still shivering from the cold water, walked over and stood next to him. He glanced at Jan, shivering in a blanket, bleeding from his head wound. Then, bending over, hands on his knees, cocking his head in an investigative pose, Joe examined the body.

"Well, Doctor, the evidence seems pretty clear. It appears Captain Swenson was the victim of a shark attack." Kronegard turned, open mouthed, and stared at Joe. But before he could speak, an emergency medical technician took Joe's arm and led him to an ambulance with the two police officers and Jan. They went to the hospital for observation and to stitch Jan's bleeding forehead wound. The other ambulance took Swenson's body to the morgue. In the commotion, no one noticed Terry leave the ship, carrying a mangled videotape cassette.

Chapter 49

May 14th

*F*emke and Terry followed the ambulance to the hospital in their faux-police car. After several hours of examinations, doctors released Joe and the policemen, but kept Jan overnight due to his wounds, blood loss, and emotional stress. They returned to their hotel in silence, each privately reflecting on the day's incredible events. "If you ladies don't mind, I'm going to take a hot shower," said Joe. "I feel like my core body temperature is one step above sending me into hibernation."

"Okay, dear. Enjoy. Well, what do we do with this?" Terry asked Femke, holding the smashed videocassette and several feet of loose videotape.

"I don't know, Terry. I really don't want to see my sister being killed. We know who is responsible and he's dead, thank God. Why keep it?" Just then the telephone rang and Femke answered it. "Jan! How are you feeling? Oh, that's wonderful. Yes, we can pick you up tomorrow morning. What? Oh just a minute. Jan, Terry wanted me to ask what we should do with the videotape you found in Swenson's safe. Yes, those were my thoughts as well. Have a good night and we'll see you tomorrow."

"What did he say?"

"He doesn't want to watch his wife being killed either. We both feel justice has been done. We can't view the tape anyway. Look, it's ruined. Just throw it away." Terry tossed the cassette and loose tape into the kitchen garbage can. Several minutes later, Joe returned.

"Boy, that hot shower really felt good. I was chilled to the bone. Hey, where's the tape?"

"We threw it away," said Terry.

"What? Terry, it's still evidence! You can't just throw the tape away!"

"It's irrelevant now, Joe. And besides, you can't watch it. The cassette is ruined."

"Terry, we still don't know what's on that tape. And we still might be able to restore it. I sure would like to see it."

"I'll pass," said Femke.

"Is there anyplace around here where you can get that cassette fixed?" asked Terry.

"Well, I wasn't going to even try locally," said Joe. "I may have to send it to a videocassette manufacturer, or maybe a special lab if the loose tape is damaged. Call me paranoid, but I don't trust anyone around here these days. Tapes can be erased too easily." Joe fished the damaged cassette and loose tape out of the garbage can and studied it. "On second thought, I have some buddies who can help me. I'll call them tomorrow morning."

After breakfast, Femke and Terry drove to the hospital and picked up Jan, while Joe took a taxi to the U.S. Embassy. Flashing his detective shield granted him access to a senior staff member. *Hope I never lose this baby. It opens more doors than Abracadabra.* "How do you do, Detective Manetta? I'm Alice McDonald, the senior duty officer. How may we assist you today?"

"Good morning, Ms. McDonald, nice to meet you. Actually I'm retired detective Manetta now, but I'm assisting an investigation and I must send sensitive material to the U.S. for examination and analysis. It has to be sent quickly and confidentially."

"Well, the embassy hasn't been informed of any ongoing investigations involving U.S. citizens. Is this an official matter or is it personal?"

Joe sensed the odds of obtaining Ms. McDonald's cooperation were a toss-up. *Time to turn on the old cop charm, Joe-boy,* said his familiar internal advisor. "Well, Alice," he said, combining his most official, police-business persona with pure sincerity, "it's partly both. I'm helping a close friend regarding his wife's suspicious death. A videotape may contain evidence proving if her death was accidental or a crime." She leaned forward, totally engrossed.

"I see. Please continue, Mr. Manetta."

"Yes. By the way, please call me Joe." *You haven't lost your personal touch, Joe-boy. You got her hooked, now reel her in.* "I need your help desperately, Alice. I can't trust anyone here to handle this tape. We've run into some, ah, shall we say, irregularities, at very high levels. I'm sending the tape to an official agency, the New York City Police Department, specifically, and I would like to send it via diplomatic pouch. If you can arrange that I, and my friend, would be extremely grateful."

"Well, Joe, I can certainly arrange that. Do you have an address?"

"Yes. If I can use a phone for a long-distance call . . . .?"

"In the next room. Help yourself."

Joe excused himself and stepped into a small conference room. He dialed a familiar number and the connection went right through. "Bill Ryan here."

"Hey Bill, what's new, buddy?"

"Joe? Is that you? Hey, how the hell are you? Long time no see, or talk."

"Well, sorry to be out of touch for so long, but I'm doing fine."

"And how's your lovely mermaid? Any little fishes yet?"

"She's great, thanks, and the answer is no, but we're tryin'. Real hard too."

"Great. How's the weather in Cozumel these days?

"Well, I wouldn't know, Bill. I'm calling from Reykjavik."

"Where?"

"Reykjavik. Iceland."

"What the hell are you doing in Iceland? I thought you and Terry were strictly warm-weather birds."

"Well I'm here on business. Kind of, officially unofficial."

"Okay, I get it. How can I help you?"

"I need to have a shattered videotape cassette reassembled so it'll work. The tape may require restoration too. I don't know how badly it's damaged. If I send it, can you run it over to the lab and have your friends see what they can do?"

"Sure. What's on the tape? It's not your honeymoon is it?"

"Evidence, but that's all I can say now, Bill."

"Okay, Joe. Send it to this address. Got a pencil?"

"Shoot."

"How're you sending it?"

"It'll be coming via U.S. diplomatic pouch. And Bill, I need quick turnaround. It's very important."

"Okay, Joe. Only the best for my ex-partner, even though you never call your pal anymore."

"Rub it in. Thanks for your help, Bill. Promise to see you soon."

"Bye, Joe, I'll hold you to your promise."

"Thanks Bill. Good bye." Returning to Alice McDonald's office, Joe handed her the tape. "Here's the address, Alice. I can't tell you how much I appreciate your assistance."

"My pleasure, Joe. I'll contact you as soon as we receive the tape back," she replied, extending her hand. "And please express my condolences to your friend."

"Thanks, Alice, I will. Take care and have a good day."

Chapter 50

One Week Later

May 21st

"*I* have invited you here today to discuss the final disposition of this case," said Judge Kristinsson. "First, I believe this belongs to you," he said to Jan, handing him his wife's gold bracelet. "Police investigators recovered it in Swenson's cabin." Jan turned it over gently and his eyes moistened as he read the inscription engraved on the inside. *To my dear Lara, I give you my love for eternity. Love, Jan.* He held it next to its matching twin, looked down at the table and said quietly, "They're together again." After a moment of silence, the judge continued.

"First of all, we are not bringing charges against Mr. Shalken in the death of Captain Swenson. We have concluded he acted in self-defense. Although Mr. Shalken may have possibly subdued Captain Swenson instead of killing him, we have concluded he was acting under extreme stress and was not responsible in the moments leading up to the terminal event."

Terminal event? Now there's a catchy phrase I'll have to remember the next time I investigate a killing, thought Joe.

"As you already know from the photographic evidence provided by Mrs. Terry Manetta, we had already concluded the *Arctic Wind*'s propeller did not strike Mrs. Shalken or cause her death. We recovered four harpoons from the ship, in addition to the one Mrs. Manetta and Miss Van der Zee removed, and we have tested their metal composition. Two harpoons, relatively new models, were composed of a different alloy from the trace sample in Mrs. Shalken's wound. However, the metal composition of the other three harpoons found on the ship is identical to the trace metal found in her neck vertebra. Even though we cannot perform a true ballistics test to determine which weapon caused her death, we can assume it was most likely one of those three. Given that no other ship was in the vicinity at the time of the incident, the only logical conclusion is that a harpoon fired from the *Arctic Wind* killed Mrs. Shalken. There is one more thing," continued the judge, his words echoing off the walls of the quiet room. "A new witness has come forward."

Everyone was silent at first, then animated as they pressed the judge for details. The judge held up his hand, quieting them, and pressed the intercom button. "Mrs. Vroost, please send in Mister Frankhurst." Terry and Femke did a double-take, recognizing the young seaman who had been standing watch on the ship when they boarded a week ago. He looked at Femke and Terry, puzzled, trying to recall where he had seen them before, but not recognizing them without a uniform. "This is Erwin Frankhurst," said the judge. "He has some important information to share with you. Please sit down, Mr. Frankhurst, and tell these people what you have told me."

"Well, that day I was below deck working in the engine room. Our ship's intercom was not working properly, so my superior told me to give the captain a message regarding the status of the engines. I ran to the pilothouse, but our first mate was at the helm because Captain Swenson was outside at the harpooner's station. It was my first voyage on a whaling ship, and I was always assigned to duties below deck. I had never seen a whale killed before. The whale was ahead of the ship but there was a small craft, a Zodiac with three people, between the whale and our ship. They kept maneuvering so our harpooner, Mister Vikinsson could not get a clear shot. I saw Captain Swenson push him aside and grab the cannon."

Jan moved to the edge of his chair. Femke was biting her lip, eyes moistening. Terry and Joe sat motionless, rapt with attention.

"Everything happened very quickly. The ship fell into the trough of a wave and the Zodiac was lifted into the line of fire by the next swell. I heard Vikinsson, the harpooner, shout, 'No!' But Captain Swenson yelled, 'Damn that bitch!' Then he fired. I saw a tall lady standing at the Zodiac's helm. Her blond hair disappeared in a spray of red. She was knocked over the side of the Zodiac." Femke put her head in her hands, weeping silently. Jan riveted his eyes on the young man. "With no one steering, the Zodiac went out of control, spun ninety degrees, and wallowed in a trough. We passed right over it. I heard the screams. I will never forget it. I ran from the pilothouse. The first mate never knew I was there, standing behind him, watching the whole thing."

"That fact probably saved your life, son," said Joe. "And you were never summoned to testify?"

"No. I am underage and have no working papers, so Captain Swenson never gave my name to the authorities as part of the crew."

"And why did you keep silent until now?" asked Jan.

"I heard that men who had been on deck and had seen everything were disappearing, or in some cases, dying in strange accidents. There was a rumor that Captain Swenson may have been involved in some way. I was afraid to let anyone know I saw anything. Now he's dead, so I decided to tell my story."

"Thank you. You may leave," said the judge. Femke and Jan made eye contact but said nothing as Erwin Frankhurst, quickly left the room. "I believe this concludes our investigation. My sincere condolences to Mrs. Shalken's family. Mr. and Mrs. Manetta, the court thanks you for your assistance." Joe and Terry nodded. "I'm glad we have finally arrived at the truth, and even though it may have been painful, I sincerely hope it will eventually bring you peace."

"Thank you," said Jan. "I believe it will."

"What about the other disappearances and killings?" inquired Joe.

"Those matters are still under investigation," replied the judge. "Inspector Hansen will continue with the case."

"I see," replied Joe. He thought, *those cases will be headed for their cold-case files.*

As they left the building, Jan said, "Joe, Femke and I are going to have a quiet dinner. We'd like to have you and Terry join us. Without your help, we never would have learned the truth."

"We'd love to, Jan," said Terry. As she accepted Jan's invitation, Joe noticed Jan had removed his bracelet from his wrist and was holding both together in his hand.

Chapter 51

Planning for the IWC conference

June 5th

*J*on Andresson waited patiently for Oshura Haigata to answer his private phone. For the first time in many months, Andresson did not dread speaking to Haigata. Just when he assumed the call would go into voicemail, Haigata picked up his phone. "Hello. Haigata here," he answered, brusquely.

"Hello, Oshura, it's Jon Andresson. Have you heard the news?"

"No, what news?"

"Swenson is dead. The woman's husband, Jan Shalken, killed him."

"He killed Swenson?" Haigata asked, incredulous at the unexpected turn of events.

"Yes. In a most gruesome fashion." Andresson recounted the details, after which several seconds of dead air hissed over the phone line. "Oshura, are you still there? Did you hear what I just said?"

"Yes, yes. Very interesting. Fascinating, in fact." He smiled. *For the first time in four years, I feel like a free man.* "Do you think there will be any repercussions at the IWC conference next week?"

"Well, I don't know for sure, but I believe our position is secure. Stig and Eric have laid a solid foundation supporting our positions. I don't think any adverse publicity can shake us now. Besides, that thorn in our side Swenson met such a grisly fate, I think our opponents are satisfied. They got their pound of flesh, so to speak."

"Good. Today I am preparing my opening and closing remarks for the conference. I fly out tomorrow. See you in a few days, Jon."

"See you soon, Oshura. Have a safe trip." Andresson leaned back, closed his eyes, and relaxed. He took a deep breath and exhaled. *Everything is going to work out after all.* The phone rang and he answered promptly. "Jon Andresson speaking."

"Jon, Stefan Valsson here."

"Hello, Stefan. You sound better than you have in quite some time."

"Yes. Well, I feel relieved with this matter closed and finally behind us."

That's the understatement of the year, thought Andresson.

"Do you think everything has been contained?"

"Yes sir, I think you can relax and forget about any repercussions."

"Well, I plan to do just that. Good luck at the conference next week."

"Thank you, sir. I am confident everything will proceed smoothly."

"Fine. Well, goodbye, Jon."

"Goodbye, sir." He reflected on how Valsson's good spirits matched Haigata's. *Interesting, how one man's death can make two people a world apart feel so wonderful,* he thought.

Terry, Joe, Femke, and Jan drove together to meet the Peaceful Seas representatives. "Terry, as I mentioned earlier, we really would like you to speak at the conference," said Sir Adam Raleigh. "Although non-governmental organizations are only permitted to observe, I can include you in Britain's official delegation. That way we can arrange for you to make a short presentation."

"Well, Mr. Chairman, I mean sir, I mean, ah, what do I call a British knight?"

"How about just Adam," he replied, laughing.

"Okay, Adam. Look, you'll have all your experts and scientists speaking, and diplomatic representatives will be presenting their governments' official positions. I would feel out of place. What could I possibly contribute?"

"That's the point, Terry. You have no economic agenda. And, while you are not a scientist or a diplomat, you do have some very unique experiences, giving you credibility as a speaker. I can assure you that no voting delegates have ever swam with humpback whales. Besides, as an expert observer, you represent millions of common people who believe our position is correct, morally, environmentally, and also economically. They have no platform. You will speak for them."

"That's quite a responsibility, speaking for so many people."

"Hey that's no problem for you, hon," Joe chimed in. "You speak for me all the time." As they all laughed, Terry threw an elbow that made Joe wince.

"You know what I mean. It's the idea of representing so *many* people that has me shaking. What would I say?"

"Just speak from your heart," advised Sir Adam Raleigh.

Chapter 52

The IWC Conference

June 15th

*T*he morning of the conference, Terry, Joe, Femke and Jan met for breakfast. "This should be a very interesting experience," said Femke.

"Yes, I hope the Peaceful Seas folks show up early. I want to see what they have planned for me," said Terry.

"Well, we have to wait for them anyway, since they have our passes and we'll be sitting together."

"There's Adam," said Joe, waving.

"Good morning, everyone," he said. "Is your presentation ready, Terry?"

"Yep, it's all here. I decided to add some slides to break up the talk and give them something to look at besides me."

"You'll do fine," said Adam, laughing. "It looks like you're scheduled to speak toward the end of the conference. Is that satisfactory?"

"Sure. It just means being on pins and needles for a few more days."

"Well, sorry about that. But there are so many presentations, speakers, and exhibits, it was quite difficult to get you on the agenda. In fact, they might cut your presentation if there isn't enough time. Looks like we can go inside. Here are your passes. Just follow me."

"Oh, I hope you get to do your presentation," said Femke.

"Well, I wouldn't mind just being a spectator," replied Terry.

The moderator called the conference to order, and after delivering some welcoming remarks, introduced the first speaker. Oshura Haigata strode purposefully to the podium and began speaking. "Ladies and gentlemen, fellow diplomats, and eminent scientists, we have assembled today for the purpose of . . . ."

After almost one hour, Haigata concluded his speech. "So, fellow delegates, as we break into working groups, presenting and analyzing our findings, let us maintain a positive spirit and tone. Remember, our goal is to better mankind and our planet. Thank you." The delegates responded with enthusiastic applause, and Haigata bowed, projecting as humble and modest an image as he could. No one saw the smirk on his face as he departed the stage; the same confident look a gambler has knowing he has fixed the game in his favor.

As the week progressed, the working groups and committees analyzed data, presented positions, and voted on recommendations. Haigata and his cronies were successful passing most of their positions. The major vote on extending the ban on commercial whaling was scheduled on the final day. The prior evening, Femke and Jan dined with the Peaceful Seas contingent. She turned to Sir Adam Raleigh. "What do you think our chances are, Adam?"

"Well, I'll be frank with all of you. Based on this week's developments, and from my conversations with the other representatives, I am not confident. By the way, where are Terry and Joe? I thought they were joining us."

"I don't know. They should be here," said Femke. "Oh, here they come now."

"Sorry we're late," apologized Joe. "We just got stuck in a little traffic."

"No problem," replied Adam. "I wanted to confirm Terry is prepared for tomorrow. The agenda is that Haigata opens the final session, there will be some concluding speakers, one of which will be Terry, and then the delegates vote. Ready?"

"Ready as I'll ever be," replied Terry.

Chapter 53

The Final Day

June 19th

Terry was reviewing her presentation when the phone rang. "Joe, it's for you," said Femke.

"Thanks. Good morning, Alice. Yes, I'll be right over. Bye now. You folks go to the conference. I'll meet you later. I have to pick up a package that just arrived at the U.S. Embassy."

"Okay, we'll see you later. Don't miss my presentation," said Terry.

"Don't worry, hon, I wouldn't miss your international debut for the world."

"Yeah, I need at least one fan planted in the audience."

"Don't forget about Jan and me," laughed Femke.

Joe arrived at the embassy and was immediately ushered into Alice McDonald's office. "Good morning, Joe. This came early this morning. I knew you were expecting it, so I instructed my assistant to inform me as soon as it arrived."

"Thanks, Alice. Let's see what we have here." He opened the sealed package and found a short note from Bill Ryan and two videocassettes. He read Bill's note aloud. "We made two copies for you. Glad to help out a pal. Hope it's what you need. All the best, your buddy, Bill." He looked at the two tapes. One was marked, *Tape #1*. The other was marked, *Tape #2, PAL*. "Looks like my pal in New York sent me a spare tape."

"Nice to have friends in the right places. Would you like to watch it now? I have a TV and VCR on my credenza right over here." Joe thought about her offer. *I don't think it would do any harm if she saw the tape. After all, she did help me and she's very curious. And I really do want to see it right away.*

"Sure, Alice, let's take a look," he said, handing her the tape marked #1. Alice turned on the TV and inserted the tape. As they waited for video to begin, Alice was mildly curious but Joe was extremely anxious. Several seconds of blank screen, were followed by unintelligible electronic clutter and no sound. "Oh no! I don't believe it. After all this work, *nothing?* Why didn't my good *pal* Bill warn me the tape was so garbled it wouldn't play?"

"Joe, may I see the other tape, please?" Alice looked at the cassette label and laughed.

"What's so funny?"

"Well, this is the one you should have given me in the first place."

"Huh?"

"When your friend wrote *PAL* on the label he wasn't trying to be friendly. He meant this tape is recorded in a format called *PAL*. It's designed to play on European television systems. The other one must be *NTSC* format, designed for American televisions. He sent you both formats so you could play it anywhere."

"Well I'll be a son of a bitch! Oops, sorry. Forgot my manners," Joe said. "You're excused," said Alice, laughing. "Let's try again." The screen remained gray for several seconds and Joe looked at Alice apprehensively. Suddenly, the picture appeared. "Look!" she said.

The tape ran less than three minutes. Stunned, they watched it again. "Oh my, that was horrible. I am truly sorry for your friend," said Alice. "What are you going to do now, Joe?"

"Well, first I have a stop to make in town, and then I have to rush over to the conference center where they're holding the IWC meeting."

"Good luck, Joe. If there is anything else we can do to help, just call."

"Thanks, Alice, I will. I gotta run. Take care and thanks again."

The Peaceful Seas contingent took their places, hoping for some miracle to halt the groundswell of support for Haigata's positions, which had swept the delegations like a tsunami. They watched apprehensively as he stood erect and confident at the podium.

"I extend my heartfelt thanks to all the delegates and attendees for their diligence this past week. You have worked hard with good will, and I am personally glad we have addressed the issues rationally, without rancor or animosity. It is my hope we will leave this conference with that same spirit. After all, while we may have differences of opinion, we are all honorable people." *Hmph,* mused Sir Adam Raleigh, reflecting on Haigata's remark. *Just how Mark Antony described Brutus and his conspirators after they murdered Caesar.* "We will go forth with a plan to manage the ocean's resources for the benefit of all mankind, not for the benefit of narrow self-interest groups. Resource sustainability must be our goal. Achieving that end requires logical policies consistent with . . . ."

As he droned on, Adam Raleigh looked at his associates, recalling all their hard work. He realized someone possessing greater political skills had outmaneuvered them. He thought, *is that all it comes down to?* Terry kept checking her watch and scanning the entrances, looking for Joe. Finally, she spotted him frantically waving to her from the other side of the hall. "Look, Adam, there's Joe! I never thought he'd make it."

"Looks like he's signaling. I think he wants you to join him."

"Let me see why he's so agitated." She excused herself and walked quickly to the other side of the large hall. "Joe, what's up? You look like you just saw Bigfoot or something." He took her by the arm and led her from the hall.

"I wouldn't be this excited if I did see Bigfoot. Terry, you have to see this tape! Come over here." He brought her to a table where he had a television with a video player.

"Where'd you get the combo TV-VCR?"

"I bought it on the way here, but that's not important. Take a look at this tape!" Joe inserted the tape marked *Tape #2PAL* into the VCR. "Watch!" Joe had already seen the tape twice, so he just watched Terry and waited for her reaction.

"Oh my God!" she exclaimed.

"That was my sentiment when I first saw it too."

"Please play it again!"

Terry could hardly believe what she saw. "Wow! What do we do now?"

"I have to call the embassy right away. After I viewed the tape, I asked them to make some arrangements and run diplomatic interference for me. I have to find out if they came through."

"Okay, I just got an idea. Give me that tape."

"What are you going to do with it?"

"Sorry, no time to explain. I think I speak soon. I have to make some last-minute adjustments to my presentation."

"Good luck. I'll be watching from the floor of the auditorium."

"Thanks. Love you!"

"Love you too."

Haigata concluded his remarks and received another enthusiastic ovation. He shook hands with the IWC board members

234

on the dais and took his seat with the Japanese delegation. The next speaker delivered some brief remarks. Then the moderator introduced Terry. Approaching the podium, she noticed the audience was restless. Delegates were checking their watches, anxious to vote on the final agenda item so they could catch planes, attend receptions and settle other business. She took a deep breath and began speaking.

"Ladies and gentlemen, fellow delegates, thank you for extending me the privilege of addressing you today. I am here to speak about the importance of saving the great whales of the world's oceans, not just to *sustain* them on some arbitrary, razor-thin balance between extinction and preservation." Terry glanced at her notes as she spoke. "If we examine the statistics, we see that in the last century, over 350,000 blue whales, almost 99 percent of their original numbers, have been killed. Today, less than several thousand remain. During this same period, finback whales became the most hunted whale species, with over 700,000 killed in the Southern Hemisphere alone. No one really knows how many remain. Humpback whales have fared no better. Whalers have killed over 200,000 in the southern oceans alone. Worldwide, perhaps only 30,000 humpbacks remain. Now that these whales, along with bowheads and right whales, hover on the brink of extinction, there is pressure to hunt other species, such as minkes and sei whales.

"If you delegates vote to resume commercial whaling, those whales will also be hunted to extinction. Furthermore, the supposedly protected species will never recover. Scientists estimate that by the end of the twenty-first century . . . ." she looked up from her notes and saw the eyes of the delegates were glazing over. They sat frozen, their arms folded across their chests, some breaking into private conversations. She looked at the observers in the gallery and their body language indicated they were equally bored. She realized she was not reaching them. She glanced toward the Japanese delegation and saw Haigata, sitting confidently, listening politely, but definitely impatient. Terry closed her eyes for a moment and Sir Adam Raleigh's words echoed in her brain. *Just speak from your heart.* She took a deep breath, leaned closer to the microphone and raised her voice. "Oh hell, I'm not a scientist, so I'm not going to bore you with more of the same statistics and arguments you've heard all week." Her change in tone surprised the audience. Even the Peaceful Seas group sat up in their chairs. She folded her notes and made eye contact with her audience.

"After a while, these numbers just don't mean a damn thing anymore, do they, ladies and gentlemen? After you talk about killing hundreds of thousands of whales, or anything else for that matter, the numbers defy comprehension, don't they? So let's talk about smaller numbers. Let's talk about *three*. I met a group of three individuals, a *family,* actually, last year in the Dominican Republic." Terry nodded to the audiovisual assistant, who switched on the slide projector. Pointing the wireless remote, Terry brought up her first slide. "This photo shows a newborn humpback whale I met earlier this year. It's only a month or two old. Notice its eye, looking right at my camera lens, looking at *me* actually. I could see it was wondering about me, exploring me intelligently. Look at it. You can see it too, can't you? This next photo shows the mother, coming toward me. I don't suppose you would care to try this with a bear or a lion, would you?" The audience laughed as she moved to the next picture. "My husband took this next photo. You can see the mother whale passed so closely that she pulled her long pectoral fin back along her body to avoid hitting him, respecting his personal space. You can see she is clearly observing him. Have you ever looked into the eye of a whale? Not a hundred thousand whales, just *one single* whale? In my line of work, I spend a lot of time in the water, but I never have before. Ladies and gentlemen, just look into that eye. Can't you see intelligence, wisdom born from years of experience and eons of evolution?" The audience sat forward, intently looking at the whale's photo. It was clearly looking at the camera with cognition.

"As she passed me and followed her baby, I took this next photograph, showing the underside of her fluke. Each humpback's marking pattern is distinct and unique, like a human fingerprint. I named her Clover, because of this cloverleaf pattern here, on her fluke," she said, pointing to it. "This next photo is her male escort, possibly the father of the baby whale. I saw the three together several more times during the week I was there. In this last sequence of photos, you can see how they interacted, affectionately touching and rubbing their bodies together." She pressed the remote control. "This next photo is the last one ever taken of Clover and her family. It's the Associated Press photo that was published in newspapers. It shows the escort whale floating next to the whaling ship, dead, awash in its own blood. The baby whale is on the deck, dead, next to its mother, also dead, partially suspended by a rope around her flukes. You can clearly see the distinctive cloverleaf pattern on her left fluke. Pirate whalers killed this family near Bermuda." Terry noticed the mood of the audience had changed. Now they were paying very close attention. Individual conversations had ceased. The room was silent.

"Earlier today, I heard your delegates talk about sustainability. Yet, all through this conference, recommendations have been made and votes taken weakening the penalties against pirate whalers and so-called 'scientific whalers' who commit these brutal acts. You have passed measures inhibiting the means to prevent these atrocities. And now, some countries have asked you to approve a proposal exposing the whales to commercial hunting. How are those positions consistent with sustainability? I have met many of you kind, sensitive, intelligent people during the past week. I cannot believe you same good people will vote today to finally allow what amounts to unrestricted killing of whales on a mass scale.

"These killers take another toll, a toll on your own humanity and decency. To those who support the resumption of commercial whaling, I ask you: If you allow yourselves to be led by murderers, what does that say about your cause?"

"Now hold on, young lady," interjected a Canadian delegate, rising from his seat. "I strongly object to your remarks. We have listened politely to you, and your remarks have been indeed moving. They certainly have given us pause for reflection. But no one has *ever* proposed that killing whales, whether or not you support it, equates to murder." There was a smattering of applause.

Terry paused, then continued. "I was not referring to killing whales, sir. Please watch the screen carefully." She nodded to the audiovisual assistant, who inserted Joe's tape and activated the videotape player. The audience, now curious, stared at the screen in silent, rapt attention. The picture faded in, showing a fuzzy, distant image. The camera focused and the fuzzy image became a ship less than a mile distant, just as dawn was breaking. The first rays of the sun pierced the horizon.

Sir Adam Raleigh's eyes focused on the screen and narrowed as the camera zoomed in. *My God! I know that ship!*

Then, the camera panned back showing a man with his back to the camera, standing at the ship's railing, holding a small square device. A voice was heard on the tape, giving instructions. "Now just flip that cap up. When you are ready, push the red button." The camera caught the movement of the man's hand. Then a click was heard. A split second later, a huge explosion of sea and foam obscured the ship that was less than a mile away. Some in the audience were startled and jumped in their seats. The camera zoomed in on the sinking ship, showing her final moments in graphic detail. The stern settled low in the water, and the bow pitched up. In less than a minute, it slid stern-first into the depths and disappeared. The audience sat transfixed. Adam, Jan, and the rest of the Peaceful Seas group realized they had just watched the destruction of the original *Sea Angel* and the murder of her crew, almost four years ago in the Pacific.

The camera panned back once again, just as the man holding the remote controlled detonating device turned. The audience gasped as they saw the camera had captured the profile of a younger but still very recognizable Oshura Haigata. With a polite bow, he handed the detonator to a tall man standing beside him. The tall man had taken great care to shield his face from the camera, but there was a clue to his identity. He bowed slightly and a shark-tooth necklace hung from his neck. The audience turned toward the Japanese delegation. Terry saw Haigata standing, looking at the screen, wide-eyed, dumfounded, his jaw hanging slack. He turned to flee, but two Interpol agents had moved in behind him, grabbed his arms, and quickly escorted him from the hall. Terry looked at Joe, standing behind the Interpol police. He threw her a wink and a smile. She made eye contact with the delegate who had objected to her remarks. He was sitting in shock. Then, she turned on her heels and left the stage.

The room was in chaos. The moderator wiped his brow as he rushed past Terry to the podium. "Ladies and gentlemen, please remain seated," he gasped, trying to restore order. "We are adjourning the meeting for one hour before voting. If you need to leave for a moment, please use the exits nearest your seats. I ask all representatives to remain with your delegation so we may resume the meeting promptly. Thank you."

Chapter 54

June 26th

"*I* don't know how we can thank you two," remarked Sir Adam Raleigh.

"Well, that luxury suite Peaceful Seas provided for our last several nights in Iceland was a very special treat. Our final night was truly magical, and *very* romantic," Terry said, smiling at Joe.

"Oh, it's the least we could do, my dear. The IWC's vote to maintain the commercial whaling moratorium until the next meeting gives the whales a reprieve. Perhaps it's only temporary, but at least it provides time to regroup and lobby for a permanent ban extending far into the future."

"I was pretty surprised we pulled it off," said Joe. "Haigata and his voting bloc had a pretty good head of steam. I didn't think we'd be able to derail them."

"Well, I'm used to these political types. They have a herd mentality. They just wanted to distance themselves from Haigata and his bunch. I think they feared voting for a position that he had personified would have made them look guilty by association. Once that mood began to spread, it became contagious. By the way, you still have time before your plane takes off to change your minds and join us."

"Thanks, Adam, but I'm a warm-weather girl. Besides, we do have a business to run. Which reminds me, I hope it's still up and running. But I promise we'll stay in touch. If Peaceful Seas ever needs help, just call us."

"Okay, it's a deal. I'll put you on our mailing list, and if we ever need . . . ."

"Terry, Joe, sorry we're late. We got caught in traffic!"

Terry turned and saw Femke and Jan running toward them. "Hi Femke, hi Jan. We were afraid we wouldn't see you before we left."

"No chance of that," said Jan, kissing Terry. Then he turned to Joe, lifting him off the ground with a massive bear hug. "And you, my friend! How can I ever thank you and your lovely wife!"

"By letting me breathe?" asked Joe, gasping for breath as everyone laughed.

"Resolving everything was painful, but it has also given me peace. I will never stop missing my sweet Lara and my brother Karel. But at least I know they can rest in peace now."

"Well, from what I've read in the local newspapers, there won't be much peace in the government here for a while. Adam, did you find out any more details about the political fallout?"

"Yes, Joe. Haigata gave up everything, and everyone, after only brief interrogation. We arrested the two accomplices who killed Vikinsson, and probably the other witnesses. I was quite surprised that he cracked so easily."

"Well, don't be. Take it from me, those Interpol guys can be pretty persuasive. And Haigata, for all his posturing, wasn't exactly what we NYPD guys would call street-smart. Under all that bluff and bluster, he was pretty soft. I've seen his kind before. They'd give up their widowed mother to avoid a day in jail."

"I see. Well, it seems Ulf Swenson was quite a devious character, in addition to being a murderer. He was blackmailing both Haigata *and* Prime Minister Valsson simultaneously. Haigata didn't realize he was on that tape, until Swenson conveniently informed him at a later date. He used it as leverage, forcing Haigata to supply muscle to resolve his problems."

"Problems such as inconvenient witnesses," remarked Joe.

"Exactly."

"But how did they ever meet each other in the first place? Coming from such different backgrounds, it seems unlikely they ever would have known each other."

"Well, Haigata told us the whole story. Several years ago, Swenson was plying the Pacific, hunting for whales. He had a reputation for being very aggressive and very good at what he did. He was freelancing at the time. Some Japanese businessmen hired him to captain the *Hakudo Maru*. Haigata was just a junior-level political appointee to the Ministry of Agriculture, Forestry and Fisheries. His government assigned him to disrupt the efforts of conservationist groups like Peaceful Seas. Japan wanted to expand its whaling activities and was losing patience using scientific research as a cover to hunt whales for economic purposes. Haigata was very ambitious. He had his eye on being appointed to the powerful Fisheries Agency of Japan, because that agency determines Japan's whaling policies. He heard about Swenson and contacted him. They never really liked each other. Haigata thought Swenson was one step removed from a barbarian, while Swenson dismissed Haigata as an ambitious political flunky. He didn't respect him but realized he might go places in his government one day, and become useful. And he was right. They got along because they had a common goal. He went on some of Swenson's whaling trips and experienced firsthand how frustrating it was to catch whales with Peaceful Seas harassing them."

"So they hatched the plan together to sink the *Sea Angel*?"

"Well, to hear Haigata tell it, the idea was all Swenson's. Haigata just had access to the resources."

"But wouldn't that have involved other branches of his government?" asked Terry.

"Yes, probably some arm of the military, like a clandestine special forces group. But don't expect Iceland or Holland to initiate investigating Japan. There are too many layers of insulation. Anyway, Swenson used the opportunity to set up Haigata. Once he caught him on tape blowing up the *Sea Angel* and sending all those young men and women to the bottom, he had him. Swenson showed Haigata an edited copy, so he had no idea he was even on the tape. Then Swenson called him one day and sent him an unedited copy. And whenever Swenson needed some assistance, Haigata would get another phone call.

"Amazing," remarked Terry.

"Swenson also pressured Prime Minister Valsson to squash the investigation," continued Adam. "That was why those early investigative findings, which you all worked so hard to overturn, didn't make sense."

"And did that involve my buddy, Inspector Hansen?" inquired Joe.

"Quite right. Prime Minister Valsson worked that angle through Jon Andresson, but he was the one behind it."

"Well that explains Hansen's contrary nature at every critical step."

"Yes. But Hansen wasn't such a bad chap. Unfortunately, he couldn't push back, with his government pension hanging in the balance."

"But what did Swenson have over Valsson?" asked Terry.

"That one is a blockbuster, my dear. You see, when he was a young married man, Stefan Valsson had an extramarital relationship with a young lady. That relationship produced a son."

"You don't mean!"

"Precisely! Besides not wanting his wife to discover his adultery and illegitimate son, there were also potential political repercussions. Can you imagine what would have happened to Valsson's support within his own party, given Swenson's unsavory character? The resumption of whaling is a contentious issue in Iceland. There is strong support for it in some quarters, but the economic pressure against it has grown considerably. Whale watching has become a major tourist industry, by some measures

243

contributing more to their economy than whaling. Valsson was sitting on the fence, trying to appease both sides."

"Looks like he got pushed off the fence," remarked Joe.

"What will you two do now, Femke?" inquired Terry.

"Well, I don't see how I can go back to Holland and continue my life as it was before," said Femke. "It would seem so boring now, after all this," she said, sharing a laugh. Then she turned serious. "I plan to join Peaceful Seas and continue Lara's work. If it was important enough that she risked, and lost, her life, then I need to be part of it. I know I'll miss my job working with the children, but I'm, ready for a change and new challenges, at least temporarily."

"That's wonderful, Femke. We'd love to have you join us," said Adam.

"And you, Jan?" asked Terry.

"I will remain here and supervise fitting out the *Sea Angel II*. We'll sail in about a month, but for where, I don't know."

"Oh we'll find a suitable assignment," remarked Adam. "By the way, we have a little something for you two," he said, turning to Terry and Joe. He pulled two windbreaker jackets from a bag. "I think we got the sizes right. I hope they're not too large."

"Don't worry, Adam. Terry can shrink anything." Joe remarked, wincing as Terry delivered one of her trademark elbows to his ribs.

"Why, Adam, how sweet of you and everyone else." As she opened her jacket, she saw the embroidered piping on the back read, *SEA ANGEL II*. Under it was an emblem of an angel holding a shield, riding on a whale's back. On the left front of the jacket was an identical, but smaller, patch with *Terry* embroidered beneath the patch.

"And this also," Adam said, handing Joe a plaque indicating he and Terry were honorary members of Peaceful Seas, as well as honorary *Sea Angel II* crewmembers.

"Why, thank you very much, Adam. That's quite an honor. I don't know what to say."

"A historic moment! My husband is speechless for the first time since I met him," Terry said to a round of laughter.

"US Airways Flight 1023 to New York is now boarding all first-class passengers."

"Hey, that's us! We'd better go," said Joe. After a last round of tearful hugs, Terry and Joe boarded the flight for the first leg of their trip to Cozumel. After settling into her seat, Terry closed her eyes and reflected on their adventure. She looked at Joe, who was reading the latest edition of the airline's monthly magazine. "Joe, do you believe in fate?"

He looked up from the magazine, surprised at her question. "I don't know, Ter. I mean, I guess so. Perhaps. But I really don't know. Do you?"

"Well, think about it. Meeting Femke in Cozumel was a pure chance occurrence. In fact, if you recall, we almost didn't even take her diving. And that encounter, by chance, unless you believe in fate, led us halfway across the world. We uncovered the mystery behind the *Sea Angel*'s sinking, solved several murders, and influenced the vote of an international organization, preventing the slaughter of countless whales. I'd say that's quite a good day's work. So what do you think, Joe? Was it all just a big coincidence, or was there some reason we were supposed to be in Iceland?"

"That's a lot to consider, Ter. Maybe we *were* supposed to travel to Iceland for some reason. It does seem like a lot happened, almost too much to leave to blind chance. But I don't know if it was fate. I don't think I believe in some kind of. . . ."

"Flight attendants please be seated. We are next for takeoff." They ceased their conversation, settled back in their seats and held hands, each lost for a moment in the private thoughts most air travelers have as their jet roars down the runway. The big Airbus 321 accelerated rapidly and lifted off smoothly. The airport was situated near the coast, away from any buildings, so there were no noise abatement procedures requiring a steep ascent. The aircraft climbed at a gentle rate and Terry looked out as the plane passed the shoreline and headed over the ocean. She looked down at the sea. Several large, dark objects moving through the water, glistening in the sun, caught her eye. A little boy sitting in the window seat behind her tugged his father's sleeve. "Daddy, look! What kind of big fish

245

are those?" Terry smiled, waiting for the father's answer. When he didn't reply, she turned to the boy.

"Excuse me, but those aren't fish. Those are whales!"

"Awesome!"

Terry smiled.

Epilogue

Cozumel

August 30th

*T*erry watched the other three divers and checked her watch. It had been a good dive, with lots of critters and hundred-foot visibility. It was also her first time underwater since her ruptured eardrum had healed. *Only two more minutes hanging at our fifteen-feet safety stop, then we can surface.* Suddenly, she felt a familiar tingling sensation in her midsection. She looked around and saw two torpedo shapes materialize out of the blue, buzzing the divers like fighter jets in formation. The other divers were startled at first, but then overjoyed realizing a pair of dolphins was visiting them. The larger dolphin, a mature female with a familiar notch in her tail, paid special attention to Terry while the smaller one, a calf, swam with the other divers. They surfaced minutes later, elated that the dolphins continued swimming with them. Terry wondered why

Notchka stayed so close to her, even allowing Terry to stroke her smooth skin. Suddenly, as if summoned by some unseen signal, the pair dove, disappearing as rapidly as they had appeared.

Terry waited in the water while the other divers climbed up the *Dorado*'s ladder. Climbing aboard, she listened to the divers' animated conversations. *Happy divers mean good tips,* thought Terry. As the *Dorado* docked and discharged the customers, Terry was surprised to see Joe waiting. "Hey, what's up?" she shouted. "You should have come diving with us! A couple of old friends paid us a visit."

"Really?"

"Yeah, really. We saw Notchka and her new daughter. We really should name her, don't you think?"

"Sure, I suppose so."

"But Notchka sure was acting strangely. I felt her scanning me continually. And then she swam real close. Weird! Hey, by the way, why are you here? I thought you were busy today."

"I was. I went to see Doctor Ortega this morning."

"Oh right. I saw him last week and he mentioned you had an appointment for a check-up today. What did he say?"

"Not too much. Just told me to lose a few pounds. I said it was difficult when my wife is such a good cook."

"You are such a BS artist. You should have been a salesman in your former life instead of a cop."

"Well, in that case I probably never would have met you. Fate, right?"

"Sure, I guess. Anything else?"

"Yes. The doctor said he wanted to see you, today if possible."

"Did he say why, or if anything was wrong"

"Nope. But he had an opening at three o'clock and he was keeping it available if you could make it. I told him I'd bring you. It's almost 2:30 now.

"Would you mind driving me? I'll never make it if I go home and change."

"Sure, that's why I came down. Dry off and jump in the car."

Thirty minutes later, Terry and Joe were called into Doctor Ortega's office.

"Hello Terry, good to see you. And Joe, I'm surprised to see you again."

"Well, Doctor, I'm just the limo driver today," he replied, laughing. "Can I stay or do you want to speak with Terry privately?"

"On no, you may stay. I don't think Terry will mind."

"No problem. It'll save me from getting the third degree later," she said, smiling at Joe.

"Excuse me?" asked Doctor Ortega.

"Oh, just a police joke," explained Joe.

"Yes, of course," said the doctor, not really understanding the humor. "Well, getting to the reason why I wanted to see you, Terry. When you were here last week, I noticed some changes. That's why we ran some blood tests. The results came back showing elevated HCG levels, so I wanted to examine you right away to confirm my suspicions." Terry looked at Doctor Ortega, her brow furrowed with concern. "Joe, would you please wait here for a moment while I examine Terry in another room?"

"Sure. Is it serious?" asked Joe, feeling worried

"Possibly. It may have long-term implications," said Doctor Ortega over his shoulder as he led Terry into a small room. Several minutes later, Joe anxiously fidgeted in his chair, reading any magazine he could find, when he heard Terry scream.

"Oh my God!"

He bolted from the chair, ran to the examination room door, and stopped, frozen. Seconds later, Doctor Ortega opened the door, inviting Joe inside. He rushed past the doctor and saw Terry looking at a sheet of paper, crying.

"Terry, honey, are you all right?" Terry said nothing but just turned the paper toward Joe. He stared at a fuzzy black and white image, puzzled.

"I just asked Terry if twins run in her family," said Doctor Ortega.

"Well, I recall she told me her aunt had twin girls, but why would you . . . . I mean, how does that . . . . I mean . . .oh my God!" echoed Joe. "Do you mean she's . . . ?"

Doctor Ortega interrupted him. "Yes, these sonogram images indicate Terry is just over two months pregnant, with twins." Terry leaped off the examination table and kissed Doctor Ortega, knocking his glasses askew. He blushed as he adjusted them. Terry turned to Joe, kissing him as they embraced. "There isn't anything else for us to do here today. You two go home and celebrate. I'll permit you one glass of champagne tonight, but then no more alcohol until the babies are born, understand?"

"Oh yes, Doctor. Thank you, thank you so much," said Terry. Joe followed up with an enthusiastic handshake as they left. When they reached their car, Joe opened the passenger-side door with a flourish.

"Let me assist you, now that you're in a *family way,* my dear." he joked.

As he started the car, Terry said, "Joe, can you believe it? Can you really believe it? After all this time!"

"Yep. How about that? And from the way you described Notchka's actions today, she probably scanned you and saw you were pregnant. She probably knew about the twins, too."

Terry glanced out the window as they drove home. She squinted at the golden sea shimmering in the late-afternoon sun, wondering if Notchka was thinking about her. She thought about how a dolphin who had once saved her life knew she was pregnant even before she did. She recalled a magical, romantic night in Iceland, just over two months ago, when she and Joe had made love. And then Terry thought once again about fate.

* * * * *

Afterword

This story is fictional, but many details are based on fact. Unfortunately, *The Whale War,* a term coined by author David Day, and the title of his 1987 book (A Sierra Club publication), still continues. Unrelenting political maneuvering by Japan, Norway, Iceland, Finland, and several other countries, to overturn the International Whaling Commission's ban on commercial whaling continues. Their attempts to use economic incentives and threats to influence other IWC members to support their position are real. Some of these nations continue using the term "scientific research" as a cover for killing whales, so they can be sold for food and other commercial products. Their efforts to undermine the development of policies and scientific tools that could determine if threatened whale species are being illegally killed are real. Several nations have already resumed limited whaling, as a precursor to full-scale commercial whaling.

The dangerous exploits of those bravely risking their lives to save whales by interposing themselves between the whalers' deadly harpoons and the hunted whales occur on the high seas today. Exciting accounts of these confrontations can be found in Kieran Mulvaney's informative book, *The Whaling Season,* published in 2003 by Island Press/Shearwater Books. Kieran's book provides a dramatic, informative account of the current struggle to stop commercial whaling.

Fortunately for the whales, a rising tide of support from both individuals as well as from some governments has helped hold the pro-whaling forces at bay, at least temporarily. In some cases, this support is driven by economic incentive, since revenue from whale watching in many areas of the world now surpasses the revenue from whale killing.

In the final analysis, whales will continue to be threatened with extinction until sufficient worldwide support is driven by the enlightened knowledge that whales are highly intelligent, sentient beings, which deserve to exist on this planet in their own right, along with humans.

* * * * *